The Saints of Belvedere Road

Written by Darke Conteur

© 2016 Dark Conteur Collection of Works

ISBN:
978-0-9879447-7-1

Special Thanks to:
Cover Art: Rebecca Poole @ Dreams2media
Karen Lawson @ The Proof is in the Reading
&
Judy Brown@ writetechniques@gmail.com

CONTENTS

Chapter One   Pg 1

Chapter Two   Pg 14

Chapter Three   Pg 30

Chapter Four   Pg 46

Chapter Five   Pg 64

Chapter Six   Pg 82

Chapter Seven   Pg 93

Chapter Eight   Pg 106

Chapter Nine   Pg 123

Chapter Ten   Pg 238

Chapter Eleven   Pg 152

Chapter Twelve   Pg 173

1

Who ever said the fastest way to a man's heart is through his stomach, obviously never thought about going through his chest.

Amelia Saint couldn't remember where she'd heard the phrase before, but it echoed her mood as another piece of carrot rolled to the edge of the counter and disappeared over the side. If this kept up, she might as well just chuck the whole dinner on the floor.

She threw the serrated knife on the counter, wincing as it clanged against the ceramic tile. She picked up her glass of Chardonnay as she ran the tip of her finger over the impact area, hoping her rash impulse didn't leave a permanent chip in the stone. With everything going on this weekend, the last thing she needed was the hassle of retiling the surface.

She turned from the cutting board and leaned against the island counter, swirling the pale liquid around in the glass. Tonight's dinner had to be special. For the first time in weeks, Henry would be dining with the family. His overtime had created a noticeable absence, but hopefully, now that the client was happy, things would return to normal.

She faced the counter, still swirling the Chardonnay, allowing it to graze the rim before taking a sip. She missed him, missed them being a family, especially now that the boys were teenagers. Kids grew up so fast. Why couldn't they just stay babies? She set the glass off to the side and reached for the partially dissected carrot when the phone rang.

Amelia glanced quickly at the clock. Henry should have been home by now. She set the carrot down and walked to the wall phone.

"Hello."

"Hey, it's me." Amelia's heart jumped into her throat at the sound of Henry's voice. "Looks like I'm not going to be home for supper."

"Are you serious?" Amelia's eyes narrowed as her grip on the receiver tightened. "I thought you said Faunt was giving you the night off."

"He wants to talk to me about something, and then I'll be home."

Her shoulders drooped. "Well, I guess you don't have much of a choice then, do you?"

The faint sound of chatter came through the receiver, as well as a female voice telling Henry to hurry. It was soft and sultry and sent a shiver through her.

Without thinking, she asked, "What's going on?"

"What are you talking about?"

"Hurry for what?"

There was a long pause on the other end. "It's nothing. Faunt's taking us out for a few drinks with the client. You know, a schmoozing sort of thing. Don't worry about it."

Don't worry about it? A surge of anger overtook her and she clenched her teeth, trying to keep calm. "Fine, but try not to be too late."

Henry's end disconnected before she had a chance to say goodbye.

She slammed the receiver down and walked back to the counter. Her anticipation for the evening, as well as her appetite, was gone. She picked up the serrated knife, but tossed it back down on the cutting board. She didn't feel like preparing this anymore.

Amelia reached for the neck of the wine bottle and filled her glass to the rim. She moved from the counter, leaning back against it and caught a glimpse of herself in the kitchen window. Her ghostly image silhouetted against outside objects only enhanced the lines on her face, as hints of grey peeked through her auburn hair. She reached up and traced one limp curl with her free hand, examining the other wisps of faded red that framed her face. Growing old and graceful was not going well.

The sudden banter of her teenage children brought a frustrated smile to her lips. Their muffled argument grew louder as they walked past the kitchen window. Even though Chad was a few years older than the twins, they bickered constantly. Lately, even more so.

The trio tumbled into the mud room, dropping their book bags on the nearest convenient place on the linoleum floor. The three roughhoused their way into the kitchen before splitting up and heading off in different directions.

"How was your day at school?" Amelia asked, resuming her place at the cutting board. "Did you have fun?"

One of the twins, Liam, shot her a sarcastic look as he headed for the couch in the attached family room. "It's school," he said, falling onto the couch. "Who has fun at school?" Out of the three, her small-boned features were most apparent on him. His oval face held signs of the child he once was, with the shaggy mess of blonde hair suggesting otherwise.

"Well, I just thought something fun might have happened today, that's all."

Morgan walked past her and toward the pantry. Even though he was Liam's twin, it always amazed her how different they looked. She could see parts of her and Henry in the other boys, but Morgan, with his sad eyes and muscular appearance, had a look uniquely his own.

"What's for supper?" Morgan asked, opening the cupboards.

"Food," Liam called out from the couch.

Morgan turned, his face scrunched up in disgust. "Shut up!"

For a split second, Amelia saw the family resemblance.

"Stop it, both of you," she said. "I don't understand why you have to fight all the time. Can't you just be nice to each other?"

Chad walked past her and opened the door to the fridge. His jet-black hair hung down over his face, partially hiding his features.

"This isn't the eighties, Mom," he said, scanning the shelves. "Life isn't one big Breakfast Club."

She bit her bottom lip and reminded herself this was only a phase.

Amelia picked up the knife with one hand and a carrot with the other and began slicing. "Did you get all the invites out to your friends?" She hoped a change of topic would lighten his mood. "The party is only a few days away now. I want to make sure I have enough food for everyone."

Chad grabbed a can of pop and let the fridge door slam shut. "I tossed 'em out."

Amelia stopped slicing. "Why?"

"Because they're stupid."

"So, how am I supposed to know who's coming to this thing?"

He mimicked Liam's sarcastic look. "You'll know when they get here."

"How many people did you invite?"

"Enough." Chad left the kitchen without saying another word.

Amelia put her knife down and hurried out of the kitchen, catching up to Chad at the foot of the staircase. "You know, this party was your idea. You're the one who wanted to have a few friends over."

Chad whipped around, tilting his head down so his gaze met Amelia's. His green eyes narrowed into slits. "Yeah, for a good time, not some high-priced social event of the year."

Amelia sighed. "Look, I know you're upset that your father invited some people from work, but these are important people, and he needs to be on their good side if he's going to make partner."

The beginnings of a sneer formed on his lips. "Not good enough."

Amelia knew Chad wasn't a fool. Henry sometimes put his ambitions before family, and it was always the boys who suffered. "What do you want me to say?" she said, defeated. "If I tell you he's doing this for the family, you won't believe me and if I agree with you that he's doing it for himself, you'll fly off about how it's always him first, and to hell with everyone else."

His sneer became more prominent. "Isn't it?"

She knew that tone, and she was tired of arguing. "He's going to make it up to you, trust me." Amelia paused, waiting for some kind of reaction. "Can't you play along, just for one night?"

Chad's glare deepened, so much so that it caused Amelia to take a step back. She felt a tightness build in the pit of her stomach, as small hairs on the back of her neck tingled. He'd never looked at her with this much animosity before.

"Play along?" He straightened his stance. "How about I ask you that when he starts paying attention to other women." He turned and stomped up the stairs. "Maybe then you'll know how I feel."

Amelia flinched as a door on the second floor slammed shut. Memories of the sultry female voice echoed through her mind.

"Way to go, Mom," Morgan said, walking past her and up the stairs.

"You watch your mouth, young man!"

"Whatever."

Amelia turned and walked back into the kitchen. She felt like crying, and would if she thought it would do any good. A few tears blurred her vision, but she brushed them away as she stepped in front of her cutting board and began slashing away. The vegetables never had a chance.

**

Amelia sat on a chair at the head of the table in the kitchen nook, rubbing a polished index finger back and forth across her top lip, gazing out the picture window in front of her. Chad's words ran through her mind over and over. As upset as he was, this was the first time he'd said anything so hurtful.

"Mom, are you all right?"

Liam's soft voice drew her attention back. She folded her hands on the table and smiled. "Yes, I'm fine. Why?"

"Well, you were sorta spaced out there for a while."

"I'm sorry." Amelia shuffled her chair closer to the table. "I guess my mind wandered." She pulled the geography textbook toward her. "Now where were we?"

Liam fiddled with his pencil. "I'm doing math."

Amelia frowned. "I thought we were on geography?"

"I'm doing geography," Morgan said, peering out from under his overgrown bangs. He held out his hand, motioning with his fingers for Amelia to give him the book.

Embarrassed, she handed back the text. "Sorry. I guess I'm more preoccupied than I thought."

"That's all right," Liam said. "You're an adult so you're allowed."

"Well, I'm focused now, so what do you two need help with?"

"I'm fine," Morgan said, flipping through the pages.

Liam moved his math notebook closer to him. "Me too."

Amelia exhaled deeply and stood. Soon they would outgrow her as well, and the idea of her and Henry rambling around the house alone, was too depressing a thought to entertain at the moment. She walked over to the sink and picked up her wine glass. Maybe now, she could finally convince Henry to spend some time up at the cabin.

A stabbing pain shot through the front of her head. Amelia braced herself against the counter with one hand as she squeezed her eyes shut. Her hold on the wine glass weakened and slowly it slipped from her grasp and smashed into the sink.

"Mom?" Liam's voice was a distant echo in her ears. "Are you all right?"

She rubbed her temple in a circular motion. A flash of lightning shone through her eyelids and she opened her eyes.

"Whoa!" Morgan said as he and his brother jumped up from their seats.

The pain subsided enough for her to focus. Both boys knelt on the bench of the nook, their faces almost plastered to the glass window.

"What's going on?"

Morgan smiled. "That is so cool!"

She glanced out the window over the sink. A strong breeze churned up a few dried leaves along the edges of the driveway and scattered them around the yard. Muffled sounds of patio furniture scraped along the ground just beyond her view as the sun faded, throwing a grey blanket over the landscape. A loud thud from the back door jolted Amelia from the window, and sent both boys to the mud room at the far end of the kitchen. Morgan pulled on the door's metal handle, and it blew open throwing him back. Several pieces of broken pottery tumbled inside, their soil contents spilled onto the floor.

"Look what you did," she said. "Why did you open the door?"

Her anger turned to shock as wind chimes hanging from the wooden archway on the back porch, tinged and spun frantically on the delicate filaments that supported them. Amelia whispered a string of swear words as she watched chaos unfold in her backyard. Small whirlwinds danced around the gardens, twisting ornamental trees and shrubs almost to the breaking point. Colourful leaves were stripped from their branches, and off in the distance the formation of threatening clouds billowed up over Calgary's downtown core. Their dark grey plumes gave an ominous look to the skyline and sent a shiver up her spine.

Two wicker patio chairs were picked up by the wind and thrown down the cobblestone driveway. Amelia darted out into the maelstrom and sprinted after them, apprehending them just before the front walkway.

Everything went calm.

Amelia scanned the neighbourhood looking for further destruction from the small whirlwinds, but the lawns and gardens of her Belvedere Road neighbours were pristine as ever. Grabbing the chairs by the backrest, she dragged them back up the driveway, giving a quick glance to her neighbour, who was washing the hull of his sailboat.

"Never fails, does it, Bud?" she asked, pulling the chairs toward the waist-high hedge that separated the properties. "Every time you go to wash something, it always rains."

The balding middle-aged man stopped in mid-wipe and frowned at her. "What are you talking about?"

Amelia tried to keep from staring at the bulge of flab that poked out from under his Hawaiian shirt. "There's a storm coming. Look at the clouds."

Bud crinkled his nose before turning his attention toward the sky, then snapped his head back around. "Are you trying to be funny, Amelia? There isn't any storm coming. There's not a cloud in the sky."

Amelia frowned as she turned her attention skyward again, ready to argue that his lack of fashion sense was messing with his mind, only to have the sunlight return, its warmth and light washed over her. Off in the distance, there was no sign of the pending storm. The dark clouds and gusts of cool wind were gone. Amelia stood by the bushes, stunned.

Bud loosened his grip on the nozzle and lowered the hose. "Are you all right, Amelia?"

Amelia looked up the driveway toward the two-car garage nestled just behind their house. The boys stared back at her looking just as confused. "I don't know. I could have sworn there was a storm coming. The wind blew these chairs down the driveway and almost took out my wind chimes." She absent-mindedly rubbed the top of her head, tracing her part with her fingers. "Didn't you see it?"

"Sorry, I didn't see anything. I didn't even notice you, until you said something."

Bud's look of empathy didn't stop her from feeling like a fool. She was sure there had been clouds heading toward them. Another chill ran through her, but she brushed it off and began hauling the chairs up to the garage. She made a mental note to watch the news tonight. A fast moving storm system would definitely make the news.

Amelia placed the chairs back on the stone terrace and looked over the railing into the backyard. Disheartened, she could only shake her head in disbelief. Only she would end up with property damage caused by a freak windstorm. She rubbed her temple again and headed toward the beveled glass doors on the terrace. This was too much. She needed a hot soak and another glass of wine.

Liam's excited voice penetrated her thoughts. "Dad's home!"

Amelia smoothed back a few strands of hair as Henry's red Porsche pulled into the vacant spot in the garage. She hustled the boys inside and crouched down to pick up the broken pottery. Footsteps on the cobblestone came toward her as she gathered up a few of the larger pieces.

"What happened?" Henry asked.

Amelia glanced over her shoulder at him. His designer suit cut perfectly to his form. "Windstorm blew them over."

He walked past her, stepping over the dirt. "Wind storm?"

Amelia frowned. "Didn't you see it?"

"See what? What are you talking about?"

She stood with the broken pieces in her hand. She couldn't have been seeing things. The boys saw it too. Baffled, Amelia followed him into the house.

"So, how did your schmoozing go?" she asked, dropping the broken pottery in the garbage.

"Faunt's nephew drinks too much." Henry walked through the kitchen, grabbed a fork off the counter and picked at the remains of a roast on the stove.

"That's never a good thing."

Even at this age, Amelia still thought he was handsome. His complexion reminded her of clay; pallid and smooth, not a wrinkle to be seen apart from the small crow's feet that appeared with the movement of his mouth. His goatee and moustache were neatly trimmed on his square jaw, and, other than a loose strand of black hair that flopped down in a curl from his forehead, nothing else about his appearance looked out of place. Yet Amelia felt something was wrong.

"You're telling me, but the little puss-fucker had to work up the courage somehow."

"The courage for what?"

Henry moved away from the stove. The muscles in his jaw clenched and relaxed a few times. "To tell me he's taking the partnership at Faunt and Associates." Henry turned from the stove and headed for the doorway to the front foyer. "I've had a really shitty day. If you need me, I'll be in the shower."

A sense of dread washed over her. She went over to the kitchen nook and placed her hands on the back of the chair. The twins were back at their homework, but she knew they were only pretending. They had heard the whole thing.

She clasped a hand over her mouth to hide her trembling lip. Henry had sacrificed too much time vying for this promotion, and she wasn't sure if he was up to the task of starting back at square one, or more precisely, if she was. His loyalty to the firm was strong, but she wasn't sure if her marriage could last another round of ass-kissing.

The ceiling above began to creak and moan. Amelia frowned, and followed the muffled noise across the ceiling with her eyes.

Annoyed with Henry's revelation, she lashed out, "Who's doing that? Is that Chad?"

"Yeah," Liam replied, looking up at the ceiling. "He's been pacing a lot lately."

"What do you mean 'a lot'?"

Liam shrugged his shoulders as he returned to his notebook. "Almost every night."

"Seriously?"

"Yeah," Morgan said, keeping his eyes on his books. "But never this early. Usually he does it late at night."

A small ache tugged at Amelia's heart, tempering her anger. She glanced at the ceiling. "How long does it go on for?"

"Not long, maybe an hour or so," Liam said.

Amelia was stunned. "An hour or so? Liam, are you sure? That's an awful long time."

"I don't know," the teen whined. "Maybe an hour, I guess. I always fall asleep."

She marched toward the front hall. "You two keep working. I'll be right back."

Amelia's face grew hot with shame. Had she been so absorbed with Henry and his work that she'd overlooked Chad's odd behaviour? Was she that blind?

The wind howled outside the front doors as she headed toward the staircase. Outside, the ornamental trees on the front lawn bent with each gust of wind. Was another freak storm about to wreak havoc?

With each step up the staircase her remorse grew, along with her curiosity. At the landing, she heard the sound of running water behind the Victorian wainscoting. Henry was in the shower, but it was the shuffling noises from the last door to her left that kept her attention. The wind outside grew stronger as she walked along the carpet in the centre of the hall, blowing hard against the set of French glass doors that led outside to the top balcony. She thought about checking to make sure the wind wasn't damaging anything, and chastised herself for taking her mind off the real problem.

Amelia peeked in through a small gap in the doorway outside one of the bedrooms. Inside, Chad sat on his bed facing away from the door, head in hands, running his fingers through his shaggy hair. Eighteen was a hard age. No longer a child and barely and adult, and to Amelia, way too young to be going to university in the fall. Her heart ached as he stood and paced back and forth, shaking and wringing out his hands and exhaling deeply.

She knocked. "Chad? Can I come in?"

He jerked around and headed for the door. He moved faster than she anticipated, and she was startled by his sudden appearance in the doorway. He didn't say anything, just stared down at her, a blank look on his face. His eyes were black pools with any hint of colour absorbed by the orbs of his pupils. Dread consumed her and her heart raced as she felt the full weight of his glare. Then he turned and walked away, allowing the door to drift open.

Amelia braced herself against the doorframe, feeling lightheaded and drained.

"Is everything all right?" she asked, and stepped cautiously into his room. The dim lighting made it hard to focus, and the shadows on the walls seemed to stretch out to touch her.

"Why wouldn't it be?" he asked, flopping himself down on the bed.

She took a few steps closer. "I was in the kitchen and could hear you pacing. I thought maybe there was something wrong."

He looked over his shoulder at her. "Nothing's wrong."

"There has to be some reason you're wearing a hole in the floor in your room. Is it about these extra classes your taking? You know, you don't have to take them all at once. I'm sure the university would—"

"There's nothing wrong, all right?" Chad got up from the bed and stood in front of his bedroom window.

She went to his side, gently placing her hand on his shoulder. "No, it's not all right."

Chad shook her hand off and faced her. His eyes were still pools of black, darker than anything she'd ever seen, and she was unable to look away. Amelia felt her forehead throb as the light around her began to dim. Her stomach heaved slightly, and she forced herself to take a few steps back.

Chad closed his eyes and slowly opened them again. "I'm telling you. There is nothing wrong." His tone was intimidating.

Amelia took a few more steps back. She'd never seen him in such a dark mood and wasn't quite sure what to make of it. A tingling sensation shot up her spine as the small hairs on the back of her neck stood on end, and she could barely contain a sudden urge to flee from the room.

"Fine," she said, turning quickly toward the door. "But if you want to talk, you know where I am."

She was inches away from the entrance when he called to her. "Mom, wait. I'm sorry. I didn't mean to snap at you like that."

Amelia took a deep breath, steadying herself before turning back around. His mood felt lighter and the shadows stayed confined, but she couldn't shake her fear, and she certainly didn't want it to show. "That's all right. I shouldn't have pushed you." She moved toward him. "If you say nothing is wrong, then nothing is wrong. I'll take your word for it, but you have to understand; I'm your mother. I'm only trying to help."

He smiled. "I know. You're just doing your mom-thing. I get it."

She walked to his bed, sat down, and then patted the spot next to her.

"Yeah," he said, taking her invitation, "maybe there is something going on." He lifted his head and smiled at her. "But you need to let me figure out how to deal with it on my own first."

"I know." She wrapped her arms around him and squeezed. "Old habits are hard to break." She held him at arm's length, brushing a few strands of wayward hair out of his eyes. "You are so much like your father, and I know you'll grow into a strong man, just like him." Amelia stood and headed toward the door. "Just do me a favour?"

"Sure, what?"

"When you figure out what's wrong, let me know. Maybe I can use it for future reference with your brothers."

His smile washed away her guilt. "No problem. You'll be the first."

She walked back into the hall and closed the door. She felt lighter, but her maternal instincts wouldn't allow her to let go of her worry. Not just yet. Chad was right; whatever was causing him to wear down his carpet was something he had to figure out for himself. He was an adult now, and she would have to reign in the familiar twinge of motherhood that gnawed at her conscience. At least she still had the other two for a while longer.

"Dammit!"

Henry's agitated voice quickly dampened her mood. He was in their bedroom now, out of the shower, and apparently still not happy.

She heard the touch-tone of his cell phone, and the long input of numbers. Her curiosity was piqued. That many digits couldn't be a local call. She stepped to the other side of the hall, bracing herself up against the doorframe, her right ear just inches from the wood-stained door. Amelia knew she shouldn't listen in, but this could be a rare look into his work, and she wouldn't mind knowing a bit more. Especially if it involved that sultry voice she heard earlier.

"Yeah, Lyla, it's me." Henry sounded apprehensive. "I can't wait until Friday to see you again. I have to see you right away. Call me when you get this message."

Amelia was taken aback. She knew the names of all the women Henry worked with. This one was new. Then the thought tugged at her; what was he doing meeting up with her on Friday?

She smoothed back a few stray hairs before grabbing a hold of the doorknob. Henry stood near the picture window that overlooked the side yard, a towel wrapped around his lower half. He still held the phone in his hand and didn't flinch as she entered the room.

She walked over to their bathroom and began straightening things up. "Calling someone?"

"Yeah, just Ben from work," he replied, his voice calm. "I was reminding him to bring the Matterson files with him on Friday."

Amelia's heart skipped. She knew Ben well enough to know his secretary's name wasn't Lyla. "What's happening Friday?"

"What are you talking about?" he asked. "You know what Friday is."

She hesitated for a moment. "I know it's our son's birthday."

"Yeah, that, but it's also that big corporate meeting." He was standing right behind her now. The faint musky scent from his soap gently hung in the air around her. It was times like this she found him irresistible.

Yet she frowned. "Meeting?"

"Don't tell me you forgot," he said. "I told you about this weeks ago. George Matterson's company is being sued by some lowlife, and our firm is representing him. We're having a big meeting this weekend to put our case together."

Amelia's mind was blank.

Henry sighed. "How could you forget?" He was more shocked than angry as he placed his brush down on the counter, and used his fingers to continue grooming. "You chewed me out for two hours when I told you, remember? Kept going on about how I put work ahead of family, and how I'm never home anymore for special occasions." He stopped fussing with his hair and put his hands on his hips. "You made me call Ben back

11

and tell him that I'd meet him in the hotel bar instead of the train station, so I could be here to celebrate Chad's birthday."

Her brow softened as the full memory of their argument floated back into her mind, and she smiled, remembering her victory. "Oh yeah, that's right."

"It's the reason I invited Jespersen and the others to Chad's party."

"I wish you weren't going." She turned around and faced him, playing with a few strands of his black hair that fell out of place. She put her arms around his waist, and leaned her head against his chest. Maybe this Lyla person had something to do with his case. After all, there was so much about his job she didn't know.

"I know," he said, and wrapped his arms tightly around her shoulders. "But this is my job, and considering I'm screwed for that partnership, I have to do this."

"But the whole weekend?"

He broke off the embrace and walked back out into their bedroom. "Actually, I may need to stay a few days longer than I originally thought."

"How much longer?"

"I don't know." He walked into their shared closet. "Probably as long as they need me."

Amelia strolled to the bed. "As long as this helps you, I don't mind," she said, sitting on the edge. "But I don't like the way they treat you. You were promised that partnership. Faunt guaranteed it. Sometimes I wonder if you should find another firm to work for."

"Are you kidding?" Amelia jumped at his harsh tone as he stormed out of the closet. "Faunt Legal is the best law office in the country. I've put all my energy into building a career with these people, and you want me to walk away?"

His eyes were black, peering at her in disgust. Another wave of fear wash over her as the room grew dark. She'd never seen him so angry before, and she felt the familiar urge to leave. Quickly.

Shaken, she swallowed a few times before speaking. "I'm just saying, it doesn't seem like Faunt respects you. To promise you something like that, then take it away and give it to his nephew, doesn't sound very—"

"Well thank you, but I don't want your opinion." He walked back into the closet, and the air in the room lightened. "That partnership is mine and no little puss-fucker of a nephew is going to stand in my way." He strolled out wearing casual clothing. Amelia felt her stomach twist into knots as he walked over and kissed her gently on the forehead. "Now stop worrying. Let me take care of it."

She stood and hurried toward the door, trying to keep her anxiety from showing. "If you're sure about this," she said, taking a quick glance back before walking into the hall.

"Don't worry," he smiled. "Come Monday everything will be the way it's supposed to be."

Amelia stepped out into the hall, struggling to keep her anxiety under control. She leaned up against the far wall and took a deep breath, holding it for several seconds before releasing.

Something *really* wasn't right.

2

The sound of rock music assaulted Amelia's senses early the next morning, as her alarm clock spewed the raunchy on-air personalities of the local radio station. A loud belch from the speaker made her smile as she got out of bed and headed toward the bathroom. Henry was already gone. A hint of his aftershave still hung in the air, mixed with the musky smell of his shower gel. Images of him draped in only a towel floated through her mind. As did his obvious lie.

All through breakfast, it gnawed at her. She burnt the twin's toast, wondering about this woman being brought in for the big meeting. Why didn't Henry tell her? She ignored their grumble about the burnt food as tightness grew in her throat. Maybe there was something going on that Henry didn't want her to know about.

She drove into the subdivision just north of Calgary, to the small bookstore where she worked. Amelia tried again to push the weird events from her mind, hoping to lose herself in the dimly lit aisles of new and used books, but the store was quieter than usual, and categorizing new arrivals on how to save your relationship brought her mind back to Henry's lie.

How did he know her? How did he meet her? Amelia found herself entertaining the thought that her husband could have a whole other life. *Did they meet in some lurid bar or other hangout?* He'd been pretty wild back in their college days: prone to spontaneous behaviour. A trait she found attractive right from the beginning. Amelia shook her head. All this guessing was putting thoughts into her head. Henry might have been a lot of things, but a cheater wasn't one of them.

The tinny sound of the gold doorbell alerted her to a new customer.

She smoothed back any strands of misplaced hair and stepped out into an open area of the bookstore. A young man cautiously walked through the entrance. His appearance took Amelia by surprise. Vagrant was not a fashion style in this area. He must be from the city. Amelia frowned. Why would he be here? The big chain stores in the city had a wider array of stock than she did.

She kept a close eye on him as he walked through the store. "Can I help you?"

His head turned in her direction and his eyes gave her a quick once-over. "Do you have any books on paranormal occurrences?" he asked, taking a few steps toward her.

The backlighting from a nearby window shadowed his face and kept Amelia from getting a good look at his features. "No, I don't think so." She squinted, trying to get a better look. "But we do have a wide selection of classic ghost stories."

The young man changed direction and walked up to the counter. Away from the sunlight, he looked a few years older than Chad, with the same shaggy haircut. The few days' growth of facial hair was the same colour as on his head. "I don't want stories," he said. His eyes focused directly into hers when he spoke. His lip curling into a slight sneer. "I was looking for documentation of the real thing. Not make-believe."

"This is a small, privately owned store, sir." Amelia hurried toward the counter. "I don't think you're going to find what you're looking for here. Sorry."

"What about the occult? Have any books on that?"

Amelia stood her ground. "No. We don't."

His brow furrowed. "But you haven't looked. How do you know if you haven't looked?"

"I work here. I know what we have and what we don't." She paused, trying to keep her calm. "Like I said, this is a small store, and our inventory is just as small. Might I suggest you visit one of the big chain stores? They might have what you're looking for."

The young man walked away. Amelia relaxed her stance but wasn't completely relieved until she heard the familiar metallic tinkling. She watched him through the storefront windows as he crossed the street and entered a coffee shop. She was accustomed to strange requests, but they were never confrontational.

Amelia picked up a magazine from the counter and realized her preoccupation with Henry was gone. For what it was worth, the stranger's distraction forced her to focus on something else, and she found herself grateful for the short, albeit odd, interaction.

With Henry's lie no longer monopolizing her thoughts, Amelia went back to work, stocking inventory and categorizing the new periodicals. It was several hours later when her boss arrived, carrying two large coffees from the shop across the street.

Amelia wanted to be Leslie Carmichael. Strong, independent, and more confident than Amelia could ever hope to be. They'd been friends since college, and Amelia was positive Leslie was meant to be tall, blonde, and beautiful, no matter what her age.

"So," Leslie said, handing the coffees to Amelia as she walked past. "Have you figured out who this Lyla woman is yet?"

Amelia took a sip from one cup and put the other on the counter. She forgot she'd told her about her eavesdropping. "Why do you think I'd be doing that?"

Leslie walked into a back room, re-emerging a few moments later minus her jacket. "We've been friends long enough for me to know how you think, Amelia Saint." Leslie reached for Amelia's hand. A hint of expensive perfume drifted along with her. "You've been wandering around here, racking your brain, trying to figure out who this person is." Her smile was warm and sympathetic. "And I don't blame you. I'd be doing the exact same thing if I were in your shoes."

Amelia slumped forward. "I don't get it. Why would he lie to me about a phone call? I'm not the jealous type. If this Lyla person is from his office, why doesn't he say so instead of lying and saying it was someone else?"

Leslie crossed her arms. "It can only mean one thing. He's cheating on you."

Amelia was stunned. "I don't buy that. If there was something . . ."she stammered, feeling a bit embarrassed as she searched for the right word, "*wrong* with our marriage, I think I would know it."

"Don't be too sure. My sister didn't know her husband was cheating on her until he walked out the door."

Amelia shook her head. "I know Henry. There's no way he would cheat on me. It's just not like him."

Leslie walked behind the counter. "The wives are always the last to know." She stopped and put her hands on her hips. "I can give you the name of my sister's divorce lawyer if you want. By the time he's finished with Henry, that bastard will wish he'd kept his dick in his pants."

Amelia tried to smile, but Chad's hurtful comments from the night before drifted back to her. Did he know something she didn't?

"He's not cheating." She took a sip of her coffee, not completely convinced by her own words. "There has to be another reason why he's keeping this from me."

"Well, whatever it is, it can't be good." Leslie looked up from the cash register. It's pretty slow today. Take the rest of the day off."

"Are you sure?"

"Go home, take a hot bath and relax. If you say Henry isn't cheating, then you have nothing to worry about, right?"

"I do have a few things I want to pick up for Chad's birthday."

Leslie motioned to the storefront. "Go. I can handle things here."

Driving to the store, Amelia's thoughts were occupied with divorce lawyers and Henry's alleged cheating. Leslie was sour on men even on a good day, and she never liked Henry. Not even when they were in college. Amelia giggled to herself as she pulled into the store parking lot. This whole thing must have solidified her hatred for the man.

The parking lot was relatively empty, and she found a spot close to the entrance. The sun finally decided to peek out from between the clouds, bringing ample warmth with a touch of humidity. The seasonal weather would go a long way in replenishing the ornamental trees that were injured in the freak windstorm.

Amelia walked into the store, swiping the arm of a passerby with her purse. "Oh, I'm sorry," she said, embarrassed at her clumsiness. It took her a moment to realize it was the young man from the bookstore.

"That's all right, no harm done," he said, and his face lit up. "Hey, you're the lady from the bookstore."

It was nice to see he wasn't all scowls and sarcasm. "Yes," she said, returning his smile. "Sorry we didn't have what you were looking for."

"Please, I should be the one to apologize. I shouldn't have been so rude."

"Don't worry about it. It happens all the time." Actually, it didn't, but after seeing he could be civilized, Amelia felt bad for her own standoffish behaviour.

"I thought Calgary was a friendly city." he chuckled. "Why do I find that hard to believe?"

"You'd be surprised at the attitude around here. Especially toward strangers."

He cocked his head to one side, giving her a lopsided grin. "Funny, I guess people are skeptics no matter where they're from." He gave a small nod. "Take care."

Amelia nodded politely and walked into the store. After chatting with several acquaintances, she headed to the baking goods and loaded up her small basket. She loved creating homemade desserts for her family, especially for their birthdays, and as she glanced over the supply of baking goods, it suddenly dawned on her she didn't have too many more opportunities. Again, the idea of Henry cheating came to mind, and she cursed herself for ever listening in on his conversation. Life would have been so much simpler if she'd just minded her own business.

She crisscrossed the store, her small red basket almost overflowing by the time she reached the checkout. The elderly man by the register smiled; his face was lost behind a bushy beard and moustache. Amelia smiled politely and waited as he tallied up her items.

"Mrs. Saint?"

Amelia turned toward the unfamiliar male voice. The man was shorter than her, with a little too much padding around the middle. His wrinkled face and dark receding hairline hinted of familiarity, but she couldn't quite put her finger on where she knew him.

She frowned. "Yes?"

His wide grin did little to jog her memory. "You don't remember me. I'm Father George, from Holy Sacrament church."

Memories flashed through Amelia's mind the old church down the road, and the few Sunday masses they'd attended.

Her face went warm with embarrassment. "Ah yes, Father George, now I remember you. How are you doing?"

The priest nodded politely. "Oh, can't complain. Wouldn't do any good if I did." He put the few items he had on the counter. "I take it you're making a cake."

"Yes, I am." There was a hint of pride in her voice. "For my oldest, Chad. It's his birthday this Friday, so I thought I'd do something special."

"Homemade cakes are always the best. Made with the one special ingredient. Love."

Amelia smiled at the corny phrase, but something about it warmed her heart.

"I'm sorry you stopped coming to church," he said. "It was so nice to see your whole family attending mass."

"I know, and I'm sorry." She opened her purse and rummaged through the contents looking for her wallet. "I tried to get them to go more, but they just don't have their hearts in it."

"Don't apologize," Father George said. "Church just isn't the 'in' thing to do, nowadays. Kids are more interested in their gadgets and games than sitting to listen to the Word of God."

She stopped rummaging and looked up at the blank stare of the store clerk. "I don't have my wallet on me." Then it dawned on her. "I left it at home on the front desk when I cleaned out my purse this morning."

"No problem, Amelia." The clerk chuckled. A wide grin appeared from under a thick, greying beard. He pushed the bag of groceries to the far end of the counter. "I'll just leave them here if you want to go back and get it."

"Are you sure it's not a problem?"

The old clerk shook his head. "Nah, no problem."

Amelia bid the priest a quick farewell, then hurried out of the store. Her face flushed from embarrassment.

She got into the car and started the engine. Shifting the car into gear, she drove onto the road and noticed the same young man from the bookstore standing on the opposite side of the street. This time, he wasn't alone. An older man with a ponytail stood next to him outside the coffee shop. They turned toward her and watched as she drove past them on the street. Amelia took a quick glance in her rearview mirror, and was stunned to see them still watching her car. There was something cold and calculating about the way they stared, and she tried hard not to look back.

First, Henry's possible infidelity, now creepy stalkers. This week couldn't end fast enough.

She tapped her finger rhythmically on the steering wheel. What would she do if Henry's indiscretion were true? Would she become one of those obsessed divorcées who stalk their exes? She'd watched several TV movies of the week about women getting even with their ex-husbands and killing them. Images of her killing Henry in all different ways began to flow through her mind. Shooting, stabbing, choking: all of them would do the trick, but she couldn't figure out which one would be the best way to make it look like an accident. The streetlight ahead turned red. Amelia slammed on the brakes, skidding to a stop just before the intersection. Then it hit her. Use the car as the weapon! She could always say it was an accident; she didn't notice him standing behind the car when she went to back up. Yet that wouldn't explain why she'd run over him several more times.

Amelia let out a disgusted sigh and rested her forehead on the steering wheel. This was getting out of hand. Here she was, sitting in her minivan trying to determine the best way to kill her husband, in retaliation for an affair he may or may not be having.

The light turned green, and she decided the best way to deal with this was to tell Henry what she'd overheard. That way he could either come clean about the affair, or he could explain to her who this Lyla was, and why he was so anxious to see her.

She reconciled her plan of action as she pulled into the driveway of her home. One of the garage doors was open, Henry's car parked inside. He was supposed to be at work. He told her he was going to be late tonight to make up for leaving early tomorrow. So why was he home?

She got out of the car and walked to the front of the house. With each step, a nauseous sensation took hold as her heart beat rapidly in her chest. The air blew stronger, felt cooler than a few moments ago, and as she approached the front door, the sunlight disappeared, draining everything around her of colour.

A shiver up her spine caused her to hesitate. Everything felt out of place, ominous, and the recurring sensation to flee was growing. She turned the key in the lock and the sensations grew stronger, but this time, there was the additional feeling she was being watched. Amelia scanned the trees and bushes blowing in the breeze. The rustling leaves added to her paranoia, and she turned the key and quietly slipped inside.

The house was still. With Henry home, Amelia assumed the television would be on or at least the stereo. Sometimes he would listen to music to ease away the stress, but there was nothing, only the ticking of the grandfather clock sitting in the front hall next to the writing desk. Which, to her relief, still had her wallet sitting on top.

She walked to the desk and reached for her wallet, checking to make sure there was money inside. She didn't need another embarrassing moment.

The phone rang, and she jumped. She reached for the receiver, her heart pounding in her throat.

Henry answered first. "Hello?"

"You called?" The female voice was sultry and deep. Amelia recognized it immediately as the female voice in the background from his call to her the day before.

"Yeah, what took you so long?" Henry's abruptness caught her off guard. "And why are you calling the house? A little risky, don't you think? My cell number is more private."

Lying. Private phone calls. Maybe Leslie was right.

"Events are unfolding quickly. Energy is building around you and will interfere with contacting you any other way."

Energy? What events?

"Well you took your sweet time getting back to me. Considering what I'm giving you, I expect you to get in touch with me a little quicker."

Typical Henry, always demanding. Amelia frowned. What was he giving her? A recommendation? A job? What did Henry have that she could possibly want?

"So, what is so important that it could not wait?" the woman asked. "Have the changes begun?"

Changes? What changes?

"I don't know," Henry said. "Chad's a teenager. He's moody and angry to start with."

Why was Henry talking about Chad? Despite Amelia's anger in herself for listening on his private conversation the last time, her curiosity now was too strong to hang up.

"You should already begin to see subtle changes with him," Lyla continued. "The closer to his birth time, the more he will be affected."

"He was born about ten thirty at night," Henry said. "Will it take over here? My wife is planning a big party for him, and there'll be too many witnesses."

"Not likely," she said matter-of-factly. "The first instinct after Korthos has taken over, will be seek us out. From there, we will instruct him on the ritual to make the transformation complete."

"Why behind our house?"

"Would you prefer it done in the middle of the street?"

"I'd prefer it not to be done anywhere near the property." He sounded annoyed. "There's going to be enough eyes watching us after I report him missing. Last thing I need are the cops finding evidence of a Satanic ritual close to my backyard."

Amelia's chest contracted so hard it felt as though the air was ripped from her lungs. She lowered the handset to the base, and then paused. If she hung up, they'd hear and know she'd overheard their conversation. Quickly, she put the phone back up to her ear.

Lyla's voice was severe. "The longer we wait, the weaker the connection will become."

"Yeah, about that. There's a snag."

"What kind of snag?"

"The kind that will keep me from that partnership," he said. "I've been passed over for the promotion. The old bastard is giving it to his nephew."

"You claimed there were no others in a position for him to promote."

"Yeah, that's what I thought too, but the bastard wants to keep it in the family."

"This will not do. You need to deal with it."

"And just how the hell am I supposed to do that? I can't change Faunt's mind on this. I don't have that kind of power."

There was a long pause. "How can I help?"

"The nephew has to be taken care of."

Amelia went cold. This wasn't her husband. This was some stranger with Henry's voice.

"How should it be done?"

"I don't know, but don't kill him." There was a slight compassion to his tone. "His family is too powerful, and any investigation could put the spotlight on me. Whatever you do, just make sure nothing touches me."

"As you wish."

"Wait!" There was an urgency to his tone that sent a shiver through her. "What about payment? Is this going to cost me another deal? Because I still have the twins."

The sultry tone of Lyla's voice vanished. "No. The agreement was for you to acquire control of Faunt & Associates, in exchange for the soul of your firstborn. You will need your twin boys for the next step."

Amelia's breath caught in her throat. Panic gripped at the thought her child was in danger. Frantically, she scanned the nearby rooms, looking to see if Henry was using a downstairs extension.

"Fine. Whatever. Just make sure none of this can be traced back to me."

"I will get back to you with the details."

"Make it quicker this time."

There was a click as Henry hung up the phone. Only when the dial tone returned did Amelia put down her receiver. Her mind was a fog. Numb, she leaned up against the desk, unsure of how to process what she just heard. It didn't seem real. She couldn't have heard them properly. The sanity of her world was crashing around her. Henry wasn't cheating, he wasn't even going through a midlife crisis. He was involved in something she couldn't take lightly. Not when he involved their children.

She clamped one hand over her mouth to contain her anxiety. Her mind raced as she desperately tried to focus on what to do. Should she run to the high school and pull the kids out of class, but then what? Put her children in danger by returning home to the arms of a madman?

She glanced at the grandfather clock. If she hurried, she could get to the school and pick up the boys before they got on the bus home. Amelia grabbed her wallet. There was a motel just down the road. She and the boys could stay there until she figured out what to do next.

The sound of running water and a gentle thud from the pipes indicated Henry was taking a shower. He hadn't noticed she was home. She turned to leave, but paused and looked down at her wallet. Henry could have seen it already, and if she took it, he would know she'd been there. Her hands shook as she removed several bills, her credit card and driver's license, and then carefully placed the wallet back in the same place. Keeping a wary eye on the second floor landing, Amelia hurried to the front door.

***

Amelia sat in the van, her hands trembling as she rubbed her thumbnail against her lower lip. She scanned the faces coming toward her. Her eyes darted between the multitudes of blond to dark-haired teens that shuffled into waiting school buses. Her anxiety over the welfare of her children climbed to almost hysterical proportions, until the familiar flash of Morgan's gold and green jacket steadied her nerves.

She beeped the horn, catching his attention and motioned him toward the vehicle.

"What are you doing?" Morgan asked, walking up to her window. "You never pick us up."

She raced through possible stories as to why she was here. None of them seemed to convey the urgency she was looking for. She forced a smile. "I got off work early and I thought you guys would appreciate the ride home instead of taking the bus."

"But I just called home," he said. "I told Dad I was going to Frankie's house to practice for the soccer game next week."

A part of her felt relieved. She could always pick him up later, when she had a better idea of what to do. "All right, that's fine, but what about your brothers? Where are they?"

Morgan shrugged. "I don't know. I think I saw Chad hanging with Tina." He turned and looked down the road. "See, there he is."

Amelia focused on the small group of teens at the far end of the street. Chad was in the middle, with several young girls hanging on his side. She smiled as she watched them laugh and stumble around. He didn't look angry at all.

"Hi Mom."

Liam's voice caused her to jump. The door on the passenger side opened and Liam threw his knapsack on the floor. "You're here to pick us up, right?"

Amelia smiled. "Yes, I am."

"Cool. You *never* pick us up."

Amelia turned back to Morgan. "So you're going to Frankie's then?"

"Yeah."

"Well, you can stay for supper if you're invited."

Morgan's eyes went wide. "Really?"

Amelia pursed her lips. At his friend's house, he'd be safe. At least he wasn't home with his father. "But only if you're invited. Understand."

A wide grin broke across Morgan's face. "You're awesome. Thanks!"

She watched him run down the road, and meet up with a small group of kids that looked to be the same age. She clenched her jaw to keep her emotions in check and then reached for the ignition. She pulled her sunglasses down over her eyes. She could feel them growing warm with tears.

"Mom, what's wrong?"

Amelia could see him looking at her from the corner of her eye. "Nothing's wrong. Why would you say that?"

He looked away from her. "The last time you picked us up was when you came back from the vet when Bucky died."

"Don't worry. No one died. It's like I said, I was finished early and thought I would pick you all up."

Liam didn't respond as she pulled away from the curb and drove slowly down the street. She stopped once they were closer to Chad and his friends. Liam waved and rolled down his window as his older brother walked to the vehicle.

Chad smiled. "This is different."

"Yeah, I thought I'd be nice for a change and drive you all home."

"I'm not going home," Chad said, giving his friends a quick glance. "Tina's invited me over to her place. Thought I would hang out with them for a while."

Amelia felt relieved and anxious at the same time. "Does your father know?"

Chad gave her a sarcastic look. "Right, like I tell him everything I do."

"So why haven't I gotten a cell call yet?" Amelia frowned. "Just because you're turning eighteen doesn't mean you can stop letting me know where you are."

A lopsided grin crossed his face. "Well, now you know."

He walked back over to his friends, giving her a quick wave goodbye. Amelia watched him as the gang headed down the street. She felt a surge of confidence. There was no way Chad was going to go anywhere with his father. No matter what Henry thought.

She relaxed into her seat as they drove off then took a quick look at Liam. "Why don't you and I go out for supper tonight?"

Liam raised his eyebrows. "What about Dad?"

Amelia smiled. "He's had dinner out without us enough times. It's our turn now."

***

Supper of restaurant pizza and pop went quickly and took up half of the money she'd grabbed from her wallet. Driving back to the village, Amelia scanned the odd motels for vacancies, but the ones with rooms available didn't look all that appealing, or maybe it was because she still couldn't believe what she'd heard. She went over the conversation again in her mind. Satanic rituals? She didn't think Henry even believed this stuff, let alone be involved with it. Leslie was right about one thing, she didn't know her husband like she thought she did. Henry was delusional, mentally unstable, and she wasn't about to have her children around someone like that, even if he was their father. This was insane, and she wanted no part of it. If she had to, she'd call the cops.

It was late in the evening when she pulled into a paved driveway next to a red bricked house. The sun was barely above the horizon and shone a deep red over the tree tops, casting long shadows across the ground. She sat in her car with the engine running, waiting for Liam to return, when something moving in the bushes caught her attention. She focused on the mint-green leaves as they moved unnaturally in the breeze. Eyes peered through the bush, red and ominous, focused solely on her. Her breath came in shallow gulps as she sat frozen, transfixed on the stare. Condensation fogged up her side of the windshield as the air grew steadily cooler.

Liam's sudden appearance from a side door of the house was enough of a distraction to pull her attention away—but he was alone. She took a second glance at the bushes as he climbed back into the car and fastened his seatbelt.

"Where's your brother?"

"Frankie said he went home about a half hour ago." He frowned at her. "Did you have the air conditioner on?"

From out of the bushes, a calico coloured cat jumped onto the hood of the van. Startled, Amelia slammed the car into reverse and sped out of the driveway.

"Mom, slow down!" Liam braced himself against the door. "It's just a cat!"

She took the corner at the end of the street a little too close, squealing the tires as the vehicle rounded the curb. The minivan hit the driveway of their house, and Amelia sped up the cobblestone brickwork. She squinted at their two-car garage. Henry's Porsche convertible was gone.

Liam opened his car door. "And I thought Chad was a crazy driver."

A dull flickering of the television in the family room shone through the kitchen window as she reached the back step. She watched Morgan through the kitchen nook window, relieved that he was sitting on the couch playing a video game. Her hands were still trembling as Liam opened the mud room door, and she tried to steady them as she followed in behind.

"Hi, Morgan," she called out. "Did you have any supper?"

She walked into the kitchen. Scattered across the counter were bags of chips, several boxes of cookies, and two open bottles of soda. That answered her question. Liam immediately became enthralled with the game, dropped his knapsack on the floor, and went to the couch.

"Hey, Mom," Morgan said, turning around and smiling at her. "Dad's gone."

Amelia let out a sigh. "Did he say where?"

"I don't know." Morgan turned back to his game. "He was gone when I got home. He left a note on the counter, though."

"Okay, thanks."

She picked up the note and gave it a quick once-over. He'd be gone until late tomorrow afternoon. Last minute work things, but he would be back in time for the party.

We're not going to be here.

Amelia headed to the front hall, trying to anticipate their questions when she told them they were spending the night at a motel. Should she tell them about the conversation between Henry and Lyla? Was telling them even a viable option? Morgan wouldn't believe her, and it would only scare Liam. As for Chad, well, she wasn't sure what he would say.

The foyer was dark with only the light from the kitchen shining outward. The front window above the door held a perfect view of an almost full moon, as the pale light reflected on the family pictures hanging on the wall. Amelia took her time as she walked up the stairs, tracing her finger along the outline of smiling faces. A stray tear tricked down her face as she recalled the day each picture was taken. Her whole life was here, wrapped up in this house. Leaving this place would be the hardest thing she'd ever done.

A cool breeze swept down the hall from the partly opened balcony doors on the second floor. The gentle pounding of the open door against its mate shifted her attention away from her sorrow. A silhouette stood on the back balcony, leaning against the railing, facing the woods behind their house.

Amelia walked toward the glass doors. "Chad?"

A sudden gust pushed the door wide open, sending chills across her body. The balcony was bathed in the final crimson rays of sunlight as she stepped out onto the porch. The figure was tall and lean, and for a brief moment, in this lighting, Amelia thought it was Henry.

"Chad?"

He turned to face her. "Hi. You just get home?"

"Yeah. I decided to take Liam out for pizza." She stepped up next to him. "What are you doing?"

"Just thinking."

She smiled and brushed a few strands of his hair out of his eyes. "About what?"

Chad kept quiet as he slumped over the railing and looked out over the backyard.

Amelia watched him, concerned. "Something is bothering you?"

"A little."

"Want to talk about it?"

He straightened up, opened his mouth a few times but didn't speak, as though he were unsure of his words, then he slumped forward again. "Tina invited me to sleep over at her house after my party tomorrow night."

Amelia's expression was blank. The intimacy of his statement caught her off guard. "Well," she paused for a moment and tried to think of something that didn't sound like a lecture, "What do you want to do?"

"I don't know, she's a nice girl and all, and I like her, but—"

"Then tell her how you feel."

"I can't. I don't like her in *that* way."

Amelia smiled. The angst of young love.

"Are you sure? You've spent a lot of time over at her house, and I'd hate to think you were leading her on."

He turned to her. "That's just it. I wasn't there to see her."

Amelia was confused. "Then why did you go over every time she called?"

Chad shuffled in place a bit, clearly struggling with an internal conflict. "I didn't go over to see her. I went over to see . . . her brother."

At first his words didn't register. Then slowly, as she stared into the awkward expression on her son's face, did the full meaning of his words sink in.

Amelia raised her eyebrows in astonishment. "Oh."

Chad stuffed his hands into the front pocket of his pants. "Oh, you're okay with that, or oh, you've just ruined my life?"

Amelia turned toward the railing. The backyard was completely awash in moonlight. She was unsure what to say next—afraid her words would come out wrong and hurt him. Chad's revelation was a shock, yes, and it would probably take some time for her to get used to seeing him with males, but truthfully, she didn't feel any differently toward him. If anything, she felt more protective and even a bit better about their relationship. He felt comfortable enough to come out and tell her, especially after he was so adamant there was nothing wrong the night before.

Amelia smiled at him. "How about 'Oh, I still love you no matter what.'?"

Chad exhaled deeply, nodding. "Okay."

"Is this what was bothering you last night?" she asked.

"A little," he said, leaning against the railing. "She was one of the first people I met when we moved here. She's my best friend, but that's all she is to me, a friend."

"I take it she doesn't know you're . . ." Amelia let her voice trail off.

"Gay? No," he said. "Hell, I didn't even figure it out until last summer."

She looked out into the darkness of the woods, trying to find the right words. "I would talk to her," she said. "Tell her how you feel. She might not like it at first, especially if you tell her you'd rather date her brother, but if she's any kind of a friend, she'll understand."

A wide grin broke across his face, and he gave her a quick bear hug. "Thanks, Mom."

She put her ear to his chest and listened to his heart beating under his clothing. Tears began to build in her eyes, and she pulled back, brushing them away. "You're welcome."

Amelia walked toward the house; a pang of guilt began to surface. Of all the weekends for their world to fall apart, it would be this one.

She reached the glass doors and decided Chad should know everything. After all, this involved him most of all, and she could confide in him about the twins' reaction. She paused, and turned to him.

A dark glow shimmered around Chad as his face melted and twisted into a grotesque distortion of itself. Her body went cold as his flesh bubbled and peeled back the hair from his skull, revealing a second face that leered at her from the side of his head. The air cooled to freezing as its black eyes focused on her, and it hissed with a forked tongue. She gasped and reached to steady herself against the door, but with a blink, everything returned to normal.

Chad snapped his head around. "Mom?"

Horrified, she hurried inside and ran down the hall, stopping just before the staircase, and leaned against the wood railing. Her body trembled and her heart pounded as she tried to convince herself what she saw was a trick caused by the moonlight.

Amelia raised her head and stared out the huge picture window above the front door. She felt the air around her grow incredibly cold again, as the wind picked up and blew strongly through the leaves on the trees, bending them back, forcing a low whistle through the dim foyer. There were people standing on the other side of the street under one of the streetlamps. She squinted to get a better look. It was the young man from the bookstore and his friend. Both locked in a hard gaze directed at her home.

"Mom!" Chad's quick footsteps came running up behind her. "You're shaking. What's wrong?"

She looked up at him, scanning his face for some evidence of what she saw, but to her relief, found nothing. "I'm fine," she said. "But call the police. I think those people are following me."

Chad looked past her and frowned. "What people?"

Amelia turned to point, but the street was empty, and she saw no sign of them anywhere within her view.

"Mom, are you all right?"

Amelia brought her hand up to her forehead, rubbing the worry lines with her fingers. "I just saw them. They were standing right across the street."

She felt Chad's arms encircle her shoulders. "I think you should go lie down."

Amelia stepped away from the railing and wrapped her arms tight around her body. A chill ran through her as she contemplated the thought that maybe Henry's plans were real.

3

Amelia turned and headed toward the balcony doors. Her conversation with Chad wasn't as revealing as she'd hoped. Something else was bothering him; she could see it in his eyes. It wasn't just this new understanding and acceptance of his sexuality. There was something else hidden just below the surface. She could feel it there ... waiting ...

She paused and then turned back. A dark crimson aura shimmered around Chad as his face melted and twisted into a grotesque distortion of itself. His flesh bubbled and peeled back the hair from his skull, revealing a second face that leered at her from the side of his head. The air cooled to freezing as its black eyes focused on her, and it hissed with a forked tongue. She gasped and reached to steady herself against the door.

Chad's head turned toward her. "Hello, Mother. Still love me now?"

Amelia bolted upright in bed gasping for air. Her heart raced as the images of a grotesque creature quickly faded from her mind, but the fear remained. Her hands trembled as she wiped the sweat away from her brow. This was more than a dream. It felt too real.

She lay on her back staring up at the ceiling. Her eyes felt puffy and swollen, and her body ached from lack of sleep. At least the morning brought an end to her nightmares, and she was grateful to find herself alone. With everything she'd seen and heard in the last twenty-four hours, it would be difficult to keep her feelings buried, and the last thing she wanted was for Henry to suspect anything.

She sat back up and looked at the alarm clock. Ten past eight. She threw back the covers and grabbed her housecoat, angry now that her alarm didn't go off.

Amelia walked into the kitchen just as the twins were shuffling through the mud room door.

"Wait! Where are you going?"

"To school," Morgan said, as he held the door open for his twin. "Where do you think?"

She glanced at Chad as he sauntered past. "Why didn't you come and get me, or wake me up?"

"Don't worry about it. I gave the little pukes breakfast."

His sarcastic look only fueled her anger. "Don't call them that."

"Okay, relax, it was just a joke." Chad tilted his head to one side. "Are you all right?"

Amelia didn't know what to say. Her dreams of his grotesque form flashed through her mind. She opened her mouth to speak, but caught herself. Should she tell him what she overheard? Would he believe her? Did she believe it? This whole situation still felt all too surreal.

Morgan slumped in frustration. "Chad, are you coming?"

"Go on, I'll catch up." He looked back at his mother and his expression softened. "You know, you were pretty freaked last night. I don't have to go to school," he said, as Morgan let the door slam behind him. "I can stay here until you're feeling better."

Amelia snorted. She doubted she would ever feel better. She needed some time to think, to figure out her next move, and she couldn't do that with Chad hovering around. He'd be asking too many questions and right now, and she had no answers. She cupped his face with her hands and smiled. "Thanks for the offer, but you've only got a few more weeks until graduation, and I don't want you to get into trouble with your teachers."

"I'm eighteen now," he chuckled. "If I don't want to go to school, they can't make me." He let his knapsack drop to the floor. "I'm worried about you. Something's going on. I know it."

She let out a sigh. "There is something I want to discuss with you, but we'll do it when you get home. All right?" She gave him a hug, and then pushed him toward the mud room. "And you're not eighteen until tonight. Besides, don't you have to talk to Tina?"

"Yeah, but I'd rather talk about whatever's bothering you."

"I told you, we'll talk about it later. Now go before you miss the bus."

Chad gave her a peck on the cheek, grabbed his knapsack and headed out the mud room door. She watched them from the window as he caught up to his siblings, and they roughhoused down the driveway.

Her lip trembled as she thought back to the phone call. She would tell them tonight, when they got home from school. They had a right to know how insane and dangerous their father had become.

Amelia worried as more teenagers congregated at the bus stop near the end of their driveway. She didn't like Chad being away from her, and she reassured herself there was safety in numbers, but she couldn't rid herself of a nagging feeling. She headed toward the mud room door. There wasn't anything wrong with her watching them as they waited, was there?

Outside, she pretended to fuss with the hedge on the other side of the driveway. She smiled as she noticed a few stripped branches. Normally she would have been upset, but this way she was able to keep her eye on them under the false guise of pruning. It was ten minutes before the bus pulled up, and she'd pruned the hedge halfway down the driveway, close enough to see the teenagers begin the slow march toward the bus entrance. She didn't take her eyes off Chad. She watched him at the back of the line with his friends as they shuffled along. Gloomy faces on them all.

"You'd think they were on a death march." She crossed her arms as Chad neared the bus doors. "Be safe," she whispered.

Chad immediately turned and looked in her direction. An odd smile crossed his face as he mouthed the words "Don't worry" back at her.

Amelia gasped. There was no way he could have heard her. No one's hearing was *that* good. No one but . . .

A few words from Henry's phone call tumbled into her mind. One in particular—*minion*—stuck with her. Was this one of the changes Lyla mentioned? Was Chad's super-hearing a minion trait? Amelia didn't know anything about the occult, and the idea still seemed ridiculous, but she couldn't deny something *was* going on.

She hurried back toward the house as the bus pulled away. Her mind filled with the odd occurrences over the last few days. The more she thought about it, the more she began to think maybe Henry was crazy. Whether he was sick or delusional, it didn't matter. She had to take the boys and get out.

She headed to the basement. The kid's suitcases were downstairs, packed away since their last trip to the cabin. She crinkled her nose at the musty smell as she opened the door. She never liked coming down here. It always felt like a tomb.

She found their suitcases tucked neatly away next to the water softener, and dragged them into the sparse light to check them over. She was sure Leslie would take them in, and she'd better keep the truth to herself. Revealing strange visions and menacing feelings wouldn't go over well. Let her think Henry was cheating. Those conversations were easier to handle than soul-selling and demon worshiping.

Amelia dragged them upstairs and rested them against the wall, then headed toward the mud room door and outside. The larger suitcases were in the loft above the garage. They were heavier, but she wanted as much of their personal belongings with them as possible. She didn't want to have any reason to return. She'd pack up the boy's stuff and have the van ready to pick them up by lunchtime.

She tugged at the rope that dropped a hidden ladder. The wind picked up, and toppled over several flowerpots along the edge of the asphalt. Startled, Amelia clamped one hand over her mouth and tried to steady her nerves, and then chastised herself for being so jumpy.

She reached up to climb the ladder and was shocked to see the young man from yesterday and his friend standing on her side of the street. Right at the end of her driveway. Their eyes focused on her.

They stepped off the curb and headed up her property. Amelia's heart pounded as she let go of the ladder and dashed for the house. She slammed against the metal door of the mud room and pushed hard with her shoulder to open it. Strong arms wrapped around her waist and pulled her away from the door, as a hand clamped down over her mouth. She struggled against her captor as the young man dragged her away from the door. Amelia smelled coffee on his breath as the bristles of his days-old beard rubbed up against her cheek.

"Did you think you could get away with it?" he said, as she struggled against him.

Get away with what? Her mind raced with possibilities. Did Henry find out about her? Did he know she'd overheard his conversations? She kept struggling, taking deep breaths through her nose, trying to get as much air as possible.

His companion quickly came up beside them. He was much older than her with hints of fading blond curls pulled back into a thin ponytail, and a receding hairline. He looked down at her along the bridge of his slightly curved nose, yet Amelia saw something familiar within the hardness of his eyes.

"Jared, ease up. You're hurting her."

"So?" The young man's tone was cynical. "With what they're going to do, don't you think she deserves it?"

"We don't know if she's even involved."

Amelia felt the sudden hot breath of Jared's laugh. "How could she not be?"

The older man's face softened. "Well, there's only one way to find out."

He motioned to the door and Amelia was dragged back through and into the kitchen. Jared's grip was strong, and when she struggled, his companion revealed the hilt of a revolver hidden by his coat.

Amelia froze, staring at the weapon. There were strange markings carved into the ivory inlay, and it sent a shiver up her spine just looking at it.

"Be good, Mrs. Saint, and I won't have to use this."

Once inside, Jared released her and shoved her toward the kitchen. Amelia didn't take her eyes off the older man as the door slammed shut behind them. Not even when the deadbolt lock clicked into place.

Amelia stumbled to the centre counter. "What do you want?"

The older man removed the gun from his coat and laid it down on the tile counter. Amelia's gaze fell on the weapon. She hated guns, always did. It was the one of the few ideals she and Henry shared. He never wanted to bring one into the house, and neither did she. Although, right now, she wished there were several and in close range.

She shifted her stance, putting herself closer to the counter. If she could grab that one, then maybe she could escape. She'd have the power. She'd be the one in charge. They'd have to get out, or she'd blow their heads off.

"My name is Homer Wakeman, and you've already met my partner, Jared Quinn." Homer leaned up against the counter. "And you're Amelia Saint, aren't you? Married to Henry Saint?"

Amelia rested her hand on the edge of the counter. "How do you know that?"

"We've been watching you," Jared said. "And we know a lot about you, and what you're up to."

Amelia spun around. "You don't know shit about me."

Her body trembled as the adrenaline raced through her veins. She wasn't afraid. They were on *her* property, and she'd taken a few self-defense classes over the years, yet despite the weapon and being dragged inside, there was something about the two that didn't seem threatening. Who introduces themselves before they rob you? Amelia wasn't taking any chances. She turned and lunged toward the counter, latching on to the cold steel barrel of the gun. Homer grabbed the hilt and pulled it toward him, but Amelia had a tight grip and wasn't about to let go.

She felt arms wrap around her waist. "Now, now, Mrs. Saint," Jared's breath was warm against her ear as his body came uncomfortably close to hers. "We can't have you trying to get away."

She bucked under his embrace, trying to move as much as possible and break his hold. She pulled the gun close to her, inching her fingers closer to the trigger. Jared reached out and gripped her one hand, trying to force it off the weapon. Amelia leaned to one side and bit into his forearm. His scream of pain was a little satisfying, but she didn't let go.

"Shit, Homer! Do something."

A vile, musty smell burned the inside of her nose and made her swoon. She let go of Jared's arm and buried her nose in the sleeve of her shirt to block out the smell.

The vapours made her eyes water and her knee's buckled slightly. She felt the young man's hold on her weaken and the adrenaline shot through her again. Amelia reared back, throwing as much of her back into it as she could. Jared's grip was firm, but she forced him back a few steps.

The horrible smell was back again, this time stronger as a small glass vile was held under her nose. The older man stood in front of her, one hand still gripped gun tight. Amelia jerked her head one way and then the other, desperate for fresh air, but the more she struggled the harder it became to focus. Her mind fell into a fog, as she collapsed backward and passed out.

***

"Mrs. Saint, can you hear me?

Amelia tried to lift her head, but it felt like there was a pile of bricks holding her down. Her head pounded with each heartbeat, as she blinked to clear her eyes and the fog in her mind.

"What did you do?" Her words slurred from her lips.

"I'm sorry I had to do that," Homer said. "But I had to get you under control."

Amelia slowly raised her head. The older man was bent down on one knee in front of her. "Why don't you just kill me now?"

"We don't want to kill you, Mrs. Saint."

There was a chortle from somewhere beside her. "Speak for yourself, dude."

There was a flash of anger in Homer's eyes. "We haven't found anything that ties her to the ritual. For all we know, she's innocent in all of this."

Amelia moved her head to one side. She was on the floor near the kitchen table. Her arms and legs felt like dead weight and her wrists were bound behind her in handcuffs. "Ritual?"

"I don't buy it! How can someone not know what's going on in their own house?"

Amelia wanted to know the answer to that herself.

She propped her head back against the wall as she worked to clear her mind. She focused on Jared as he paced back and forth in front of her. "She said it would happen in the woods out back." The words tumbled out of her mouth. She wasn't even aware she was talking until she heard her own voice.

Jared stopped. "What?"

Amelia glanced at Jared before focusing on his friend. What was going on? Why wasn't she dead, or raped, or assaulted in some other way? Why were they standing around talking instead of robbing her blind? "The woman Henry's been talking too. Layla or something like that."

"Lyla?" Homer asked.

Amelia frowned. "Yeah. You know her?"

Homer glanced down at the floor before standing up. "We need to search the house again."

Jared exhaled deeply. "It's a big house. It could be anywhere, if it's even here at all."

"He'd want to keep it here. Close to the vessel."

Jared rested his hands on his hips. "Where it could be discovered? I don't know about that."

"Yeah but if anyone does come across it, they're not going to know what it really is."

Amelia tried to shift positions. The fog in her mind was clearing out enough that she could focus on their conversation, even though she had no idea what the hell they were talking about. "If you're not here to rob me or kill me, then why are you here?"

Homer looked down at her. "Because we know your children are in grave danger."

Amelia lifted her chin. She wanted to know what kind of danger, or how they knew, but one question was at the forefront of her mind. "Henry's not crazy, is he? He's really planning on doing some kind of satanic ritual with Chad?"

Homer's brow lifted. "You know what we're talking about?"

Jared's stance became rigid. "I knew it!"

"I don't know anything, not really." Her gaze fell away. "But I'm not involved. Whatever sick and twisted plans Henry has, I'm not a part of it."

"Why should we believe you?"

Amelia glared at Jared. "Because if you did know anything about me, like you claim, you'd know I could never let anything happen to my children." Amelia gave him a smug grin as Jared shrank away and faced Homer. "I was about to start packing when you two showed up. I'm going to be out of this house and long gone before Henry and that bitch can do anything to hurt my family."

Homer's green eyes gazed at her sympathetically as he shifted his weight from one foot to the other. "You have to know, Mrs. Saint, you can't just run away from this. You're dealing with a situation that's beyond your comprehension."

Amelia frowned. "What are you talking about? It's some stupid—"

"This is a demonic possession," Jared cut her off. "Henry sacrificed the soul of your first born to a demon named Korthos, and it takes possession of his body tonight."

Amelia swallowed a couple times, trying to remove the tightness developing in her throat, remembering the twisted grotesque face from the night before. "But if I take Chad away from here—"

"He will still die," Homer said, his tone soft and compassionate. "Chad's your oldest?"

Amelia nodded. She felt a lone tear trickled down her cheek. "There has to be something I can do."

"There's nothing," Jared said, leaning up against the island counter. "He's been marked as the vessel. Once the pact was created, his fate was sealed."

Amelia sniffed. "And taking him away won't help?"

Homer exhaled. "I wish it did."

She struggled in her cuffs, trying to pull her arms free. Homer pulled a set of keys from his pocket and bent down. He was close, and the thought of biting into his cheek flashed through her mind, but Amelia quickly lost her anger as she heard the cuffs snap open.

Homer jumped back as she brought her arms forward and began rubbing her wrists. The white hilt of his gun poked out from the waist of his pants.

"So why are you here?" she asked, trying not to look at the weapon.

"We try to hunt these things down," Jared said. "Take them out before they kill innocent people."

She braced herself against the kitchen table as she stood up. "Take out? What, do you mean kill?"

Jared's gaze darted toward his partner then back at her. "Yes ma'am."

"NO." Amelia lunged at Homer hitting him as hard as she could with her fists. She slapped at his chest, clawed at his face, and when she noticed Jared heading toward her, she reached in and grabbed the gun.

She stepped back and pointed it directly at Homer. "Get the fuck out of my house now!"

Jared froze next to Homer. "Mrs. Saint, you don't understand—"

"Oh, I understand perfectly. You two are just as crazy as Henry, and there's no way in hell I'm going to let you hurt my child!"

"He's not going to be your child for much longer," Jared said. "The vessel will be consumed on the anniversary of his birth, and anyone who is stupid enough to stick around for it, will be the creature's first victims."

Jared moved toward her, and she pointed the gun at him. Homer held up his arm, blocking him from going forward. "Mrs. Saint, please, we have to get you and your other children someplace safe."

"Do you think I'm stupid? I'm not going anywhere with you."

Homer took a step toward her, and she focused the barrel of the gun back on him. "Mrs. Saint . . . Amelia . . . please listen to us. We're not going to hurt you. We just want to help."

Amelia took a step back. "Don't come any closer."

Homer put his hands up as he took another step. "I'm not armed. Are you going to shoot me?"

She could feel her grip on the hilt slip a bit as her palms became moist. "If I have to."

Homer took another step and Amelia pulled gently on the trigger. "Don't make me hurt you."

Her heart pounded with each step closer he took. She didn't look at his face, she didn't want to see the shock and pain that would erupt once the gun went off. Amelia squeezed the trigger harder, felt the rotating of the barrel. She squinted as she pulled a little harder, bracing herself for the noise.

Click.

Her eyes went wide with shock. No loud noise. No bullet and the intruder was now less than a foot away from her. He reached out and put his hand on the barrel of the gun and yanked it out of her grasp.

"Despite what you see in the movies, Mrs. Saint, not a lot of people walk around with a loaded weapon shoved down their pants." He turned away and walked back over to the counter. "Go check the upstairs again."

Amelia braced herself against the door, dumbfounded. It didn't go off. It wasn't loaded. "Why would you bring a gun that wasn't loaded?"

Homer turned as Jared walked out of the kitchen. "I told you, we're not here to hurt you."

"Then you're here to"

"To get your family to safety."

Amelia covered her face with her hands. "This isn't happening. None of this is real." She tensed up as she heard footsteps come closer.

"I'm afraid this is all too real," Homer said. "I really wish it wasn't. They seem like great kids. They don't deserve this." He turned away from her and fiddled with the gun. "No one does."

Amelia's mind was blank, her whole body felt numb. She shuffled over to the kitchen table and fell onto the bench seat.

"You know about this stuff?"

Homer nodded. "Yes ma'am."

"Then maybe you know how to save my son?"

"Honestly, Mrs. Saint, I wish I had the answers for you, but we've never caught up to a vessel *before* it was possessed."

Amelia frowned. "Never? But you're here now, and nothing has happened to my son."

Homer smiled weakly. "We got a heads up this time. Usually, we follow the omens, but by the time we get to a house, the creature has taken possession or is long gone."

She tilted her head to one side. "Omens?"

"Signs," Homer said, a little more relaxed. "Strange visions, weird weather, that sort of thing. It's caused by minions as they move through our plane of existence."

Amelia thought back to the other day. "We had a freak windstorm here a couple days ago."

"Yeah, we know. There's been a bunch of strange things going on for a while. Mostly focused around this neighbourhood. Minions gathering and waiting for their leader to enter this world"

Amelia inhaled deeply. It was like something out of a movie, but she had to admit it was the only explanation that made sense. The windstorm, the foreboding feelings, she couldn't dismiss them. They were real. She felt them, but it didn't make it any easier for her to accept the situation either.

Jared came back into the room and shook his head. "Well, if there's anything here, it's hidden well. There's no way we'll find it." He looked over at Amelia. "Is she all right?"

Amelia glanced up at him with a blank look. She frowned at the absurdity of his question. "What do you think? This has been going on right under my nose, and I didn't even know."

"Don't blame yourself, Mrs. Saint," Jared said. "Most people don't even believe in Hell or demons. If it's not something tangible that affects them every day, why should they?"

Amelia gazed out the window. "I thought I was imagining things. That everything I saw or heard was due to stress." She glanced back over at the men. "I'm sorry. I can't just let Chad die."

Jared sat on the bench seat across from her. "That's not a choice. You have two other children you have to think about now. When this all goes down, they're going to need you more than ever. You have to think about them and their safety."

Amelia looked helplessly over at Homer. Her heart ached too much for her to even think straight. "I can't do it," she whispered. "I can't throw away my son."

The room went silent. Amelia saw sympathy in Jared's eyes, but she knew he would fight her on this.

Homer leaned back on the counter. "We may be able to help him," he said, concentrating on one spot on the floor.

Amelia's eyes widened. "How?"

Jared frowned, shaking his head. "That's just a theory, Homer. Ancient legends. It's never been put to the test, and you know it."

Homer kept his focus on the floor. "But she's right. We can't let this kid die. We have to at least try to save him."

Jared ran his hands through his hair then slammed them down on the table. "I get that you're sick of watching innocent people die, I am too, but I think we have a better chance of getting through this by protecting her and the other children, rather than sacrificing our escape window to save the vessel."

Amelia leaned across the table, took Jared's hand and looked into his eyes. "Please, if there's a way you could help Chad . . ."

Jared slumped forward. "I'm sorry, Mrs. Saint, there's not enough time. Maybe if we were here sooner we could have done something, like a reversal ritual or something, but as it is, we should concentrate on protecting the rest of your family."

"No. The vessel is her family," Homer said.

She gripped Jared's hand tighter, looking deep into his eyes. Slowly, the hardness in his face softened. "We don't have the right supplies."

"We can get them," Homer shot back. "Aslin's Wiccan friend Brianna owns a little shop on the edge of town that should have what we need."

Amelia saw Jared's expression change, and for a moment, she thought he would give in. Then he frowned and faced his partner. "Do you have any idea the shit we'll unleash if we try to do this? This is Lyla we're dealing with, Homer. The Overlord of the Ninth Realm. Her husband has Lyla's patronage, and when they find out what we're up to, we're as good as dead."

"So, we don't let him find out." Homer walked to the table and sat in the chair. "Look, think of the opportunity we have here. If this works, we could stop more minions from entering this world. Save lives for a change."

Amelia felt a glimmer of hope. "What is this theory?"

Homer leaned forward. "The veil between this world and Hell is too strong. Minions need help to break through, and it's done with the aid of a Talisman. It's thought if you read the ancient language out loud along the edge before the minion takes possession, then the pact will be broken and the vessel will be freed."

Amelia frowned. "But if it's in an ancient language, how are you supposed to know what it says?"

"That's the problem," Jared said. "We'd need a few hours just to decipher the markings. That, and then there's the problem of getting to the Talisman."

Homer pursed his lips. "We can't let this opportunity pass. We have to try and get a hold of that Talisman before Chad's birth time." He looked at Amelia. "Has Henry given Chad any strange jewelry lately?"

"Not that I know of, but he did say he had something extra special for him for his birthday."

Homer flashed an excited smile. "That could be it."

Jared sat straight in his seat. "We don't know what could happen," he said. "It may help, or it may make it worse." He faced Amelia. "You still need to think about your other children."

"I can't," she said, wringing her hands. "I know that sounds awful, but right now, I can't focus on anyone but Chad."

Homer held up one hand. "The other kids will be fine. We'll make sure they're out of the house and someplace safe before any of this happens."

Jared shook his head. "I don't know. What about her husband? If he suspects anything, it could blow this wide open."

Homer turned to Amelia. "I know you want to leave, but you can't, not now. We need you to stay and keep a close eye on your husband. Chad only has a few hours left, and if we want to break that pact we can't let Henry know you've found out."

Amelia put her head in her hands. "I don't like the idea of being anywhere near that man right now."

"We know, Mrs. Saint, but this whole plan hinges on that Talisman. If Henry is at all suspicious that you know, well, I just hate to think what he would do."

Amelia raised her head. "You think he'd hurt us, don't you?"

Jared shrugged. "A man who sacrifices his child's soul is capable of doing anything."

She nodded. "So what do you want me to do?"

"Keep going on with your day. Do whatever it was you were planning on doing."

"I was going to make Chad a cake."

"Then do that," Homer said. "It'll go a long way in keeping up the appearance that things are normal."

"I think I can do that." As Amelia's anxiety grew, she knew she had to maintain the appearance of normality, in order to help try to save her son.

"What about your other children?" Jared asked. "Do you have a place for them to stay for the night?"

"I can ask my friend Leslie if they can come over after the birthday party."

"Party?" The pitch of Jared's voice rose an octave. "You can't have a birthday party for him here."

"Why not? It's been planned for weeks."

"If she cancels the party, Henry could become suspicious," Homer said.

Jared went to speak, but got more stern looks from his companion. "Fine," he said. "But I hope everyone is gone before the fun starts."

The men stood, and Jared headed for the back door. Amelia followed, picking up the gun off the counter and handed it to Homer. "Don't forget this."

Homer smiled. "I can leave it here, if you think it'll make you feel safer."

Amelia glanced nervously at the weapon. "What can a gun do against minions?"

Jared opened the mud-room door. "You'd be surprised how the right bullet can mess them up."

"Minions are flesh and bone, just like us," Homer said. "They're stronger than us, faster, but they're not impossible to kill."

Amelia felt a weight lift from her shoulders. These people knew more about what was happening, and could possibly help, but it was draining her mentally. Not to mention the heartache she knew would never go away. She was tired, and her head hurt from the immense gravity and weirdness of the situation. She welcomed the quiet afternoon to gather her thoughts and try to prepare.

Jared took a quick scan of the area before stepping out onto the driveway. Clouds rolled in, making the sky grey.

"We will get in touch with you later on today," Homer said, before he walked outside. "Try to stay strong, and don't let on that you know anything. If Henry suspects anything . . ."

"I know." Amelia gave him a weak smile and found herself reaching out to embrace him. She felt his body tense, and then he pulled back and smiled.

"Here." He handed her a small bag from his pocket. "Take this."

Amelia looked inside. "Grass?"

"Protective herbs. A repellent, and a strong one. There's not a lot, but it should go a long way to protect you and the other kids, just in case anything unexpected happens."

"What should I do with them?"

Homer shrugged. "Dump some in their pockets. It creates a protective aura around the wearer. Anything evil will be kept at bay as long as these herbs are somewhere on their body." He leaned in to her. "But keep it hidden from sight. If it can be seen, it can be removed."

She nodded and folded up the bag.

Amelia shut the door and stepped back into the kitchen, watching them through the window over the sink. She inhaled deeply, allowing the air to slowly drain away and take her apprehension with it. She felt a giddiness building. She wasn't going crazy after all, but as she watched them climb into a beat-up van, her happiness faded, replaced with the cold hard fact that everything she was experiencing was very real.

***

Amelia lost track of time surfing the internet. She'd spent most of the day looking up information about demons and evil creatures, protective herbs, and anything else she could find on the occult. Most of it was discouraging. She could find very little about minions. Demon possessions, yes, but she would have to go through the Catholic church for any help, and she didn't have the time to wait for the Vatican to decide whether or not her case was valid. The only piece of information she found on protection herbs was to create sachets. It wasn't much, but at least it was something.

The day became dull and drizzly; a steady mist hung over the entire neighbourhood. Amelia got the cake ingredients and began measuring things out. She'd been making the sachets and had three done before she remembered the birthday cake. Making any more would have to wait.

The small bundles and materials sat on the other side of the centre counter. Amelia would periodically look at the bag of herbs while mixing the cake ingredients. She was finding it hard to concentrate on just one thing; her mind torn between what she was doing, and what she wanted to do, which was to look for more information, but the cake had to be made, and she wanted to make a few more sachets, just in case. She could surf the net once those were taken care of.

She placed the ingredients into her electric mixer and turned it on. One more step and she could get back to the sachets. Then there was the problem of getting the boys to wear them. What would she say? Keep these on you, so you can live? They'd probably think their mother was losing her mind. Again, she focused on the herbs, and she reached across the counter and picked up the small bags. Amelia opened it slightly, careful not to spill the contents, and shook some of the dried mixture into the palm of her hand.

They didn't look special. The broken twigs and pieces of dried leaf reminded her of the homegrown pot her college roommates used to smoke. She gave them a quick sniff, but there was no distinct aroma, just a heavy musky smell mixed with dirt, but with all the crying she'd done earlier, her nose was still slightly stuffed. She was amazed she could smell anything.

She rubbed the herbs around in her palm with her index finger, feeling their texture and getting more of an aroma; the faint hint of lavender calmed her mind.

The sound of an engine revving in the driveway caught her attention. Amelia took a few steps back to look out the kitchen window. Henry's red Porsche pulled into the empty space in the garage. Panic set in. What would he do if he saw her with the herbs? Would he know what they were? Would it be enough for him to know she was suspicious? Amelia wasn't sure what he would do, but standing around with a palm full of dried twigs didn't look good.

She remembered what Homer had said about their protectiveness and glanced down at the cake batter.

Wouldn't hurt, would it? She brushed the herbs off her hand and into the batter.

"You'd better work, dammit," she said, as the mixer blend in the herbs. Hopefully, they wouldn't taint the taste of the cake.

She stepped back to the counter, gathered up the small pieces of material and the remaining sachets, and stuffed everything into her sewing kit. She had just enough time to straighten herself out before Henry walked into the mud room.

"Well," she smiled at him, hoping he wouldn't notice how fake it was. "You're home early."

"I told you I would be," he said, giving her a quick kiss on the cheek as he walked by.

Amelia felt the nausea rise at his touch. She clenched her fists as she fought off thoughts of hitting him with something heavy.

"Did you get everything straightened out at the office?"

"Of course."

He poured himself a cup of coffee and walked to the other side of the counter. Amelia hid her smile as he made an odd detour around her sewing kit.

"Something funny?" he asked.

"No, just thinking about tonight."

Henry frowned. "What about it?"

"How it's going to be a good night."

"You can say that again." He walked over to the couch and sat down.

"When is everyone supposed to get here?"

"Probably after supper. Around seven."

"Good, that gives me time to do some work."

"More work?" She tried to sound interested, but nothing about him interested her anymore.

"Yeah, this meeting over the weekend is really big. I have to be prepared."

I bet you do.

Amelia glared at the back of his head and walked around the centre island to her sewing kit. She knew a pair of cutting shears lay inside underneath the sachet material, and slowly reached inside for the handle. *I could end this right now,* she thought, but then caught herself. Would she really be ending it? As much as she loathed him, this wasn't the plan.

She pulled her hand out and fastened the latch. "Well, at least you're doing it before the party. It's bad enough you have to leave right afterward. It would crush Chad if you worked all the way through his party too."

Henry read his newspaper without commenting. Amelia stood a few feet behind him, clenching her jaw, trying to keep her homicidal thoughts, just thoughts.

4

There were more people wandering through Amelia's home than she would have liked. The mixture of cheap perfume and expensive aftershave irritated the inside of her nose, and with the large crowd, it was difficult to keep an eye on all the teenagers. She picked up an empty can of soda shoved behind a plant stand, immediately noticing the smell. Rum was not the most discreet of liquors and a small growl escaped from the back of her throat as her grip on the can tightened.

Amelia wandered into the kitchen and put the can in the sink. She took a quick glance outside, looking past the row of expensive cars in the driveway, hoping to see one of her new acquaintances. Homer said they'd return, but she hadn't heard a word from them all day. Fear and the idea that maybe their offer to help was nothing more than a ruse set in. Maybe they were acquaintances of Henry's sent to spy on her to find out how much she knew. *If* she knew.

She brought her thumb to her lips, nibbling gently on the edge of her nail as she glanced quickly around the room. Her stomach clenched at the thought of her collaborating with Henry's cronies. They would have told him by now about their hastily conceived plan to save Chad, or maybe that was the point. Lull her into a false sense of security with a few well-timed lies, concealing the fact they had no interest in helping her at all. Amelia frowned. If that was their plan, Henry would have done something by now. Wouldn't he? Her pulse raced, and the walls felt like they were closing in around her. Maybe he was waiting until later, or when she was alone? Her breath came in hungry gulps and she cupped one hand over her mouth and headed for the patio doors. She had to get away before she lost it completely.

"Could I have everyone's attention?" Henry's voice boomed over the sound of gently clinking glass. Amelia stopped just before the beveled doors and quickly turned around. The family area and kitchen grew quiet as all attention shifted toward the living room and Henry, who stood in front of the oversized marble fireplace. It took a few moments for the crowd to completely quiet down, but once they did, he had their undivided attention.

"First," he began, holding a glass of red wine in one hand and extending the other toward Chad. "I'd like to thank everyone for coming out tonight and celebrating a very special moment in our family's life."

Amelia could taste bile at the back of her throat as she watched Henry play the proud father. It gnawed at her that he could be so deceitful, standing there, with his arm around Chad's shoulder and look so innocent. She wanted to scream, let the entire neighbourhood know what kind of a lowlife scum Henry really was, but they wouldn't believe her. Not in a million years, so she clenched her jaw tight and tried to keep her emotions in check.

"It isn't every day that your oldest child becomes an adult," Henry said. "And even though his mother and I still feel like he's our baby, we have to let him go and allow him to become the man he's meant to be."

A heartfelt murmur of 'Awws' filled the room, and Amelia quickly found herself the focus of attention. Uncomfortable, she smiled at a few guests, tilting her head to one side in acknowledge of their kindness, her anger still seething just below the surface.

"That is why," Henry continued, "I have an extra important gift for my son." He reached into the breast pocket of his tux, and brought out a set of car keys, dangling them in front of Chad. "There's a fully loaded Ford One-Fifty on the lot with your name on it."

The room broke into applause as Henry dropped the keys into Chad's palm. Amelia placed her hand over her mouth as she tried to blink back the tears.

Henry raised his hands. "Wait, I have one more gift for my son. This is to show how proud I am of him going to university." He reached into his opposite breast pocket and pulled out a small flat box. Henry faced her and motioned for her to come closer.

Amelia pushed through the crowd and stood next to Chad. There was nothing special about the box: white cardboard with a red ribbon tied neatly into a bow on top.

She glanced over at Henry. "When did you get that?"

"I ordered it from an Asian catalogue online a few weeks ago." He handed the box to Chad. "Happy Birthday."

Chad took the box. "What is it?"

"Well, open it up and find out."

Amelia saw the look of excitement in Chad's eyes as he tore into the gift. Opening the lid revealed a palm-size disk made of dark metal. Strange markings were etched along the edges, with a quarter-size dark red crystal embedded within the centre.

Chad picked up the disk, examining the front and back. "What is it?"

"It's an ancient Chinese good luck amulet," Henry said, patting him on his back. "It's for when you're studying at university. It's supposed to help the wearer with all aspects of his or her life. Let's just hope it has a positive effect on your grades. I wouldn't mind having you work next to me one day. "

Amelia took the disk from Chad and examined it closely. "That doesn't look like Chinese writing."

She glanced at Henry and found him glaring at her. "Since when do you know anything about ancient Chinese writing?"

The room dimmed and the air cooled, and Amelia's instinct to flee raced through her again. She shoved the disk back at Chad and turned away.

He knows!

Amelia pushed through the crowd. Several hands reached out to her, causing her to hesitate, but she politely brushed them off and continued to the downstairs washroom.

Amelia slammed the bathroom door and leaned back. She took a deep breath, holding it for a few seconds before releasing it. Her fear didn't subside, only manifested itself as tears, and once she started, she couldn't hold back. She felt an emotional release as the tears streamed down her face, replacing it with an almost exhausting calm. She took another deep breath as the tears subsided and slowly let the air trickle from her lungs.

A knock at the door caused her to choke out her remaining breath.

"Are you all right?" Henry's concerned voice was barely audible through the wood. He didn't sound angry, but then, she didn't know what to expect from him anymore.

"I'm fine," she replied, wiping the wetness from her cheeks. "Just a little emotional, that's all."

"Well clean yourself up and hurry back out. You're the hostess, remember. I can't have you disappearing for no reason."

Maybe it was the absurdity of recent events, but his comment struck her as humorous, and she clamped one hand over her mouth, to keep her laughter contained.

She took a look at herself in the mirror: bloodshot eyes, nose red and running. A splash of cold water reduced some the effects of her emotions, but not enough to avoid questions.

Suddenly there was another knock on the door. "Amelia, are you all right?" It was Leslie.

"I'm fine. I'm just a little emotional."

"Can I come in?"

Amelia unlocked the door then turned back to the mirror, pretending to fix her hair.

"Things not going so well?" Leslie spoke to Amelia's reflection.

Amelia sniffed. "No, everything's fine."

Leslie crossed her arms in front of her. "Yeah, and that's why you're standing in the bathroom crying."

Amelia gave a weak smile. "Really, I'm fine. It was just Henry's speech. It really got to me."

There was a long pause.

"How is everything else?"

Amelia frowned, trying to look perplexed. "Everything else?"

"You know, him cheating on you."

Amelia didn't know what to say. Leslie was a friend who was willing to help, but would she believe her? Or worse, would she be putting her friend in danger? Henry was unstable, and there was no telling what he would do. "He's not cheating on me."

Leslie didn't look convinced. "You know this for a fact?"

"It was all a big misunderstanding," Amelia said, hoping Leslie wouldn't push the subject. "Lyla is working with him on some big case. She was brought in a few weeks ago. She deals with some special aspect of the law, so they want to make sure everything goes in their favour." Amelia stomach did a flip. She hated lying to her best friend, but until this was over, it was better than revealing the truth.

Amelia watched for some sign that her lie wasn't taking, but after a few tense moments, Leslie's attitude lightened and she checked her appearance in the mirror. "So what's her specialty?"

Amelia thought fast. "Henry says she's one of those new IT specialists."

"So why did he want to see her so badly?"

"I don't know," Amelia said, and ran a washcloth under the stream of water. "Henry tried to explain it to me, but these things go right over my head."

Amelia could feel Leslie's eyes on her, and she tried not to let it bother her as she dabbed the wet cloth on her face.

Leslie turned to her. "Are you sure there's nothing more you want to tell me?"

Amelia let a small laugh escape her lips "Trust me Leslie, the last thing Henry is thinking about right now, is cheating on me."

Leslie faced the mirror again. "Well as long as you know I'm here for you. You can tell me anything."

Amelia lowered her hands and stared at her friend's reflection. "I promise you, if there was anything worth telling, you'd be the first to know."

Amelia gave Leslie a quick hug, then left the bathroom and headed back to the party. She tried to enjoy herself, talking to friends, laughing with neighbours, hoping her enjoyment didn't look forced. She even said a few words to Henry in passing, as she kept a close eye on him while he promoted himself to his guests. Chad seemed to be having a good time, despite his earlier protests. She found him in the backyard, showing off the amulet. He didn't look any different, did he?

The party began to break up close to eight forty-five. Amelia and Chad saw each guest to their car, making sure they weren't intoxicated. She hadn't served that much alcohol, but the last thing she wanted was for the police to show up later and stumble across whatever was going to happen.

What is going to happen? She glanced up at the sky as another guest drove away. With no word from either Homer or Jared the entire night, she felt as isolated as the twinkling stars above, and made up her mind to take matters into her own hands, even though she had no idea where to begin.

Around ten the last of the guests drove off. With everyone gone the place was eerily still. She watched Chad joke around with the few remaining friends he'd invited. The faint sound of late-night television suddenly broke the silence as Amelia stepped back into the house.

She scanned the nearby rooms looking for Henry. She couldn't do anything while he was here. He could stop her. She gathered up a few dirty dishes and brought them out to the kitchen. "All right, Morgan, Liam," she said, taking a quick look at the clock. "Time to get ready for bed."

"Aw, come on, Mom," Liam whined, watching the television. "It's a special occasion. Can't we stay up a little while longer?"

The twins turned and looked at her with pleading eyes from over the back of the couch. Their looks caused a sudden sense of hopelessness to wash over her, and Amelia tried hard not to burst into tears. She covered her mouth as their feigned acts of begging intensified. She hoped they thought she was only laughing.

"So?" Morgan pressed. "Can we?"

Amelia turned and read the clock on the wall.

Ten ten.

Her heart raced. If this had been any other weekend, she would have said no, but she could feel it coming, the feeling something was not right. Tingling sensations travelled up one side of her body, followed by a sense of dread. Despite the warm temperature, her skin felt cool to the touch, and for a brief moment, she thought she saw wisps of steam escape from her lips. She needed a few moments alone to figure out what to do.

"Fine," she said, trying to keep calm. "You can stay up for a while longer, so go upstairs and say goodbye to your father."

As they bounded up the stairs, Amelia wasn't sure if she was doing the right thing by keeping them here. Maybe Leslie would take them in, but what kind of an explanation could she give her best friend that wouldn't result in another discussion about Henry cheating?

The sudden ring of the phone caused her to jump. She ran to answer it before anyone else could pick up the extension.

"Hello."

"Mrs. Saint?"

"Yes."

"It's Jared."

Amelia turned toward the foyer as she cupped her hand gently over the receiver "Hello, Jared. Nice of you to call, considering I've been waiting all night."

"Sorry," he said. "I've been trying, but the calls wouldn't go through." She could hear the panic in his voice.

"Why didn't you just come over? I could have made some excuse for you being here?"

Jared sighed. "I suggested that to Homer, but he was dead set against it."

"What? Why?"

"I don't know. He never really gave me a reason. Listen, how are things going? Is everything all right?"

"No, everything is not all right," Amelia said, turning to face the window. "Have you managed to find anything that can help you decipher the markings?"

Jared sighed heavily on the other end. "No. The book we need can't get here until the day after tomorrow."

Another wave of hopelessness washed over her. "So you're saying there's nothing we can do?"

"If we only knew what kind of amulet Chad is supposed to get," Jared said, frustrated. "We *might* be able to delay the onset of the minion's arrival."

Amelia's heart skipped a beat. "I saw it. Henry gave it to Chad earlier tonight for his birthday present."

"What did it look like?"

She heard Jared talking to Homer as she tried to recall as much information about disk as possible. "It was flat, made of some kind of dark metal with strange markings all around the edge and a dark red crystal in the centre." She stopped as Jared repeated the description out loud.

"What else?"

"I don't know. That's all I saw." She paused, remembering her confrontation with Henry. She got a chill as she recalled his dark glare. "Is that going to be enough?"

"I don't know." Jared sounded as bad as she felt. "Where is the amulet now?"

"I think Chad's wearing it. Why?"

"See if you can get it away from him. The amulet is the only doorway for the minion. It has to be on his body in order for the creature to come through. If we can keep it away from his flesh, maybe we can stall the creature, and buy some time."

Amelia was pacing back and forth. "Okay. Anything else?"

"We're on our way over. We should be there in about ten minutes. Is your husband still there?"

"Yes," Amelia glanced up at the ceiling. "He's packing for his trip."

"Get him out of the house as quickly as possible," Jared said. "We can't do anything with him there."

"I don't know," she said. Crackles of static began over the line. Amelia moved her ear away from the phone. "Where are you? This line is starting to break up."

"We're at a motel about ten minutes away from you."

The wind picked up and Amelia jumped as something hit the mud room door. She looked at the digital clock on the microwave.

Ten fifteen

"Please hurry."

"We'll do our—"

Amelia snapped her head away from the phone as the loud volume of static abruptly ended their conversation. The air was cooler and she felt tiny goose bumps inch their way up her arms. Frantic, she hung the up the receiver and scanned the area for something big enough to put the amulet in. She spied a medium-sized gift box in the family room next to an uneaten portion of birthday cake and headed for it. Opening the box she discarded a stack of heavy metal CDs that were inside. It looked about the right size to hold the amulet. She took a piece of cake and popped it into her mouth, hoping the herbs inside didn't lose their potency when they were baked. She grabbed another piece as she headed toward the stairs, just in time to see Morgan and Liam race back down to the family room.

"Where's your father?" she asked, passing them on the stairs.

"In your room," Liam said, reaching the last step first. "He's finished packing and ready to go. You'd better hurry."

Amelia raced up the stairs. "No kidding."

She had no intention of going anywhere near Henry, instead, she headed straight for Chad's bedroom, but as she got halfway down the hall, Henry appeared in the doorway, his carry-on bag over his shoulder. She ignored him and continued on to Chad's room.

"Aren't you going to say goodbye?" he asked, as she passed by.

Amelia didn't look back as she shoved another piece of cake into her mouth. "Goodbye." *You fucking bastard!*

"What's wrong with you? Don't tell me you're mad because of the present I gave him?"

Amelia ignored his question and pushed open Chad's bedroom door. The room was vacant. "Where's Chad?" she asked, walking back out into the hall.

"Probably still outside with his friends," Henry said, walking down the stairs.

She followed Henry down the stairs and through the kitchen, glaring at the back of his head. Amelia didn't hesitate as she removed a serrated knife from its wooden holder on the counter. She could do it, wanted to do it, and was just unstable enough right now to plunge the blade into his back. She pictured it in her mind, how easy it would be, and felt a twinge of satisfaction as she imagined the knife slicing through his clothing and deep into his flesh.

She flipped the knife in her hand, positioning it blade down. *Like carving a roast.*

The boys' shouts of laughter stopped her dead in her tracks. Her anger and hatred melted away. She rubbed her eyes with her free hand; her face flushed hot with mixed emotions.

Amelia threw the knife into the sink and continued to follow Henry toward the door. Outside, Chad was waving to his friends as he walked up the driveway and met them beside the red Porsche.

"I'll be back early Monday evening," Henry said, putting his bag in the back seat before getting into the car. "If I'm going to be any later, I'll call you."

"Okay," Amelia said. She felt drained from her ever shifting gauntlet of emotions. "See you Monday evening then."

Suddenly Chad jumped toward the car. "Dad," he leaned down, closer to Henry. "Thanks for the gifts, especially the disc thing. It's really cool."

"Glad you like it, son." Henry smiled. "Do you still have it on you?"

Chad reached for a gold chain around his neck, and pulled the amulet out from inside his shirt.

Amelia frowned. "When did you give him the chain?"

"Earlier, while you were in the bathroom," Henry said, and then focused on Chad. "Now take care of that. It's expensive and rare. Something you should keep with you for the rest of your life."

Chad nodded as Henry started up his car.

Henry revved the engine a few times and gave them both a curt nod before pulling away. Amelia's anger seethed just below the surface as she watched him back down the driveway and onto the road.

A scowl formed on her lips. "Bastard," she whispered.

Chad frowned. "Mom?"

As the whine of the engine diminished, Amelia turned to Chad with her hand out. "Give me that and I'll put it in a safe place for you."

Chad gripped the metal disk, hugging it tightly to his chest. "No, I want to wear it for a while."

A gust of cool wind blew through the yard, and Amelia shivered from the change in temperature. She glanced skyward as the outline of dark clouds bubbled over the treetops, and when she looked back, Chad was already halfway to the front door.

"Chad, please, you don't understand."

"Understand what?"

"It could hurt you."

He stopped and turned around. "How? It's just a hunk of metal."

Amelia toyed with the idea of telling him. "You don't know that. It could be more—" She reached out and grabbed the amulet tight. A searing pain shot through her fingers and up her arm. Amelia shrieked and pulled her hand away.

Chad grabbed her arm and pulled it toward him. "Are you all right?"

Amelia opened her palm. The tips of her fingers were bright red and throbbed. "They feel burnt," she said. She could see small welts developing at the balls of her fingertips.

Chad shrugged. "They look fine to me."

Amelia's anger boiled over. "Well, they're not! Now give me that damn thing."

Chad pulled away. "No." He looked at her with a mixture of confusion and anger. "What's wrong with you? You've been acting all weird lately."

Amelia extended her other hand. "Chad, please."

Chad headed to the front door, shaking his head. "I'm not a kid, Mom. I can look after my own stuff."

Amelia raced to catch up, but the heavy wood door slammed in her face as she approached the entrance. She turned the doorknob and swung it the door open, catching a glimpse of Chad as he stomped up the last few stairs to the second floor landing.

Amelia hesitated before walking inside. Her home felt different, looked darker. The air around her felt cold, as though it were trying to embrace her, disconnect her from the warmth of the outside. The wind grew stronger as rapid flashes of lightning lit up the clouds off on the horizon. It didn't look like a normal storm coming in, and she couldn't help but wonder if this had anything to do with the changes Lyla mentioned.

Amelia looked at the grandfather clock.

Ten twenty-seven.

She was running out of time.

"Chad," she called, stepping into the foyer. "Please come here. I want to talk to you."

"No!"

"Something wrong, Mom?"

Amelia didn't know how long Morgan and Liam had been watching from the kitchen, but from the looks on their faces, they knew something wasn't right.

"No," she lied, smiling. "Everything's fine. Go back to your game."

Liam looked at his twin and shoved a piece of cake into his mouth. "Now I know something's wrong."

"What's with Chad?" Morgan asked. "Why'd he slam the door in your face?"

"You know how he can be," She took a few steps toward them. "Chad's just going through a hard time right now, but don't worry, everything is fine."

Liam looked at her funny. "When isn't he? What is it this time, his girlfriend dump him?"

Both boys snickered until the lights in the house started to flicker. Lightning flashes encircled the house, and Amelia could feel the darkness of the clouds looming over her home. Liam went quickly to Amelia's side, wrapping his arms around her waist.

"I hate storms," he said.

She smiled as she caught the smell of chocolate on his breath and rubbed the top of his head. "I know." She glanced over at Morgan. She had to get them out of the house. "I want you boys to follow me."

Morgan frowned. "Where are we going?"

"Just upstairs, I want to give you each something."

Liam perked up. "What?"

Amelia cocked her head to one side, trying to get a good look at him. "It's a surprise."

The boys followed her up the stairs. Amelia took a quick glance at Chad's bedroom door and hurried down the hall. She had to get that amulet away from him, but the twins needed to be protected too.

Liam ran into her bedroom and threw himself on top of the bed, throwing the pillows at Morgan. Amelia went to her sewing kit on the nightstand, opened it and took out the herb sachets.

"I'm taking you over to Louise's place for the night," she said, holding out two sachets. "I want you to take these, and go wait in the car."

"I don't wanna go," Liam whined, bouncing over to one side. "Her place smells."

Morgan took the sachet and gave it a quick once-over. "Why? What's going on?"

"Morgan, please, for once, just do as I say." She didn't want to get into this fight with him. Not now. "I'll explain everything later, I promise." She reached for Liam and pulled him off the bed. "Put these someplace safe. Don't ever let it leave your person."

"Your person?" Liam looked at her strangely. "What is it?"

She took them by the shoulders and forced them toward the door. The lightning flashed more rapidly now, and Amelia knew she had to get the boys out of the house as soon as possible. "It's an herb sachet, now enough talking. Go get in the car now."

They stuffed them into their front pockets and rushed out into the hall as the lights continued to flicker. Thunder rattled the windows so hard Amelia thought they would burst. Morgan headed toward his room, but Liam stayed by Amelia's side, reaching for her as a thunderous bolt of lightning struck someplace near the house.

Morgan stopped just before his bedroom door. "That was too close."

Liam buried his head in her shoulder. "Mom, I don't want to go."

With both the lightning and thunder intensifying, Morgan quickly returned to her side.

Amelia wrapped her arms around their waists and pulled them toward the staircase. "Come on."

"Are you crazy?" Morgan said, pulling away from her. "I'm not going outside in that."

"Morgan, please! You'll be safe in the car."

Another crack of lightning. This time right outside the balcony door.

The sound wave blasted the glass inlay, sending shards of debris inward and down the hall. Amelia and the boys fell to the floor, covering their heads. Winds whipped around inside, bouncing leaves and broken twigs off the walls.

Amelia tried to keep calm as her boys shouted and grabbed hold of her. Light bulbs and fixtures exploded around them, plunging the hall into a darkness that was only broken by the intense flashes of lightning. She felt the boys tremble in her arms and pulled them closer, to shelter them from the sharp debris.

The wind howled through the broken door as the temperature dropped below freezing. Amelia saw her breath come as pale wisps, as she shivered on the floor. She raised her head slightly and looked down the hall toward the balcony. Beyond the railing was nothing but black, as debris caught in the wind, whipped past the railing at an astonishing speed. Even the lightning became less intense, and the occasional flash revealed damage to the hall.

Then everything went still.

Amelia gripped her children tight, afraid of letting them go. The winds stopped, the thunder and lightning were gone, and they were left crouching in the hall, half buried by leaves and pieces of the doorframe. She leaned back, pulling the boys with her, and they clung to her side, knees bent to their chests and shivering.

"Was that a tornado?" Morgan asked. Dirt mixed with tears streaked his face as he turned his head toward the gaping hole at the end of the hall.

Amelia nuzzled him gently by his ear. "I don't know, but we're all right."

Suddenly Liam's tear-streaked face popped up next to hers. "Chad! What about Chad!"

Before she had a chance to answer, both boys scrambled to their feet and ran to the entrance of Chad's room.

"Guys, wait!" She jumped to her feet and followed, but they threw open his door and ran inside before she could stop them.

"Chad?" Liam called into the darkness. "Are you all right?"

Amelia ran in front of them, pushing them toward the hall as she tried to scan the room for any sign of movement. Light from an overturned desk lamp revealed overturned furniture and debris scattered around the room.

"What's that sound?" Morgan asked, barely above a whisper.

"Sounds like a dog," Liam replied. "A really angry dog."

Amelia heard it too. "Get downstairs. Both of you."

She felt Morgan pull away. "No, Chad could be hurt."

Liam was the first to the doorway and stopped to wait for his brother. "Morgan, you heard what Mom said. Come on!"

Morgan didn't follow. Instead he stayed by Amelia's side, hanging on to her arm. "No, I'm not leaving."

Amelia heard rustling come from someplace on the floor, then another growl. The low menacing tone sent shivers up her spine, and she felt Morgan brush her arm as he took a step behind her.

"Mom?" Morgan said. The bravado gone in his voice.

"Mom," Liam whispered. "I'm scared."

She took one step back, frantically scanning the room for anything moving. *So am I.*

Sounds came at her from all angles, shuffling around in the debris until it seemed to settle down in one spot on the floor. A sudden throbbing in her head weakened her eyesight as she tried to focus in the partial light.

"Chad, are you in here?" Her voice cracked. "Are you all right?"

A groan came from the far corner. Amelia shifted in front of Morgan. Squinting, she saw a lump within the shadows as it rocked back and forth, low to the floor.

"Morgan, go get a flashlight from downstairs."

"Is Chad all right?" Liam asked, from the doorway.

"I don't know."

The lump moved and growled. Amelia kept her attention on the darkness as Morgan ran from the room. She knew they wouldn't leave the house now. Not if they thought Chad was injured.

She could hear Morgan rooting through the cupboards in the kitchen counters. With each sound, Amelia saw the form twitch, as the growls and snorts continued. With rapid footsteps on the stairs and floor, Morgan was back by her side, and handed her a small plastic flashlight.

"Do both of you have those sachets I gave you?" she asked, taking a quick glance at them.

Morgan frowned. "Yeah. Why?"

"Good." She turned on the light, moving the beam toward the corner of the room. Gasps of shock came from behind her as the light fell on Chad sitting on the floor, crouched in the corner, his body covered in sweat. Pieces of wet hair clung to the side of his face and his head was bent toward the floor. He was entangled in blankets and other pieces of material and his body twitched in between heavy gasps for air. Shocked, the air escape from Amelia's lungs in one breath.

Chad's head snapped up at her exhale, revealing eyes as red as the crystal embedded within the amulet. The flashlight reflected beads of sweat glistening from his face and chest as he bared his teeth, breathing heavily.

Morgan stared at his brother. "What the fuck—?"

"Chad!" Liam ran toward his older brother, but both Morgan and Amelia grabbed hold of him before he got too close.

"Don't go near him," Amelia said.

"But he's hurt! Look at his eyes, they're bleeding."

Morgan wrapped his arm around Liam's waist. "I don't think that's blood, bro."

"Of course it is," Liam said, trying to break free. "Why else would his eyes be red like that?"

"He's sick," Amelia said.

"Sick?" Morgan questioned. "What kind of disease gives you red eyes like that?"

Amelia kept quiet as her thoughts came into conflict. The minion was beginning to take over, but if there was a chance her son could be saved, then maybe she didn't have to explain any of this to them. At least not in any great detail. What they didn't know wouldn't hurt them. Right? "I want both of you to go downstairs, and stay there."

"Like hell," Morgan argued.

Amelia faced him. "Morgan, don't fight with me on this."

"No, Mom, something's wrong with Chad. No one gets eyes like that from a disease."

Just then, Chad cleared himself of his trappings, maneuvering onto the balls of his feet and sat hunched over, his gaze switching between her and his brothers. His eyes glowed and he snarled like a wild animal. He opened his mouth wide, distorting his face and revealing full set of sharp fangs. Amelia felt the boys move behind her, and she extended her arms back, embracing them as they backed toward the door.

Without warning, Chad leaped into the air; mouth open, arms extended forward with fingernails grown out into sharp claws. Both boys screamed and fell to the floor, and Amelia fell back, shielding them with her body. Terrified, she watched the creature fall toward them. The stench of rotting meat filled the air as the creature came closer. Suddenly Amelia felt a force push through her body as a blinding flash of light came in contact with the creature, forcing it backward to hit the wall hard enough to leave an indent.

It happened so fast Amelia didn't have time to think.

"Is everyone all right?" she asked, looking for any signs of injury on the boys, but neither replied and stayed huddled together on the floor.

She felt around their bodies to check if the sachets were still on them. She wasn't sure why the creature was repelled, but she guessed it had to do with the herbs. Her intense relief caused tears to roll down her cheeks. Finally she had a way to keep her younger children safe.

"Mom," Liam's voice was shaky as he spoke to her from just behind her. "What happened to Chad?"

Amelia faced the creature as it sat against the wall, staring at them. His once thick, black hair now receded past his forehead, with facial features so grotesque she barely recognized her son.

The face contorted as its back arched and arms flew outward, tearing at the walls with its claws. Its skull morphed into two separate faces: one of the creature, the other of Chad. Amelia watched in horror as both screamed in pain, throwing their body violently against the wall. The skin around the minion's face stretched out from one side, then snapped back, disappearing and allowing Chad's features to completely reassert themselves. There was a moment of calm and Amelia saw a hint of recognition in Chad's eyes. Her son was still here, but the minion soon reappeared and the transformation began again.

This time the minion didn't attack. Instead, it crawled into the corner, leaving Amelia to watch with morbid fascination as the torso switched between the emaciated creature and her son.

"What's happening to him?" Morgan asked, as tears trickled over his cheeks.

"He's changing." Amelia barely spoke above a whisper. "Or trying to."

"Changing into what?"

She pulled them to their feet, and backed them slowly toward the doorway. "Come on."

The creature showed no interest in her or the boys, but Amelia didn't take her eyes off it. She forced herself to watch the internal struggle. Powerless to help.

"Is it going to attack us again?" Liam asked, reaching for the doorframe.

"I don't know," Amelia said. "But I think it was those sachets I gave you that protected us." She looked into its dark red eyes. "And I think it knows that."

Morgan felt around for the small sachet in his pocket. "Good herbs."

"Keep those on you. Don't take them out of your pockets."

The boys stuffed the herbs pouches deeper into their front pockets, and then turned their attention back to the creature. They got a few feet away when it looked as though Chad was winning. He snapped his head up, gulping for air, and looking at them in that all too familiar way.

"Look, Mom," Liam motioned toward it. "I think Chad's coming back."

Amelia held her breath as Chad appeared back in his own body. He was panting and his face strained as he tried to keep whatever it was from taking over.

"Mom," he said, tears ran down his face as he spoke between clenched teeth. "Mom, what's happening to me?"

Amelia pushed Morgan toward the hall, and then took a few steps forward, stopping just feet away and knelt to the floor. "You're changing," she said, trying to hold back her tears, "into some kind of a creature."

He looked confused. "Why?"

Amelia looked back at the hall, and then faced Chad again. "I'm so sorry," she whispered. "I tried to keep this from happening, but I didn't know what to do."

Chad tilted his head to one side, as though he didn't understand, then his eyes grew wide and he screamed. He ripped open his shirt, revealing the grotesque chest of the creature, as emaciated ribs pushed forward under his skin. Amelia couldn't take her eyes of the amulet as it burned red hot, bubbling the skin around the edges and welded itself to his chest. The smell of burnt flesh was overpowering as the skin fastened itself around the edges of the metal, sealing it in place.

Amelia lunged forward but an invisible barrier flashed and stopped her from getting any closer. Chad clawed at his chest, tearing into the soft flesh with his nails. She reached out to him, desperately pounding on the invisible obstacle that kept her from getting anywhere near her son.

Suddenly Morgan was by her side, tugging on her shoulder. "Mom, get away."

Amelia yanked her shoulder out from his grip. She couldn't leave. She wouldn't abandon her child to this creature, and she pushed Morgan toward the door.

"Whatever happens," she said, trying to keep her voice calm. "Don't come in here."

She heard them whimper from the hall as they watched their brother writhe around in pain. After a moment, Chad regained control, and looked at her, exhausted and frightened.

"Mom, help," he cried, reaching out to her. "It hurts so much. I can feel something trying to take over."

She turned back and knelt down as close to him as she could. "I know," she said, reaching out. "I tried to stop it, but we didn't have enough time . . ."

Chad tilted his head and frowned. "It's strong." He clenched his teeth as he strained to keep control. "I feel what it feels. Know what it knows."

Amelia clasped her hands over her mouth as her son's body meld with the creature.

"It wants to kill." Chad arched his back as the creature pushed forward. "That's all it wants to do."

"Fight it, Chad!"

He collapsed on to the floor, gasping for air. "I don't know if I can."

"You have to."

Struggling, Chad pushed himself up the wall into a standing position. A long forked tongue slid across sharp fangs, and he gave his brothers a smile that chilled her to the bone.

Chad grabbed his head and fell back down to the floor. "I can't stay here, I have to get out."

"NO!" Amelia jumped to her feet. "You leave here and I'll never see you again."

Chad raised his head and looked at her with his own eyes. "If I stay here, I'll end up killing you." He looked past her, to his brothers cowering behind the doorframe. "All of you."

"You don't know that."

"Yes I do."

With a powerful thrust, he leaped into the air, over her head, and landed perfectly on the floor between Amelia and the twins. Liam and Morgan screamed and dove away from the door, covering their heads with their arms.

"I have to get out." Chad's voice dropped an octave. It was ominous. Cold. His eyes were now completely red and glowing as vividly as the amulet that burned in his chest. "I don't want to hurt you."

He ran into the hall and Amelia scrambled after him. She heard the sound of breaking glass but, as frightened as she was, couldn't let him leave.

She found him on the back balcony, standing on what was left of the wooden railing. "Chad, please, don't leave."

"I have to," he said, tears streaking down his face. "It wants to leave, to get away from here, and I can't stop it."

Tears blurred Amelia's eyesight. "Keep fighting—"

"I can't!"

"Please!"

They heard a car pull up in the driveway, and car doors slam.

"Amelia!" Homer's frantic voice came from somewhere downstairs. A wave of relief swept over Amelia as she realized Jared and Homer finally made it, but she didn't take her eyes off Chad.

"Who are they?" Chad asked.

"Friends," Amelia said. "People who understand this much better than I do. Stay, please. If anyone can help you, it's them."

Homer's voice rang down the hall. "Amelia."

She turned to look inside the house. "I'm all right. We're out on the back porch."

"I love you, Mom." Chad's voice was soft, calmer than she'd heard it in years. Amelia turned back to the railing as Chad jumped into the darkness of the backyard, and disappeared.

Heartache surged through her, exiting her body as a loud moan as she collapsed to the balcony floor. It felt as though her heart exploded, and she screamed as loud as she could, calling his name over and over in between her sobs as the tears flowed down her face. She failed. Her son was gone, and there was no way to help him now.

5

Amelia sat at the kitchen table, head in hands, her mind a fog of uncertainty. She tried to accept what happened; her son was gone. Replaced by a creature from hell because of her husband. Henry won. He got what he wanted. How could she pick up the pieces of her life knowing she was married to a monster?

Her heart ached as she thought of Chad on the balcony. How soft his voice was, and the sentimental way he looked at her only deepened her anguish and guilt.

Homer draped a shawl over her shoulders and seated himself on the corner of the kitchen nook's bench. His hand rested on her shoulder, but she didn't look up. She couldn't pull herself away from her remorse to even thank him for his kind gesture. She cringed as he rubbed her back; feeling undeserving of his compassion.

"It's not your fault," he said, as though he could read her mind. His voice was soothing, but did little to remove the pain. "Please stop blaming yourself. There was nothing you could have done to save him. If anything, we're to blame. I promised to help you, and fell seriously short of that mark."

"If only I did more," Amelia's voice cracked. "I should have taken that damn amulet away from him the moment Henry pulled out of the driveway." She raised her head. Her hands trembled as she pulled the shawl tight around her shoulders. "Chad would be here right now if I'd just stood up to him and taken the damn thing away."

Jared sat down on the other side of the table. "You and the boys are lucky to have survived this long," he said. "That minion could have killed all three of you upstairs, but it didn't. I'd consider that a victory."

"A victory?" Her eyes narrowed, focusing on him through a few loose strands of auburn hair. "My son is dead and his brothers are frightened beyond belief, Mister Quinn. How do you consider that a victory?"

Jared leaned against the table. "Look, I'm sorry about what happened, and I wish we'd been able to stop it, but you're not out of this yet. You and the twins are still in danger. You need to know how to protect yourself if these things come back."

Amelia frowned and glanced over at Homer. "What does he mean come back? Henry got what he wanted. Won't they leave us alone?"

Homer took her hand off her shoulder. "Not always. We've heard of some incidences where the minion comes back to kill the rest of the family."

Panic gripped her again. She didn't think she could bear that thing returning in her son's body. "What if that happens?"

Homer and Jared exchanged worried glances.

Amelia knew what it meant. "You want to kill him, don't you?"

"I'm sorry," Jared looked away. "But now that he's turned, the only way to protect other innocent people is to destroy the vessel."

"You mean Chad!" A tightness choked the back of her throat. "You want to kill my son all over again."

"That *thing* isn't your son, Mrs. Saint," Jared said, sternly. "The moment that minion reared its ugly head, your son was gone."

"Jared, please," Homer said. "Try to be a little more understanding."

"No, I'm tired of this bullshit!" Jared got up from the table and stormed over to the counter. "It doesn't do her or anyone else any good, to pussyfoot around the fact that this may not be over. That minion is still out there, and there's a good chance it'll come back and finish them off if we don't try to kill it first."

"It's coming back?"

Liam's small voice cut through Amelia like a knife. She stood, but froze once she saw the boys standing in the entrance way to the kitchen, their arms full of blankets and pillows. They looked so young and helpless. Not even Morgan's tough guy attitude could mask his fear.

Homer jumped up from the table and went to them. "No, Jared was just being silly. He's just afraid—"

"Don't lie to them," Amelia cut him off, keeping her focus on the boys. "Jared's right. If I'd been honest with Chad from the beginning, maybe we could have saved him."

Amelia walked over to the twins and embraced them through the padding of pillows. They looked fine physically, but she knew what they'd seen would haunt their dreams for the rest of their lives.

"So, Chad is coming back?" Liam asked, trying his best not to sound scared.

"It's a possibility." Amelia cupped his face with her hands. "And I think Jared is right. It's something we should be prepared for."

Morgan looked nervously at Jared. "Really?"

Amelia tousled their hair and gave them a weak smile. It was the best she could do under the circumstances, to give them the strength they needed.

Jared pursed his lips and walked past them. "Let's hope not."

Homer led the boys into the living room as Amelia put on some coffee. She rubbed her eyes, trying to clear the fog from her mind, and slowly, she began focusing back on what was important. Chad was gone and she would have to live with that pain for the rest of her life, but Jared was right too. They had to be prepared, not only if the minion came back, but in case Henry did as well.

"We'll all stay in these two rooms tonight," Homer said, dividing up the blankets and then looking over at Amelia. "These rooms are big enough for us to set up and protect ourselves for the next few hours."

"I don't like it here anymore, can't we just leave?" Liam asked.

"We could," Jared said, searching the cupboards, "But we'd be leaving ourselves open for an attack if we did."

Homer spread out one of the blankets. "It'll be safer for us to move around in the daytime. Minions are weakened by sunlight. We'll set up here tonight, and then tomorrow we'll head to our motel room."

"But what if Chad does come back?" Morgan asked, grabbing a corner of the pull-out couch. "What if he comes back to kill us?"

Homer grabbed the other corner and pulled. "Don't worry. We'll be ready if he does."

"That's right," Jared said, walking back into the kitchen with two knapsacks and throwing them on the table. "He's a minion now, and *that* we know how to deal with."

Homer smiled at the boys. "We have things in those knapsacks that will keep away the strongest of nasty creatures."

Jared dumped the contents onto the table. Several small caliber hand guns, bags of herbs, dirt, salt and other things, dropped into a large pile and almost covered the tabletop. Amelia walked over to Jared, who looked more at ease now, and motioned her sons to join them.

"Wow," Liam's eyes were wide, "that's a lot of stuff."

"And it's all for fighting minions," Jared said, sorting out the items into piles.

Homer walked up to them and rummaged through the items. "Where is the herb salt mixture? I want to set up a perimeter as soon as possible."

Jared reached back into one of the book bags. "There's some here, but we're going to have to make more."

Amelia saw Homer frown as he held up a large plastic bag. "Just as long as there are enough ingredients to make more."

"What do you need?" Amelia couldn't believe the question leapt from her mouth.

Jared seemed at a loss for words. "Ah . . . the main ingredient we need is salt. Table salt, sea salt—"

"Rock salt?" she asked.

"That'll do. You have some?"

"We have four bags in the basement. For the water softener."

"We'll get it," Morgan said. "Me and Liam."

"No!" Her sudden outburst startled her. "I don't want you going where I can't see you."

Morgan's shoulders slump. "It's just to the basement, Mom."

Amelia felt a pang of anxiety. She walked to his side and flicked a few loose strands of hair away from his eyes. "I know, but—" She stopped talking as she looked into his face. "Fine. Do you still have those sachets?"

They showed her the corners of the pouches in their front pockets.

She nodded and stepped back, keeping her eyes trained at the floor. She didn't want them to see the fear in her eyes. "For Heaven's sake, child, tie your shoelaces properly before you trip and break your neck."

Morgan bent down, as Amelia tried to hide her trembling lip with her hand.

"It's all right," Homer smiled. "I'll go with them. They'll need my help anyway.

"Keep those herbs on you," Jared said, as he headed toward the fireplace.

Morgan huffed slightly as they walked toward the front hall. "Yeah, like I was going to take it out once we got downstairs."

A wide grin broke across Amelia's face. His sarcastic remark felt like a breath of fresh air. With her smile, she noticed the tension ease as well, but it was a fleeting moment of joy before the guilt set back in.

Amelia walked back to the table and opened a large brown book. The cover was battered and torn. "These are frightening pictures. Are these all minions?"

Jared took a quick look back. "Yup, minions and their overlords," he said, and bent down in front of the fireplace.

Amelia looked up at him and frowned. "And this Lyla woman is an overlord?"

Jared gave a curt laugh. "Lyla hasn't been a woman for centuries. At least, not a human woman," he said, feeding kindling to a small flame. "And from what I've read, she was pretty nasty when she was."

"She was human?"

"According to the legends she was. Some poor servant or slave. One story I heard cited her as the reason Rome fell."

Amelia sighed. "I can't believe Henry would get mixed up with someone like this."

Jared stoked the emerging flames. "Doesn't take much. A lie here, a promise there. Soon contracts are forged and before you know it, your entire world is being sucked into Hell."

Amelia closed the book. "Why do I have a feeling you're speaking from experience?"

Jared turned to her. "I did two tours in Afghanistan. A few weeks before my last tour was up, I was reassigned to a new company. One night, on patrol, we drove past an abandoned village where we heard these kids screaming. We turned, and headed back and found this family, huddled in the corner of a blown out building. They were hysterical and talking so fast our interpreter had a hard time translating." He paused for a moment. "We heard gunfire, and I figured this was an ambush, so I ran back outside, but this—" Jared shook his head. "—thing grabbed me and threw me up against a wall. The whole thing crashed down on top of me, almost buried me alive, and I remember hearing weapons fire and screaming from every direction, but the thing I remember the most, was watching that huge creature tear into the bodies of the other soldiers. Ripping them apart . . ." Jared turned away from her. "Medics found me the next day. Said I was the only one to survive."

"Did you tell anybody?"

"I did, but they thought it was stress and gave me a medical discharge."

"So how did you get mixed up with Homer?"

"Luck, I guess," Jared said. "Had to go to group therapy meeting when I got back, and one of the others in my group introduced us."

"How long has he been doing this?"

Jared stood up and walked over to her. "Don't know. A long time, I know that much."

Liam came crashing into the kitchen. Amelia smiled as she watched her boys interact in a way they hadn't done since they were small, and she clenched her jaw to keep her emotions from taking control.

"Those were heavier than I thought," Homer said, dropping his bag of rock salt on the linoleum. "These bags should be enough to safeguard the house."

She motioned both boys to her side before turning her attention to Homer. "I want you to teach us, all of us, Morgan and Liam included, everything you know about this. Knowledge is power, and maybe the more knowledge we have, the more power we'll have to keep this thing away." She looked over at Jared. "Like you said, this thing could come back for us."

It was a little weight off her shoulders, and this was something that would keep them isolated from the rest of their world. At least they'd be safe.

"Come on, boys," Jared said, grabbing a large bag from one of the piles. "Minions travel through shadows, so they can appear just about anywhere. That's why we have to set up a perimeter around this room." He pointed to the kitchen. "And that one."

"What if they do get in?" Liam asked, as he and Morgan dragged a bag into the rec room.

"As long as they're outside the salt line, they can't hurt us, and they won't be able to use the shadows inside the perimeter either."

Jared cut open the bag of salt, and then picked up several small containers from the table. "Remember this recipe. It'll save your life." He spread the salt out over the floor and grabbed one of the containers. "First, one tablespoon of Dragon's blood." He sprinkled the herb over the salt. "Second, one tablespoon of sandalwood. One teaspoon of crushed moonstone, one teaspoon of holy water, and finally, and this is the most important part," he reached in and brought out a small vial, "one teaspoon of magnesium."

Amelia frowned. "What's that for?"

A wicked smile flashed across his face. "You'll see."

Homer leaned toward her. "Magnesium infuses the salt with the herb mixture."

"It does? How?"

Homer suddenly looked uncomfortable. "It'll light the salt on fire when you drip water on it."

"Put those work gloves on," Jared pointed to a couple pairs on the floor, "and mix the herbs with the salt. We're going to need a lot of it to cover all the entrances into this part of the house."

Amelia opened her mouth to protest, but a sensation of dread crawled up her spine. The wind picked up and slammed hard against the windows. She reached out and grabbed Homer's hand. It was hot to the touch, as though the heat from her body had drained away. He turned his head toward her.

"You feel that," Homer said. "Don't you?"

Amelia nodded, realizing they must be sharing the same sensation.

Jared grabbed a small hand shovel from the bag and dug it into the salt. He jumped to his feet and laid a salt line across the floor in front of the balcony doors. "Quick, grab something and start making a perimeter."

Amelia turned toward rec room, focusing her gaze on the balcony doors. "Something's coming."

***

Sounds of the night reached out to Chad from all around. A hoot owl swooped and dove toward the ground, scooping up its prey in one pass. The frightened squeal from the rodent distracted him. Its high-pitched cry pierced through him like a bolt of electricity. He couldn't help but feel for the poor creature.

He could hear his mother's anguished cries as they echoed through the forest, piercing his mind like the tips of hot knives. He ached to return to her side, wanted it more than anything, but the creature that wrestled within him hungered for her flesh, sought the warmth of her blood to trickle through its fingers. Just the thought gave the creature strength, and Chad could feel it attempt to take control again.

It didn't succeed then, and it wouldn't succeed now.

He paused when she called his name in that familiar way she had of lingering on the vowel. He heard her pain, felt it with every breath. It tugged at him, caused him to stop and look back. Through the trees he saw her on the back balcony, held by a stranger whose scent came at him on the evening breeze. Tears blurred his vision as he realized he would never be able to return. Ever.

With a heavy heart, Chad turned his back on his home and walked into the obscurity of the woods. The night was different to him now. His eyes revealed a new world, one that hid within the darkness and gloom. Shadows moved with the wind, sliding from place to place along the ground as easily as autumn leaves drifted on the breeze. He could hear murmurs and whispers, recognized voices of those he once called neighbours and friends, and, as the clouds gradually sulked away from the moon, forms appeared, if just for an instant. Beings from other realms, appearing only when summoned.

He noticed the small nocturnal animals stayed a good distance away from him. Even the night owls flew off at his approach, making him feel miserable and alone. With each step a new instinct drew him deeper into the woods. It tugged at him, this irresistible urge to travel that he had to follow, if only out of curiosity.

Ten minutes of straight walking brought Chad to a clearing. At first he didn't recognize it, but soon memories of stolen nights with his friend quickly came to mind. He smiled as he sniffed the air, noticing a familiar scent. He wandered around the clearing, trying to pinpoint its exact location, and settled on a patch of dirt near a fallen log. It was strongest here, and could only be from one person—Tony. Axe body spray and cigarettes with a slight hint of whiskey from where Chad spilt the bottle the last time they were here. He'd been so nervous, finally scraping together the courage to tell Tina's older brother how he felt. They skipped school that day to spend some private time together before Tony left for college. The scent was still strong, and for a moment, he was content.

"It's about time you showed up."

Chad whipped around into a defensive crouch, as a young blonde woman stepped out from the shadows. She was attractive, lean, like a runway model, with a sultry cat-like walk that reeked of sexual fantasies. Oddly, he found her arousing, but knew she wasn't what she appeared to be, and there was something about the way the shadows fell across her face . . .

She snapped her boney fingers and instantly a line of green fire encircled him. "We've been waiting for you."

He could sense power within the flames, a force that pushed at him from all directions, restricting him to a small area within the circle. A memory of her in another place came to his mind. It was an old memory, centuries old. New and yet familiar.

Lyla.

"We?" Even his voice was foreign to him, and for a brief moment, he thought someone else spoke.

"Yes," she smiled, her lips forming a mocking snarl. "Myself, and someone you know quite well."

She moved off to one side, allowing Henry to step into the clearing. Even with his face partially hidden, Chad could see the cold glare of his father's eyes radiate from the firelight.

"I'm going to rip your heart out," Chad said.

Henry eyed him carefully. "You don't seem surprised."

"Mom said you did this to me." Chad rocked slightly on the balls of his toes. The urge to tear at Henry's flesh grew as his father walked around the circle of fire. "She told me you sacrificed my soul."

Henry's cold glare was quickly replaced with anger. "How did she find out?"

Chad focused on the woman, and then returned to Henry. "Why do you care?"

"Doesn't matter anyway," Henry said. "It's done and there's nothing anyone can do about it."

Chad gave a quick glance to the woman. Her posture stiffened, just slightly. Just enough to let him sense her irritation over this information.

"I don't think your new friend agrees with you."

There was a flash of concern in Henry's eyes before the cold stare returned. "Nice try, but once Korthos takes over, the sacrifice is complete, and then what she knows won't matter." He looked over at Lyla. "Agreed?"

Lyla inhaled deeply. "Nothing is final until Korthos is in complete control."

Chad felt a moment of relief, the force restraining him eased slightly.

"And that'll happen any time now," Henry said, a look of smugness on his face.

Lyla took a few steps toward the fire. "Sometimes the possession can take longer than anticipated." Chad felt her eyes on him, and he slinked away from her gaze. "Especially when the vessel has a strong spirit."

"Doesn't matter. Everything's going the way DeJont said it would. Korthos will surface, and when he does the gateway will be opened, and we can take out the Acheron Guardians."

"Only if Korthos appears within three days."

Henry looked stunned. "You have doubt?"

"This is a strong vessel. He is not as . . . weak as I hoped."

"Yeah? Well then you should have picked someone else."

She gave him a cold stare. "I did, but you claimed *your* child would be a better vessel." Lyla extended her arm toward the shadows in the woods. A long black tendril slinked out from the darkness and deposited a scroll in her hand. Her fingers appeared long and thin as she unrolled the parchment in front of her. "Nonetheless, if the minion does not have complete control over the vessel within seventy-two hours, then this agreement becomes void," she lowered the scroll slightly, focusing her gaze on Henry, "and you will take the vessel's place in hell."

Henry's body stiffened. "You don't need to remind me."

Lyla rolled up the parchment. "Good. Then I suggest you expedite the situation."

Chad smirked. "You're not only shitty at being a father, you're shitty at everything."

Henry glared at him. Chad never saw his father look so hateful and wondered if the man ever loved him, or any of them for that matter. He felt his rage build and struggled against the tight grasp of the invisible force. His mouth became dry as a burning sensation slowly forced its way up his throat.

Henry turned his back to the fire, but Chad's new senses let him overhear the conversation. "We'll keep him locked in the binding spell until Korthos completely emerges."

She raised her head skyward. "The lunar cycle is peaking. Once the moon starts to wane we will have until the Dark Moon to complete our task."

"So what's that? Three weeks?"

"Four, but the strength of the cycle now could work against us and weaken Korthos arrival."

"So how can we speed this up?"

Lyla glared at Chad from over Henry's shoulder. "It's thoughts of family and home that keep most vessels tethered to this realm," she said. "Break those ties, and he will have nothing to hold him to this world."

Chad didn't take his eyes off his father as Henry turned back to the fire. "I have no problem with that. I'll be more than happy to rid myself of all of them."

Chad frowned. "All of them? I thought you just wanted my soul?"

"Originally." Henry kept his focus on Chad. "But when Satan regains his place in this world I'm not going to be some junior partner in a shitty law firm. I'm meant for better things than wallowing around in other people's shit, so I've set my sights on something a little more . . . influential."

The way Henry looked at him stirred his suspicions. "You can't make deals with the Devil without a soul for payment. I always knew your younger brothers would come in handy for something."

Chad swallowed hard as the faces of the twins flashed through his mind. "You're sick."

"I'm powerful and I plan on staying that way."

Chad's gaze darted between the two. "You'll never get away with it. Someone will catch on. Mom already has—"

"Are you fucking deaf?" Henry interrupted. "It's already a done deal."

Chad's anger rose. The urge to slash at his father's face and rip him to shreds was growing stronger. He lunged toward Henry, only to have the ring of fire ignite and intensify. A low growl escaped his throat as Henry stood there and smiled.

"See, that's the best thing about these deals," Henry said, as Chad pushed back against the invisible barrier. "No one can stop me because I have all the power, and anyone who thinks something odd is happening, can easily be taken care of."

Chad hunched to the ground. He would be doing the world a favour by killing this hateful bag of flesh, especially where his family was concerned, but that would be giving in to his anger, allowing the creature to act through him, making it stronger. Chad closed his eyes and concentrated on the one thing that kept him calm—his mother's face. He pictured her at his party, with dark red curls framing her face and eyes glistening with tears. She smelled of wine and the cheap perfume he'd given her years ago for Christmas, and he knew no matter how much he may have hurt her, she loved him unconditionally. Her look of horror when the creature first appeared flashed through his mind, but he sensed it wasn't him she was reacting too, rather, her terror at what was happening. She wasn't repulsed; she was a mother horrified for her child.

Another image of a woman flashed into his mind. He didn't recognize the face, but she *felt* familiar. Chad forced the image to stay in his mind. Something about the way the eyes of this woman looked at him . . . but it wasn't him she was looking at . . .

Slowly the blood urges began to subside, and the heaviness that pushed against his body diminished enough to let him stand.

Lyla frowned. "What is happening?" She stepped past Henry and held her arms out over the ring of fire. "The binding spell is weakening."

The amulet burned brightly on his chest, but no longer hurt as it did before. Chad felt the creature try to rise again, but this time it wasn't fighting against him. He felt its strength and power course through his body as the amulet glowed.

Chad felt the sharp teeth return, the lust to kill was also there, but it was easier to keep under control. Thoughts of his mother filled his mind, and suddenly, he knew what he had to do.

With a wide grin, Chad bared his fangs. "Hate to talk and run."

He jumped high into the air, his body contorting into a back flip as he sprung out of the ring of fire. He felt the release of pressure against his body, and the air currents pushed him toward the edge of the clearing. He hit the ground on the balls of his feet and returned to his hunched position. The night was alive with living creatures, and he could hear them scamper through the underbrush as his presence returned to the woods. It felt good to be free of the fire, and he drank in the musty dirt smell that lingered in the air.

The minion inside was calm, or at least not struggling to control. Chad straightened himself up and stared hard at the two on the other side of the clearing. He smiled, and without saying another word stepped back into the shadows, becoming one with them as easily as breathing. Nothing felt better than seeing the confused look on his father's face. Chad vowed to stop him at any cost.

Within the safety of the shadows, the world flashed before his eyes at a dizzying rate. Different cities, countries, even continents exploded in front of him, in any bright places where shadows were present. He saw much of the world in just a few moments, but longed to be home, at his mother's side. New instincts told Chad to focus on his parent's house, the home his mother made for them. Instantly, he was standing in the shadow of the large oak tree near the far end of their property. He was slightly disappointed to not see her standing on the balcony, but he could hear her voice from somewhere inside the house.

There were other voices too. Chad recognized one male voice as the one who called to his mother earlier. A memory of his mother talking about them came to his mind. They wouldn't be here unless they could help, right? He moved through the shadows, close to the back door. Maybe they could help him find a way to stop Henry.

***

Homer grabbed the boys roughly by the back of their shirts, causing them to drop the handfuls of salt all over the floor, and dragged them next to Amelia. Jared ran over with a large scoop and hastily encircled them with salt.

"Don't leave this circle," Homer said. "It may be the only thing that saves your life."

Amelia was disoriented. Everything around her was happening too fast. Something was close, she could feel it, and the thought of the minions returning to finish them off, set off a new wave of anxiety.

She felt arms around her waist, and she and the boys sank to the floor. It wasn't fair. They weren't ready. They barely knew anything about defending themselves.

She heard Morgan speak. "What about you two?"

"Don't worry about us," Jared said, reaching for a material sack in the centre of the table. "Just make sure you stay in that circle."

Suddenly Homer was crouched in front of her. "Amelia, whatever happens, whatever you see, don't leave this area. Do you understand?"

She stared into his eyes. Their intense green glistened slightly and Amelia saw a hint of trepidation. Homer snapped his fingers in front of Amelia's eyes. "Do you understand me, Amelia?"

Amelia blinked and nodded.

Small pieces of debris slammed against the windows as the lights in the family room flickered. The wind howled through gaps in the doors and windows as dried leaves and dust flew into the kitchen and family room from the front foyer.

Amelia stood up, but kept her hands on the twin's shoulders, forcing them to stay down. The temperature dropped quickly, and she felt cold, as though her body heat were being sucked from her core. If there were more than one minion coming for them, Homer and Jared wouldn't stand a chance.

She turned to Jared. "Give me a weapon."

Their eyes locked for only a moment, but it was enough time for her to convey that she meant business.

Homer stepped over to her. "You don't have to do this."

Amelia held out her hand. "Yes, I do."

A steady stream of loose debris flew into the area as the lights flickered a final time and went out. The rooms were washed with an eerie glow from the small fire in the family room hearth, as Amelia held out her hand, waiting for a weapon.

Jared opened the cloth bag, pulled out two small caliber guns, and handed one to her. "Do you know how to fire a gun?"

"Nope," Amelia said, gripping the hilt. "But I'm guessing it's just point and shoot."

Jared smiled. "Yeah, something like that."

"Stay low," Homer said, motioning her to stay back. "And keep an eye on the shadows."

Amelia crouched down as the boys lay curled up on the floor. She cocked her weapon, keeping it trained on an area just ahead of Jared. She didn't like being out in the open, too much space to keep an eye on as her eyes darted from one shadow to another all around the room.

She kept a close eye on Jared as he took a step toward the patio doors. The burning embers from the fire flickered making shadows dance on the walls. She felt the boys move closer to her, and reached out with her free hand to rub the top of their heads.

"See anything?" Amelia asked.

"There is something moving toward the house," he whispered. "But it's too dark. I can't make it out. Homer, you got a flashlight handy?"

Morgan bolted for the kitchen table. "I saw one in here," he said, rummaging through the piles on the table.

Amelia's fear reared up, and she dove out of the circle, grabbing Morgan by the scruff of his shirt and yanking him hard, away from the table.

"What did Homer say?" she yelled, as he fell to the floor.

"But I just—"

"No buts! You do as you're told, or so help me God the minions won't be the worst of your problems."

Amelia's body trembled as Morgan crawled back inside the circle, one arm up, shielding his face. She stepped back next to him and tried to calm herself enough to stop shaking, but it was hard. She was too angry, too full of fear at the thought of how easily he could have been attacked and killed. Then she would have failed twice.

Homer found the flashlight on the table and tossed it to Jared. Amelia tried to keep her focus on the walls just ahead of them, but her head started to throb, causing her to lose focus. She saw Homer put his gun down and head to the family room.

Jared frowned. "What are you doing?"

Homer grabbed a measuring cup full of salt mixture and headed toward the entrance. "We're vulnerable," he said. "The perimeter isn't complete."

Amelia glanced down at the boys. "Stay here."

She ignored the protests from her children as she followed Homer's lead, and headed to the kitchen entrance. If Jared was right, their only threat right now was coming from the backyard. Amelia poured a line of salt along the baseboard following the wall, empting the last bit just as she got to the kitchen window. She turned to head back to the family room and found Morgan standing behind her, holding another full container.

She threw her empty one on the counter and grabbed him by the arm. "Get back in that circle."

His look of defiance was as strong as ever as he jerked his arm free of her grasp. "No, I wanna help."

Amelia reached for him again, but he pulled back and headed to the mud room entrance. She glanced back at the circle and found it empty. Liam was back at his place on the couch, preparing more mixture.

She marched toward him. "Liam, get back in the circle."

"Can't right now, Mom," he said, handing Homer another full container. "Kinda busy."

"Amelia." Homer's strong tone startled her. "You wanted them to learn how to protect themselves; that's what they're doing. Help them or leave them. We don't have the luxury of time anymore."

Amelia's shoulders slumped as she lowered her weapon. "But they're so young . . ."

Homer went to her side. "I know, and it isn't fair, but we need to protect this room by sealing it off."

Amelia rubbed her forehead, exhausted from the gauntlet of emotions. "All right. I understand." She didn't really. With everything happening around her, her concentration was waning.

Homer laid his hand on her shoulder. "Demons can't cross the salt lines. We'll be safe once it's laid out."

"Quickly," Jared said. "It's on the deck, just outside the door."

A wave of relief washed over Amelia as both boys dove for the centre of the circle. She stepped over the salt line, and aimed her weapon at the door.

"Will these bullets kill the minions?" she asked.

"If enough of them hit their mark," Homer said.

She steadied her aim as Jared turned on the flashlight and pointed it toward one of the small rectangular windows. He moved it slowly across the pane, and in the last frame, it illuminated Chad's face as the teen stared back inside the house.

Amelia's heart jumped into her throat.

"He's back," Jared shouted and fired his weapon at the door.

As quickly as the face appeared, it disappeared, and the room fell silent. Amelia's heart pounded as her eyes darted from one shadow to another, looking for any sign of odd movement. The beam from the flashlight travelled along the wall toward the kitchen nook, and again illuminated Chad's face in a window.

Bullets rang out from Jared's weapon again, shattering the glass but missing their target. Amelia held her gun straight out but couldn't bring herself to pull the trigger. Visions of Chad struggling in his bedroom swept through her mind. She knew what was at stake, knew what would happen, but didn't have the resolve to shoot.

Then Homer was at her side and yanked the weapon from her grip, pointing it toward the window. She felt the boys tug hard at her clothing and let herself be pulled down onto the floor.

Amelia turned away as Homer and Jared fired several more rounds at different windows. She couldn't watch them shoot her child.

Thuds were heard from somewhere upstairs along with the sounds of breaking glass. Amelia glanced up, a tear trickling down her cheek. "He's coming in through the upstairs balcony."

Homer and Jared repositioned themselves closer to the entrances to the foyer. She reached out and wrapped her arms around the boys, pulling them closer to her. She was tired and her body ached all over. She could feel the cold air drift along the floor, filling the room with a death-like chill.

"Why is there only one?" Jared asked, from the family room as he reloaded his weapon. "We should be overrun with minions by now."

Amelia saw a shadow move in the foyer. "He's coming down the stairs."

Homer was standing behind her. "Don't worry, the rest will show up soon enough."

Amelia couldn't see the minion, but her eyes fell on the wall straight ahead, and she watched and waited for it to attack from the entranceway to the living room. She heard the clicks of multiple guns and waited for the inevitable.

Nothing happened.

"Mom?" It was Chad's voice, there was no mistaking it. It was same soft tone he'd used the last time he spoke to her. "Mom, are you all right?"

Homer fired several shots into the wall. "She's not your mother."

"Mom, it's me, Chad. I'm still here. I haven't changed."

Amelia didn't reply as she pulled Morgan and Liam closer to her.

"Mom, please, I need your help."

"I've got your help right here," Jared said, and fired several shots into shadows of the living room.

"Stop shooting at me. I'm trying to talk to my mother!"

A cold gust of air blew over them. He didn't sound possessed, and she jerked forward, only to feel a strong hand grip her shoulder.

"She's not falling for that trick," Jared said, as his grip tightened. "Chad Saint is dead. We know you're a minion, and we're ready for you. You can't get to anyone in this room, so go back and tell your master to leave this family alone."

Amelia barely heard Homer's whispers as he bolted out from behind her. Startled, Amelia watched him grab a container full of salt and headed for the balcony doors. The only area they didn't have protected with a salt line.

Amelia saw Chad peek around the corner and knew it would happen. A strong gust of wind threw open the doors and blew Homer back onto the floor. Dirt and debris filled the family room and surrounded Homer until he was completely engulfed in darkness. Shadows disappeared as the wind blew the fire out, throwing the room into a thick blackness that choked any of Amelia's remaining hope.

Everything went still. Amelia knew where everyone was, and now there was one extra body. Like accelerant on a flame, the hearth suddenly exploded in a radiant blaze that lit up the room before dying down into a more reasonable fire.

No one moved but Amelia. Slowly, she rose to her feet, her heart aching at the sight of her son on the other side of the room. He was holding Homer in front of the fireplace, their bodies bathed in shadows. His one arm was draped across his chest, holding him tight with a dagger in the other, held to the older man's throat. Chad looked frightened, anxious, not the way he did when the minion was trying to take control before, and Amelia felt something odd about his presence.

"Let them go, son," Homer said, as he lowered the gun slightly. "Kill me if you want, but let them live."

Jared made a move toward them, only to have Chad tighten his grip and press the blade into his flesh.

"I don't want to kill anyone," Chad said, his eyes darting between Jared and Amelia. "At least, not anyone in this room."

Jared aimed his weapon. "Then let him go."

Amelia felt the tension rise as both young men glared at each other. "Only if you promise to stop shooting at me."

Jared cocked the weapon. "I don't make promises to minions."

"I'm not a minion!"

Amelia held out her hand. "Jared, please, put the weapon down."

"Are you insane?' Jared asked, taking aim. "He's a minion, Amelia. A killer!"

"No he isn't. At least, not yet."

Amelia took a step toward them. She could see its presence, the evil that lurked within her child, but there was something else there too. Something a little more familiar. "It's Chad," she said. "That's Chad . . ."

Jared grabbed her arm. "He's not your son anymore, Amelia."

"Jared, she's right," Homer said, struggling under the tight grip. "We'd all be dead now if the minion was in control."

Jared raised his weapon again and took a step forward. "I don't trust him."

"I'm still in control," Chad said, looking directly at her.

Jared kept his weapon trained on the teen as he stepped in front of Amelia. "It could be a trick. A way to make us lower our guard to make us think—"

"Minions don't trick people, Jared," Homer said. "They're vicious killing machines. You *know* that."

There was a look of confusion on Jared's face. "So what are you saying? That we just give over because he says he's in control?"

Amelia kept her focus on Chad as she stepped out of the circle. "Let him go, sweetie. I promise no one will hurt you."

She inched her way forward, cautious of every move that was made. Right now, it didn't matter to her if Chad was in control or not; Homer was in danger and besides, if what her gut was telling her, Chad wouldn't hurt her anyway.

With each step Amelia's heart pounded. She kept a close eye on him, watching for any sign that he would attack, but the closer she came, the more he calmed. As if her close proximity helped to keep the minion restrained.

Amelia reached out one hand to Homer. "Let him go." She kept her eyes locked with Chad, saw the anguish and fear. She exhaled slowly as he eased his hold on Homer a bit more, enough that the dagger fell away from his throat.

A few steps closer. "No one is going to hurt you, Chad." Both his arms fell to his side and Homer hastily stepped away from him.

Then Chad was in her arms, trembling. She embraced him tightly around his body and placed her head against his chest, listening to the familiar beat of his heart. His torso felt thin and small in her arms, and his full weight pushed against her for a moment as he fell to his knees, his arms still wrapped around her waist.

Amelia stroked the top of his head with one hand clasped over her mouth. Her breath came in shallow gasps as she closed her eyes tight. The warmth of her tears trickled down her cheeks, chasing off the chill of the room. Everything around her was growing warm as an overwhelming flood of giddiness filled her heart.

The minion was probably still inside Chad, lurking, subdued in some invisible crevice within his body, but right now, she didn't care. Right now, she had her son back, and that's all that mattered.

6

Amelia could do nothing but stare at her son. Chad sat restrained, his arms tied behind his back and his ankles securely fastened to the legs of a dining room chair. She stepped back, allowing Homer to finish encircling a large area around the chair with the protective herb and salt mixture, as Jared kept two weapons trained on the teen.

She studied his face. He still looked like her son, although small lines and creases around his mouth made him look older. His hair, shaggy, and damp with sweat, clung to the sides of his face. A hint of dark facial hair was barely visible in the dim firelight. Everything told her this was her child, but something deep down inside challenged her instinct.

"I think that should do it," Homer said, finishing the circle. "He's facing east with Holy Water and protection salt circling him." He turned to Jared. "I doubt you'll let your guard down."

There was animosity in the young man's eyes. "I'll stay awake all night if I have to."

"Good." Homer turned to Chad. "Let's get down to business." He bent down and grabbed two daggers that lay on the coffee table, and then faced the teen again. "What are you doing here? And why is it you're not a minion?"

Chad's gaze darted between Jared to Homer, and then rested on Amelia. She was caught by the intensity of his glare. His eyes were cold, lifeless, and Amelia wondered if any part of her child was still in there.

"You can't stop it," he said. His tone sent chills up her spine. "I'm still going to turn. I just came back to warn you. You have to know what Henry is planning."

Amelia's breath caught in her throat. "You've seen your father?"

Chad's eyes shone a deep crimson. "Don't ever call him that again.

No parent would ever do this to their child."

Homer lowered one dagger. "How are you doing that?"

Chad turned to him. "How am I doing what?"

"Keeping the minion from taking control?"

"I don't know. Right now it just doesn't want to fight me."

Amelia heard shuffling from behind as the twins came up and stood next to her.

"Mom," Morgan whispered. "What's going on?"

Amelia frowned. "That's what I'd like to know."

Homer stepped over the salt ring. "This isn't right," Homer said, examining the teen more closely.

Jared lowered his weapon. "Dude, don't be stupid."

Homer took a step closer. "The minion should have taken control by now. This is more like . . . shared custody." He bent down, examining Chad's face more carefully and then turned to Amelia. "I've never heard of this happening before."

"I say it's a rouse," Jared said, aiming the guns. "Maybe it wants to trick us into letting our guard down."

Amelia watched Homer closely. "What are you thinking?"

Homer straightened up. "I think somehow he's tamed the creature."

Amelia's heart skipped a beat. "Is that possible?"

"I don't know, but the fact Chad is still in control, what, almost an hour after the minion was supposed to take possession, says something."

The familiar sarcastic gesture wash over Chad's face. "Henry and that . . . woman were wondering the same thing." His eyes twinkled in the firelight. "But whatever control I have, I don't think it's permanent. Not from the way they were talking."

"So why risk putting your family in danger by coming back?" Jared asked.

Chad rolled his eyes. "I told you, to warn you about Henry." He glanced at Amelia. "He's not finished yet. They have plans for you," he looked past her to his brothers, "and them."

"A second sacrifice?" The words caught in her throat.

Chad nodded. "Yeah."

Homer sprinted to the kitchen table and picked up one of the worn books and flipped through the pages. Jared immediately took his place in the circle. "Did you hear anything about how or when?"

Chad pursed his lips. "They didn't discuss any details, but he seems to think he's meant for better things. I think getting this partnership was the first step to something more."

Amelia's gaze fell away. How could Henry have hidden this side of his personality from her for so long?

"Whatever it is," Chad continued, "he's going to do the same thing to Morgan and Liam that he did to me."

She heard the boys gasp behind her, and her gaze shifted back to Chad. "Are you serious?" She looked anxiously at Jared. "Can he do that?"

Jared snorted. "Henry Saint can do anything he wants. He has the powers of Hell at his fingertips."

"Yeah," Chad scoffed. "He made that clear too."

Amelia felt two sets of hands grab her arms as the twins came up behind her.

"Mom," Liam's voice was weak, "I'm scared."

Amelia wrapped her arms around them and drew them closer. "I know hon, we all are."

"Anything else?" Jared asked. "Like maybe something useful to try and stop him?"

Chad's eyes narrowed. "Yeah, something about the minion having three days to take complete control."

This caught Homer's attention, and he lower the book he was reading. "What about it?"

"If it doesn't happen in three days, Henry takes my place in Hell."

"Diabolus Clarus," Homer said. "The Devil's Clause."

Amelia felt a jolt of excitement course through her body. "So you're saying we could actually beat this? That he could be normal again?"

Homer sighed. "I don't know about normal. His body is an open gateway right now. If he does survive, there's no telling what could lodge itself in his body."

Amelia went to Homer's side. Herbs and salt aside, this was the first real acknowledgement they could win. "But if we help him survive the next three days, the minion would go away, and I would have my son back?"

Jared frowned at the older man. "It's not possible."

Homer looked down at the book in his hand. "It's a rare procedure. We won't be able to do it on our own."

"Then what are we waiting for?" Amelia grabbed some of the items on the kitchen table. "We'll just use all this stuff for now, and in the morning I'll go to the store and—"

Homer grabbed her by the arm. "Amelia, wait."

She whipped around, staring him straight in the eyes. "Why are you standing there? You know more about this than I do. Help me."

"Not here." He glanced back at the teen. "If we're going to do this, we have to do it right. We'll need to be in a sanctuary. Someplace the powers of Hell can't touch. It'll have everything we'll need to keep Chad safe for the next three days."

Amelia glanced at the clock. "Seventy-one and a half hours."

Homer smiled. "It's late. We'll stay here tonight, get a little rest, figure out our next move, and leave first thing in the morning. Preferably as soon as the sun rises. I don't want your neighbours nosing about."

There was a knock at the door and Amelia felt the tension in the room mount. Homer moved quickly to the living room, cloaking himself within the shadows

"Cops," he whispered, from the darkness. "Neighbours must have heard the gun fire."

Amelia's gaze darted between Jared and Homer. "What should I do?"

"Find out why they're here. It could be nothing."

Amelia headed for the front door. It was the last thing they needed. How would she explain what was going on? Could she? She hesitated before stepping over the salt line that crossed the doorway. "What if it's a trap?"

"It's a chance we have to take," Homer said. "We can't have those cops hanging around."

She took a deep breath, closed her eyes and stepped over the line. Another knock, this one more intense, urgent. She opened her eyes and scanned the foyer. Amelia didn't see anything lurking in the shadows and quickly headed to the front door.

The knob was cool in her hand as she gripped it tightly and pulled. Her stomach lurched at the thought of what could be on the other side. Cautiously, she opened it a foot and peered out. Two police officers stood a few feet back from the house. At first glance they didn't appear threatening, but Amelia wasn't sure of anything anymore. One officer appeared preoccupied with the outside of her home, moving his head back and forth, looking carefully at the front of her house. The second officer quickly acknowledged her presence and lifted his head, looking directly into Amelia's eyes.

"Mrs. Saint?"

Amelia braced one foot against the back of the door. "Yes."

"We had a complaint about shots fired at this address."

She feigned a look of concern. "Really?"

"Yes ma'am." He placed his hands on his hips. "If you don't mind, we'd like to come in and look around."

Amelia felt her mouth go dry. "Do you really need to, I mean it's so late and—"

"Ma'am, I understand that, but we have to follow procedure, and that means checking the property to make sure . . ."

The officer's words trailed off into a distorted voice. Amelia's vision began to blur. Her head throbbed with such intensity it felt like daggers slashing at her skull from the inside. She could barely hear as a dark shadow fell across the front step, but she saw the officers react, drawing their weapons and aiming directly above her head.

A gust of wind blew the door open, and Amelia was thrown to the floor. Her eyesight cleared enough to see a set of leathery wings descend from above, blocking any escape from the front step. The body attached was strong and lean, and as ugly as the creature that possessed her son. Sharp talons on the end of muscular legs reached out and grasped the officers around the waist. It squeezed their bodies in a grip so tight, their screams caught in their throats. Blood trailed from the corners of their mouths as they choked on their own fluids and bodies succumbed to the pressure of the grasp. The soft skin of their torsos ruptured, spewing out the decimated remains of internal organs and flesh through the claws. Amelia struggled to get away as blood and bone fragments splattered the tile floor around her. Her hands and feet slipped in the pools of tissue that coated the front entrance.

The creature then lifted into the air, taking the gruesome remains with it, and Amelia was left in shock, gasping for air.

Homer and Jared raced to her side. "Shit! Amelia, are you all right?"

She sat up and stared out the door. "What the hell was that?"

"A scrayling," Jared said, helping her to her feet. "Flying demons."

Amelia's mind reeled from the attack. "They fly?"

Jared shut the door as the intense throbbing returned. Amelia pressed the palms of her hands against her temples, hoping to ease some of the pain.

"What's wrong?" Morgan's voice came at them from the living room.

Homer ran to the kitchen entrance and pointed. "Stay there!"

Glass shattered from the huge window above, raining sharp debris. Amelia fell to the floor, shielding her head under one arm. She could hear the twins calling to her, and she lifted her head as something warm hit her hand. The metallic scent of blood was strong as she gazed on a small red lump that landed just inches from her.

"Oh God," Jared whispered, next to her. "I think I'm going to be sick."

Amelia's eyes trailed off to a large bloody mass a few feet away. She knew it had once been the torso of one of the officers at her front door, but it was unrecognizable now. Her eyes focused on the piece of flesh that lay near her hand, and felt the sting of bile rise in the back of her throat as she saw the ear lobe on one side of the flesh.

Homer pulled her to her feet. "We're not waiting for morning. We leave now!"

Amelia rubbed the blood off the back of her hand, onto her pant leg. "What happened to being safe here?"

"That was before the scraylings showed up."

Homer tugged on her arm and she lurched forward, but caught herself before stepping on a dismembered body part. She examined the foyer: pieces of wood and dried leaves lay scattered across the floor, mixed with tissue and blood. Spatters of crimson dotted the wall in front of her, and dribbled down toward the floor. Amelia took a few deep breaths, trying to calm the sickening feeling in her stomach.

"Come on," Homer said. "We have to leave before more show up."

She followed them into the kitchen, walking to the sink and turning on the tap. The water was cool and refreshing as she splashed some over her face. She looked down at her hands, rubbing her fingers over the area where the flesh had landed. Amelia could still feel the warmth and how it had trickled slightly down the side of her hand. Her hands trembled, and she clenched them tight, hoping to make it stop.

"What happened?" Morgan asked.

"Scraylings," Amelia said.

Amelia felt arms wrap around her waist and turned her head to find Liam smiling at her. "Are you all right?"

She motioned Morgan to come to her and gripped both boys tight. "I am now."

Jared stomped to the kitchen table. "Shit, Homer, how the fuck are we supposed to protect ourselves from a scrayling?"

"What's a scrayling?" Liam asked.

"A flying demon," Amelia replied.

"It's more than that," Jared said, looking at them. "Scrayling are like the ultimate killing machine, and they aren't limited to the shadows like minions."

"Can they cross the salt line?" Amelia asked.

"No, but they can tear at the floorboards and break it. If anything happens to the salt perimeter, the barrier comes down."

Homer picked up a knapsack and handed it to him. "Look, we both knew what kind of danger we'd be walking into if we did this. We need to get this family—including Chad—to a shelter as soon as possible, before Henry or Lyla discover a weak spot and throw everything they have at us."

"Are you serious?" Jared asked. "You still want to save the kid? I say we leave him here. It's him they're after."

"Chad is coming with us."

"He's a minion."

"Not yet he isn't."

Amelia stepped in between them. "STOP! Both of you." Amelia glared at each of them before focusing on Jared. "I get that you're upset, but understand, I am not going to abandon my child. So you're just going to have to deal with it."

"We won't make it," Jared said, in a calmer state, but she could hear the fear in his voice. "Those things are fast as hell and twice as deadly. They'll rip us apart before we even get to the car."

Homer picked up the second sack off the floor. "That may be, but we have the advantage tonight." He paused for a moment, turning his attention to the windows. "It's a full moon, remember."

"Moon magic is not going to give us enough protection."

"That's true, but we can see them better and have extra hands ready to shoot." He glanced at the twins. "With their help, we could make it."

Amelia's maternal instinct reared up. "I don't like the idea of my sons carrying guns."

Jared gave her a sarcastic look. "Do you want to make it to the shelter alive?"

Homer walked over to the boys and handed them each a handgun. "Sorry, Amelia, I know how you feel, but you don't have a say in this. We need to leave this place now, and that means everyone has a weapon." He held out a third gun to Amelia. "Including you."

Amelia looked down at the weapon, hesitating before taking it out of his hand. "I don't like this," she said, as both Liam and Morgan lit up with excitement. "Guns can go off prematurely." She looked up at Homer. "What about those sachets? Won't that protect them?"

"It'll keep them at bay, but it won't stop them from coming after us."

Jared loaded up one of the knapsacks. "Maybe if we take a few of them out, show them we can hurt them, they'll back off."

Amelia looked over the gun without saying another word.

"What about clothes and stuff?" Morgan asked.

"Leave it for now," Homer said, stuffing another knapsack with items from the table. "There should be a change of clothing where we're headed."

Amelia grabbed a serrated knife from the wooden holder on the counter, and then went to Chad's side. She bent down and began cutting into one of the knots that held his ankle tight to the chair leg. A low growl caused her to stop. She took a quick look up at Chad, a part of her hoping she was doing the right thing.

"Homer," Jared's voice held a hint of panic, "the kid's chest is glowing."

Amelia stopped fidgeting with the knot. Under the ripped material of the flimsy shirt, was the unmistakable glow of the amulet.

Chad looked down at her, his eyes shone in the same eerie glow as the amulet, sweat beading on his forehead. "They're coming."

Jared pointed the barrel of his gun at Chad's chest, and backed up to the counter. "Who's coming?"

"More of those things." Chad struggled to keep calm. "I can hear them whispering to each other. To Henry."

Jared ran to Chad's side as Homer threw one of the knapsacks over his shoulder. "What direction?"

"Southeast. From the woods."

"We'll have to go out the front door," Homer said, walking up to the twins. "I'll take the boys out to the van and stay with them." He glanced over at Amelia. "Don't take long. I want you right behind me."

Amelia nodded. She saw the panic in Liam's eyes, and gave them a reassuring smile. Homer took the gun from Liam's hand, in exchange for the knapsack, and checked to make sure it was loaded.

"Now, whatever you do," he said, gripping them by their shoulders, "just stay focused on the front door. Do you hear me? Keep your eyes straight ahead. Don't look anywhere except the front door."

Amelia saw them disappear into the darkness and went back to cutting the knot.

"Go." Chad's voice was harsh and throaty. "Leave me here."

"Not when I have a chance to get you back."

"Mom, please. Go!"

A flash of reflected light caught Amelia's attention as Jared pulled one of the daggers from its sheath and sliced through the rope.

"Stay with us Chad," Amelia said, working on the back knot. "You fought it off before, you can do it again. I know you can. You just have to be strong."

Chad looked up at the ceiling and nodded. "I can hear them," he said. "Hear what they're planning. I can help you get away from them."

Amelia wiped a few strands of matted hair out of his eyes. "Good. We're going to need all the help we can get."

Amelia worked on the knot around Chad's wrists. The throbbing in her head returned and she clenched her jaw to control the pain and to help her concentrate. She felt a rush of relief when the rope fell to the floor.

Chad cocked his head to one side. "Henry's summoned more scraylings. They're gathering in the woods, near the clearing where the kids go to drink."

"Great," Jared said. "Now there's a whole flock after us."

Amelia stood and grabbed Chad by the arm. "Come on, we have to leave."

She felt the full weight of his body as he rested against her. He looked tired and worn, and she reached out and cupped his face gently with her hand, making eye contact. "I still love you, no matter what."

"And what if he turns while in the car?" Jared asked.

Amelia looked at her son. She could see him fighting to keep control, but what about a moment of weakness? Would it try to overtake him again? They were heading into confined quarters for who knows how long. It would be the perfect time for the minion to rise.

Chad's eyes softened as he looked into hers. "Then shoot me."

Jared picked up his gun. "Fair enough."

Jared put Chad's arm around his shoulders as both he and Amelia helped the teen walk out of the living room. Even in the dim light, Amelia had no problem distinguishing the body parts that lay scattered on the floor. The smell of blood was stronger now, and she felt Chad grip her arm as the glow in his chest grew brighter.

Amelia spoke softly. "I don't think I'll ever forget how putrid the smell of blood is."

"Actually," Chad smiled, "I kinda like it."

Outside, a strong breeze whipped through the leaves and the noise played games with her mind. The whole neighbourhood was dark and draped in shadows. No doubt, Amelia assumed, from the intense storm that accompanied the minion's arrival. She looked up into the night sky. The light from the city core hung like a haze in the horizon, and the full moon obscured what little starlight there was. On any other night, she would have loved this tranquil evening, but she knew with the wind there would be trouble. There'd be plenty of other nights like this to enjoy. If they survived the weekend.

The police car stood silent at the end of the driveway. Amelia closed her eyes and whispered a small prayer for the officers, knowing their families would never learn the truth about their deaths. She clenched her jaw in anger. They didn't deserve to die. Just more victims of Henry's twisted scheme.

Homer opened the driver's side door of a beat up minivan. "You're going to have to drive, Amelia," he said. "You know these roads better than we do."

Morgan slid open the side door as Chad tumbled onto the floor. His body convulsed as he rolled over onto his back. Liam and Morgan crouched down between the seats, staying close to their brother's side.

Amelia watched Liam as he tried to make his older brother comfortable. "Don't worry," he said. "Mom'll figure it out."

Amelia frowned. "How is it they can get so close to him?"

"I took the herbs off them," Homer said, climbing into the van.

Amelia and Jared were stunned.

"Are you crazy, old man?" Jared asked. "Right now those herbs are the only thing keeping them safe, and you took it away from them?"

"How else were we all going to fit in the car, Jared?" Homer asked. "The barrier those herbs create is strong enough to push him away." He looked over at Amelia. "And we need him as close to us as possible."

"Fine." Jared handed Morgan a handgun and got into the van. "But I'm going on record as this being a bad idea."

Homer took the passenger seat as Amelia got in behind the steering wheel and took a quick glance over the dash. It was the same layout as her car, just a bit older.

She turned the ignition. "Okay, where am I going?"

Homer took a quick look out the window. "Head to the end of the street and turn right."

Amelia put the car in reverse and turned in her seat to back out of the driveway. She hesitated for a moment, at the confused expressions on both Chad and Liam as they stared out through the windshield.

"What's wrong?"

She followed their gaze skyward, squinting to get a better look. There was a dark outline of something large hovering in the night sky, slowly moving over them.

"It's not a demon," Homer said. "Or we would have heard it coming."

Amelia faced forward, confused. Her gaze fell on the entrance to the two-car garage. Something didn't look right.

"Where's my car?"

Homer slammed his foot on the gas pedal, throwing Amelia hard against the steering wheel. She pushed against the dash, trying to brace herself as the van sped backward and crashed into the side of the police cruiser. Thrown back against the seat, she barely had time to take in what happened when a second vehicle fell from the sky—landing exactly where they'd been parked.

With a thunderous crash, the windows in her vehicle shattered, blowing glass and small pieces of metal outward, pelting their crowded, beat-up van. Amelia could barely breathe. Her hands shook as she watched wisps of smoke rise up from the engine block of her demolished car. She gripped the steering wheel tightly in an effort to steady her shaking.

"They're coming," Chad said, barely above a whisper.

Amelia shut her eyes tight and rested her forehead on the steering wheel, trying to regain control.

"Amelia." She jumped as Homer's hand touched her shoulder, and she forcefully brushed it away. "Amelia," he said again. "We have to get out of here now."

Small twigs and garbage hit the side of the van as the wind picked up. She took a deep breath through her nose, slowly letting it drain through her mouth.

"Amelia!" Homer's tone was harsh. "Any time now."

"I just needed a moment."

Chad leaned through the gap in the front seats, pointing out through the windshield. "We don't have any."

Amelia heard the high-pitched scream as several scrayling landed on the roof of her house. The moonlight illuminated their muscular bodies, with their wingspan stretched out full. Two were tossing a round object back and forth.

"What are they playing with?" Morgan whispered, from behind her. "Never mind, I don't wanna know."

Amelia kept her eyes focused on the scraylings. "I don't think they know we're here."

"They don't," Homer said. "Scraylings aren't the brightest bulbs in the pack, but if we make any sudden moves, they'll come after us."

"We're trapped?" The fearful tone in Liam's voice tugged at Amelia.

"Not yet," Homer said, turning around to the back seat. "We're in the car, we have weapons. We just need to use them."

Amelia saw his determined look as Liam and Jared scrounged through several sacks under the seats. Her eyes went wide as she watched Jared remove a large shotgun and load it.

"We're going to fight them right here? In the van?" she asked, as more weapons came out.

"As soon as this van moves, they'll be all over us. We don't have a choice." He turned to the group. "Aim for the head or chest. Direct blows will kill them."

"And easy on the ammo," Jared said. "Make every shot count."

"Don't you have enough?" Morgan asked.

"Yeah, but that doesn't mean you fire randomly."

"Besides," Homer said, reading his weapon. "With the amount of scrayling that could be on our ass," he gripped the gun, looking out the window, "not even the military has that much ammo."

Amelia took a quick look at her boys, then face forward. "I hope you're right about this."

Homer readied his weapon. "Well, we'll find out soon enough."

7

Friday, 11:05 p.m.

Amelia checked her rear view mirror. Morgan and Jared took defensive positions at the back of the van as Chad switched places with Liam, keeping his younger brother on the floor and next to a pile of loose ammo.

Amelia's pulse raced as her foot hovered over the gas pedal. "Where am I going?"

"There's a small Catholic church right at the end of Range Road."

Amelia chuckled. "Well, Father George did hint he wanted to see us again."

She took a deep breath and rechecked the rear view mirror. She'd have to hit the police car again, there was no way around it, and she prayed the engine had enough power to throw them free.

The tires squealed as Amelia tromped on the accelerator. The beat-up van bounced off the side of the police car, shattering the windows on one side of the cruiser. The grinding of metal on metal threw sparks into the air as the van scrapped along the door panels, then bounced out of the driveway, hitting the street full force. Amelia yanked on the steering wheel and straightened out the wheels.

Homer gripped his gun. "They're taking flight!"

Amelia didn't look back as she shifted into gear and slammed on the accelerator again. The van lurched forward and sped down the road. She didn't stop. Not even when she came to the corner.

Tires squealed as she turned onto the main road of the subdivision. The church was on the other side, just past the golf course. The streets should be clear this time of night, and hopefully there weren't any other police in the area.

"Way to drive, Mom," Morgan said. "Didn't think you had it in you."

Amelia glanced in her rear view mirror. "To be honest, neither did I."

Liam grinned. "I did."

She caught Jared moving from one window to the next, keeping his gaze upward. The boys seemed calm and relaxed, but Amelia knew their calm demeanor was out of fear more than anything else.

"It shouldn't take us long to get there," she said, focusing back on the road. "I hope Father George will be able to help us."

"I gave him a heads up earlier," Homer said, keeping his focus on the outside.

Amelia was shocked. "You mean he already knows about this?"

Homer opened his mouth to answer, but Jared's voice filled the van. "Incoming!"

A scrayling screeched as it landed on the roof of the van. Amelia was thrown hard against her door, banging her head against the window as the vehicle swerved to one side of the road. Her eyesight blurred, and she blinked rapidly, trying to focus on the white line. She gripped the steering wheel tight, feeling the pull from the creature as it dragged the van from one side of the roadway to the other. Tires screeched under the pressure of being forced in the opposite direction as Amelia struggled to keep the van away from the curb.

"Don't slow down," Homer said, as he was thrown against his door. "If we stop, we're dead."

Amelia clenched her jaw and grabbed one side of the wheel. "I trying to keep control, but they're too powerful."

Gunshots caused Amelia to momentarily release her grip, and the body of the scrayling dropped off the roof and tumbled into the ditch. Shaken, she grasped the wheel again, and stomped on the accelerator.

The ringing in her ears barely let her hear Homer, as he turned in his seat and braced himself against the dash. "Good job, Morgan."

Amelia grabbed the rear view mirror and scanned the back seats. They were all holding their ears and grimacing, including Morgan, who looked more embarrassed than anything. "Thanks."

Homer rolled his window down a few inches and aimed the tip of his shotgun out the opening. "I'll try to keep them off, but it anything gets too close, don't hesitate to shoot."

Amelia turned onto Range Road and headed toward the golf course. They flew past a few houses at a speed she didn't even think the van could manage. Every few moments, her gaze would wander from the road to the scattered rooftops and skyward. She could see the scraylings in the moonlight, their wide wingspan and grotesque bodies shimmering in the moonlight as they kept pace with them, but stayed far enough away to keep out of their range.

Amelia jumped as Homer's weapon went off, but she brushed it off and kept her mind on the road, driving the vehicle at a fast, but a more manageable speed.

"You're driving too slow," Jared said. "You're letting them catch up."

Amelia snapped her head around. "Are you driving? No. So shut the fuck up!"

She turned onto a side road just before the main highway. She took a quick glance in the side mirror. The horde of scraylings was still behind them.

"What are you doing?" Jared asked, almost jumping into the front seat.

"The main highway doesn't have the exit we need to get to the church. We'd have to drive almost to the city."

"It's faster to take the highway."

"No it isn't, and we'd have to slow down to exit." She stepped on the gas. "This road takes us to where we need to go, and we don't have to slow down."

Homer looked out the window. "They're not attacking. I don't like it."

"Neither do I," Jared said. "Chad, are you getting anything?"

Amelia took a quick look at her son. He was sitting on the floor just behind her, a tranquil look on his face.

"Someone's not pleased we've made it this far."

"Someone?" Amelia questioned. "Who? Henry?"

Chad shook his head. "No, I don't know who it is. It's faint, like an aftertaste or something."

Amelia frowned at Homer, who looked just as confused. "What?"

Then something hard hit the side of the van, leaving a dent in the panel and jerking it off course. The winds picked up, bending the tree tops back enough that a few branches snapped off and fell to the road.

"What the hell was that?" Amelia asked, as she steered the van back on track.

"Minions," Jared said, pointing out one of the windows.

Jared moved in behind Chad. "They're trying to do what the scrayling couldn't. Force us off the road."

"How much longer till we get to the church?" Homer asked.

Amelia motioned ahead of her. "Another few minutes, once we hit the Twelve Mile."

"Can't you shoot them too?" Liam asked.

Amelia's heart skipped a beat. He'd been so quiet she forgot he was there.

"They're coming in too low," Jared said. "We'd have to open a door to get them."

Amelia watched the unnatural movement of shadows as they jumped from treetop to building, illuminating the minions in places the moonlight shone brightest. She let out a sigh of relief as she turned onto Mile Coulee Road and stepped hard on the gas pedal.

The back door suddenly ripped open and filled the van with a putrid wind, riddled with dirt and debris. Screams ripped through the confined space, and Amelia turned to see a desperate Jared clinging to the legs of the bench seats, her sons struggling to keep the young man in the van, as a minion held tight and pulled on his legs.

"Keep driving," Homer said, pulling the barrel of the shotgun back inside.

The van jolted sideways as glass shattered and pelted Amelia from behind. Another minion broke through and grabbed Morgan around the neck, pulling him toward the shattered window. Amelia panicked as her sons' frightened screams shifted her focus from the road to the attacking minions. Her head reeled from pain, and the smell of rotting flesh was overpowering. A third minion landed hard on the hood and dove toward the windshield, fracturing the glass on impact.

The van sideswiped into a guardrail, throwing Homer back, and tossing the shotgun from his hands.

The minion in front blocked her view and reached around to Homer's side, ripping the glass from the door. It grabbed him by the neck, and he struggled for air.

Frantically, she reached over and tried to break the minion's grip on Homer's throat, but the creature was too strong, and she was at too awkward a position to do any good, she only succeeded in swerving the van from one side of the bridge to the other.

A second shotgun blast rang out from behind, followed by the sound of shattering glass. Chad dove toward Homer. The glint of a blade caught her eye as it sliced into the flesh of the minion's arm, cutting it clean off and releasing Homer from its grasp. The creature reared up and screamed as black ooze sprayed the inside, some splattering along the side of Amelia's cheek, burning her skin.

Amelia gripped the side of her face. She could smell burnt flesh as the ooze ate away at her skin. She couldn't focus on the road, but two arms reached out from behind her seat and took the steering wheel.

"It's okay, Mom," Liam whispered in her ear. "I've got it."

Amelia eased up her foot on the gas. She couldn't stop the vehicle altogether, not with them out in the open and so many minions all around.

The throbbing in her head began to ease, but her shoulders ached, and the one side of her body felt blistered and raw. Not to mention there was a constant ringing in her ears from the confined shotgun blasts. After a few blinks her eyesight returned to normal, and she took the steering wheel back from Liam.

"Here," Homer said, and touched the sores on her hand with a cloth. She could barely hear him over the ringing.

Amelia winced as her hand jerked at the sudden contact. The cloth felt cold and wet, and oddly soothing. "What's on that?"

"Holy water mixed with herbs," Homer said, and dabbed a few spots on her face. "It'll keep you from getting an infection."

Amelia sat straight and fixed the rear view mirror. She caught a glimpse of Jared in the back, lying on the floor with Chad and Morgan tending the wounds.

"Is Jared all right?" she asked.

"Yeah," Jared replied, and placed his forearm over his eyes. "Just a little beat-up."

Chad took a shotgun and poised it, ready to shoot.

"That was you shooting?" she asked.

Chad turned to her. "I had to do something."

Amelia stepped on the accelerator. The smell of fresh air was a welcome relief. She kept her eyes focused straight ahead, occasionally seeing a minion lurking in the shadows. The wind blew strong thought the trees. The minions weren't attacking, but Amelia knew that didn't mean they were safe. Far from it.

Homer checked the stock of ammunition. "I don't like this. They should have torn this vehicle apart." He took a quick look out the window "Where's the church?"

"Shouldn't be too far away."

He pointed out the window, straight ahead of her. "Do you see that beam of light off in the distance?"

Amelia squinted into the darkness. "Barely. What is it? A search light?"

"It's awful bright," Chad said, holding his hand up to his eyes. "What is it?"

"The Light of God." Homer smiled. "Normal people can't see it that well, it comes to them more like a feeling, but it radiates from churches, synagogue, temples. Basically all places where people come to practice their faith."

"Why haven't I seen it before?"

A sympathetic smile crossed his face. "Because you haven't had to deal with anything like this before now."

"And we'll be safe there?" Liam asked.

"For now. Evil can't penetrate the Light. Not while it's strong, but it can corrupt it, and weaken it. We'll need to be careful."

Amelia took a quick glance back at Chad through the rear view mirror. "What about Chad? With that thing inside him, will that corrupt the Light? I mean, we didn't just drive out here and go through all this crap for nothing, did we?"

"It's the only safe place right now, Amelia," Homer said, placing the shotgun on his lap. "I spoke to Father George the other day, and we went through all the scenarios."

Chad snickered. "Even this one?"

Amelia felt a sense of frustration building. "And what did he say? What did you two plan in case something like this happened?"

"Amelia, you have to understand. I've never seen a case where the minion didn't take control. This is brand new territory for me, and Father George wasn't too convinced this particular scenario would play out."

"Oh, this should be interesting," Morgan said.

Amelia saw the light from the church grow the closer they came. She always thought it was a pretty church, the way it sat on top of a hill, looking down over the town. The architecture and the cemetery at the back of the church showed the building was old, and Amelia felt comfortable the few times she and the kids went for mass.

"The wind's dying down," Jared said. "Do any of you see a minion or scrayling around?"

"No," Homer said. "And with the moon still out, we should have no problem spotting them."

Amelia smiled. "Maybe they just gave up."

Jared let out a bit of a laugh. "They don't just give up. Something's going on."

"Maybe they're waiting for another chance to come after us," Morgan said.

Amelia caught his attention in the mirror. "I'd like to see them try."

Suddenly, Liam pointed toward the windshield. "DAD!"

Amelia's gaze flew to the road ahead of her, and her heart leaped into her throat. The headlights shone directly ahead and on Henry, standing in the middle of the road just a few yards ahead of them.

She slammed on the brakes, swerving the vehicle and throwing everyone to one side of the van. The back end fishtailed as she tried to regain control, but a scream from a minion accompanied by another jolt to the side, threw the vehicle into a tailspin. Amelia lost her grasp on the steering as the van descended into the small gully next to the road. The front airbags deployed, knocking her back into her seat as the sound of grinding metal signaled the end of their road trip.

Amelia could barely focus on the voices coming at her from all directions. She heard her children; they were frantic, and her need to keep them safe forced her to come to her senses. With a loud groan the driver-side door opened, and she felt strong hands pull her from the vehicle.

"Amelia." She focused on Homer's voice. "Amelia, are you all right?"

She slumped to the ground, feeling the cool of the night air all around her, but the musty smell of dirt and swamp was nauseating, and her stomach heaved slightly.

Liam's dirty sneakers came up next to her, and slowly Amelia raised her head.

"Mom?"

"I'm fine." She took a deep breath and reached out to him as she tried to stand. "Nothing's broken. What about you?"

"We're fine. Good thing we weren't going that fast when we hit the tree."

She leaned up against the front wheel well, rubbed her eyes, and looked around. A sudden jolt of fear gripped her as she realized they were out in the open and very much vulnerable.

"Here," Homer came up behind her, and grabbed her by the arm, yanking her to her feet. "Come on. We need to keep moving."

She searched the area frantically. "Where's Henry?"

"Gone," Jared said from the back of the van. "Disappeared."

Amelia gasped as she saw the claw marks that ran the length of Jared's legs. "You're hurt badly."

"I'm fine." The young man smiled and threw a knapsack over his shoulder, leaning up against Morgan for support. "Stings, but I won't let that stop us."

Homer put his arm around her waist and led Amelia back up to the road. The moon was still bright, but lower in the sky, just over the treetops. She gripped Homer's arm tightly as she watched a horde of scraylings circle the area.

"The moon is setting," she said, climbing out of the gully.

"I know," Homer checked the guns he carried with him.

"I can hear them whispering," Chad said, coming up behind them.

Amelia looked at the tree canopy and noticed several minions lurking on the higher branches. Scraylings circled above, but not one made a more toward them.

She took one of the shotguns from Homer and started down the road.

"Stay in the middle," Homer said, as they shifted toward the white line. "We're safe as long as we stay away from the shadows. I don't want to give them any chance to reach out and grab you."

"Oh, perfect," Morgan said, in a dry tone put a smile on Amelia's face.

Amelia walked next to Liam, with Homer and Morgan in front, helping Jared, and Chad in the middle. She watched the expressions on Chad's face as his focus switched between the creatures that hovered in the sky and shadows. They flickered between utter disgust and envy, and she wondered just what he was reacting to.

Shadows moving through the trees pulled her attention back to the road. The setting moon cast shadows that reached out to the middle of the road and Amelia could see the minions lurking in the dark, waiting.

"They can't attack," she said, as a few reached out, only to be repulsed by the light.

"I think we're gonna make it," Jared said, smiling.

The wind began to pick up as more scraylings joined the horde above them. The creatures no longer circled them, instead, hung in groups above the treetops, watching them as they made their way up the road.

Liam stopped. "What are they doing?"

"Keep going," Homer said.

It was a low rumble that caused Amelia to turn around. At first she wasn't sure where it was coming from, but, as the clouds on the horizon drew closer, she realized this was no ordinary weather. The dark clouds billowed up, spewing forked lightning that split the ground open on impact, creating tunnels that glowed with the fires of Hell. Black ooze bubbled up from the sides of the holes, coming together to form skinless corpses. Their twisted bodies scampered across the ground like crabs, their mouths open as they charged toward them.

"Shit," Homer said. "Imps! Run!"

Amelia grabbed Liam's arm as they raced toward the stone fence of the church. A flash of lightning impacted the ground a few feet from Liam, forcing open a rift that quickly spread toward them.

"They can't get us from the air or shadows, so they're going to rip the ground out from under us," Homer yelled.

Amelia fell back as Liam lost his footing and fell partially over the edge of the chasm. She dropped her gun and gripped his arm with both hands as he clawed at the ground to get out.

Lightning stabbed the ground around them, opening more holes and releasing more creatures.

"Get to the church," Homer said to Morgan, as he grabbed Liam by the arm and pulled him forward.

The boney arm of an imp reached up and grabbed Liam by the ankle. Liam screamed in pain as the lower end of his pant leg burst into flames.

"Leave him alone," Amelia said, and stomped down on the wrist of the creature, breaking its grip.

Homer lifted the teen from the chasm as more lightning hit the ground, but the imps stayed in their holes. Amelia grabbed her gun and made a dash for the church. She hit the wrought iron gate and pulled it open, pushing Liam across the threshold.

She turned back and aimed the shotgun at several imps close to Morgan's side, as he and Jared stumbled toward them. She pulled the trigger and a creature several feet away exploded, dissolving back into the black ooze. Bone-chilling screams from the scraylings above disoriented her, and she had to focus hard on her next shot. More scraylings screamed, and Amelia felt lightheaded as the energy drained from her body.

"Hurry!" Amelia fired off a few more rounds, but her aim was off, and she hit trees or nothing at all.

"Stop shooting here."

Amelia turned to find Father George racing toward them, waving his arms in the air.

"You have crossed onto Holy ground," he said, stopping just a few feet from her. "Violence is not permitted!"

Amelia looked back at the road. Chad and the others were trapped on the other side of a large tear in the ground. They were close enough to the property that the creatures halted their assault, but more lightning strikes were opening new holes and making the gulf wider.

"We can't get around it," Jared said, aiming his shotgun at the closer imps.

"Fine." Homer pulled Morgan close to him. "Then we go over them."

Amelia's heart leapt into her throat as she watched Morgan take a few steps back then run and leap over the chasm. Skeletal arms reached up toward his legs, but a shot from Homer's gun kept them from getting a grip.

Amelia turned to Liam. "Stay here, and I mean it this time."

She stepped past the gate and took aim at the growing pit as Morgan ran past her and stood next to his brother.

"I can't jump that," Jared said. "I don't have enough strength in my legs to get a good running start at it."

An amused expression appeared on Chad's face. "Fine."

Chad grabbed Jared on both sides of his waist and threw the young man across the pit as if he were weightless. Amelia shot a few rounds, as

Jared tumbled to the other side and rolled along the ground.

"Give me your gun and help him into the church," she shouted at her sons.

Morgan handed her is weapon. "What about you?"

"I'm coming, but not without your brother."

She watched as the twins helped Jared up the steps and into the church and then poised herself to shoot off another round, as Homer motioned Chad to go. Scraylings swooped down from the treetops, coming closer to both with each pass.

"Hurry!" she yelled.

"Go, now," Homer said. "Before it gets too wide."

"No, you have to go. I can jump this, no problem, but you won't be able to make it across if it gets any wider."

Homer grabbed Chad by his shoulders. "Don't worry about me, it's you they're after. You're the one that needs to be protected."

Chad brushed free of his grip. "I'm already screwed, but Mom is going to need your help to keep my brothers safe."

Amelia shot off another round, clearing a path as Homer took a few steps back. Several more imps rose to the surface, and the tear expanded.

Homer took a running leap over the chasm, landing just on the edge of the other side. Amelia grabbed hold of his shirt as he hit the ground, steadying his landing and pulling him away from the pit.

"Come on, boy," Homer said, and took aim at several imps.

Amelia's fear grew as the tears merged together, creating wide chasms that stretched out along the edge of the stone fence. She watched Chad take a few steps back, and to her amazement, effortlessly leap to her side.

He smiled wide as he looked back at the road. "See, told you."

Amelia grabbed her eldest son and pulled him toward her. She could feel the amulet press against her chest, and for a moment she thought about the creature inside, but as his arms went around her waist, her fear subsided, and she held him tight.

The night filled with screams from all creatures as they tried to push their way through the Light and toward the stone fence. Amelia backed up, grasping his hand and pulled Chad as she moved toward the gate. A few steps from the property, Chad was suddenly thrown to the ground, and slid on his back to the edge of the chasm.

"Chad," Amelia shouted. "What happened?"

Amelia saw the amulet glowing as he struggled to get up. "It won't let me in." he said. "The Light won't let me pass through the gate."

Amelia took a few steps toward him, but Homer's grip on her arm kept her from getting any closer. She sunk to the ground and reached out to her son. She watched as Chad struggled to push his arm through the Light.

"I told you this would happen, Homer," Father George said. "He is a servant of Hell. He cannot pass through these gates."

"He's a child," Homer lashed out. "He didn't bring this on himself. It was done to him."

"I'm sorry, I don't make the rules," the old priest said. "He is an abomination to God's love. My hands are tied on this."

"Bullshit! You get that damn shroud and bring it out here, now," Homer said. "And don't tell me you don't know what I'm talking about, because I know all Catholic churches have one!"

Amelia looked back. "What shroud?"

Father George didn't look impressed. "It is a Holy Relic, and I'm not about to pollute it because—"

Homer raised his weapon and pointed it at the priest. "Get off your high horse. There's only one reason the church has that relic, and if you don't go and get it, I'll personally rip that building apart until I find it."

Father George held no expression as he turned and walked up the stone walkway to the church steps. Amelia quickly went to his side.

"What shroud are you talking about?"

Homer lowered his gun. "It's the one weapon the Catholic church has, that actually has any effect on minions or their overlords." He pushed Amelia past the gate and onto the stone walkway. "It's a sash, the source for this protective Light."

"Why haven't I heard of this before?"

Homer smiled. "There are a lot of things people don't know about. This is just the tip of the iceberg."

It felt like hours before the priest returned. He carried a gold-leaf box in his hands, but didn't come any farther than the entrance to the gate.

"You must place this over his body," he said to Amelia.

"I'll do it," Homer said. "I don't want her off church property."

Father George yanked the box away. "No, her love for the child is stronger than yours. She has to do it."

Homer opened his mouth to argue, but Amelia stopped him.

"I can do this." She lifted the lid and removed an embroidered cloth several yards long. "Just keep me covered."

Her legs felt weak as she walked toward Chad. There was something about the feel of the material in her hands that brought her a sense of peace, and she could tell from the look on her son's face that it was having the opposite effect. He winced in pain with each step she took, and pushed himself away.

"I can feel it," he said. "It hurts."

Amelia unfolded the shroud. "It's the only way."

She reached out to drape it over his shoulders, and felt a wave of dizziness wash over her.

"Amelia?" Homer asked. "What's going on? Why did you stop?"

Amelia closed her eyes as Homer's voice trailed away in her mind. The air grew warm and moist, and she could smell Henry's scent all around her. The musky aroma brought back memories of a few days ago, in their ensuite and how handsome she thought he looked.

Henry's voice was soft in her ear. "You're still my wife."

She forced her eyes open and found herself in their bedroom, naked, with Henry standing just inches away. One of her good towels was the only thing between them. She looked into his eyes, and her heart skipped as she saw his affection. His hand was at the small of her back, pressing her closer to his body. His skin was warm and wet from the shower as small beads of water trickled down his skin.

He gave her a look that made her feel weak in the knees. "Let go of it, Amelia. I don't want anything to come between us."

Amelia placed her hands on his chest as he lowered his head. His breath was hot on her neck and sent shivers through her body. Warm lips touched her skin, gently moving toward her chin, and she pressed herself tighter up against his body.

She slid her hands along his chest, felt his muscles tense up under her touch as she wrapped her arms around his neck. She smiled as Henry nibbled playfully at her chin. His eyes met hers as he nibbled on her bottom lip.

"You'll always be my wife."

She closed her eyes, ready to accept his lips, but instead, a rough jolt pulled her backward and ripped her from Henry's embrace. The air grew cold, and when she opened her eyes she was back in front of the church, standing in front of Homer with the shroud on the ground at her feet.

"What the hell?"

Shocked and disoriented, Amelia searched Homer's face for some kind of explanation. "What happened? I was just in my bathroom, then—"

"Yeah, I thought so. Forced hallucination," Homer said, and put a cork back on a small vile. "It's used when the servants of Hell get desperate for their soul. Nothing a few drops of Holy Water to the head couldn't clear up."

Amelia noticed the shroud on the ground and Chad still cowering just a few feet away. She picked up the shroud and gently placed it over his shoulders. Wisps of smoke rose from underneath the shroud as Chad struggled to his feet. Homer went to Chad's side and helped the young man through the gate.

Amelia turned to follow, when a sense of dread washed over her. She turned to the road, the chasms slowly retreating back into the earth. Through the smoke and glow, Amelia saw Henry emerge from the shadows and walk toward her. He looked different, younger, like he did when they were in college. Even the clothes he wore were different. More stylish.

"Shit," Homer said.

Amelia felt the weight of Henry's stare as he came closer. She felt lightheaded, disoriented, and there was a small part of her that was happy to see him again. She smiled weakly and took a few steps forward.

Homer's hand gripped her shoulder. "Don't get any closer, Amelia."

"Homer?" Henry said, slightly amused. "Well, haven't you aged? The years have not been kind to you."

Amelia looked up at Homer. "I think we know who gave you the forced hallucination," he said.

Amelia faced Henry. "You did that? You put that vision into my head?"

His condescending smile sliced through Amelia. "Wasn't hard. You were always looking for something better. I just gave it to you."

Amelia looked at the man standing in front of her, and for the first time, saw him for what he was.

"Everything was a lie, wasn't it?" she asked, but she knew the answer.

"You're a means to an end," Henry said. "Henry giveth, and now Henry taketh away."

"You won't win," she said. "I have friends."

"You can't stop me, Amelia. You know I always get what I want."

She took a few steps back. "Not this time."

Henry raised an eyebrow. "Are you sure about that?

Amelia stepped behind the gate and closed it. "Go to hell, Henry."

His callous smile resonated in his reply. "You first."

8

Amelia sat in the last pew, her eyes unfocused as she stared toward the floor. Her stomach ached as though she'd been hit with a lead ball. Her life with Henry was nothing but a lie. A means to an end, he'd said, and she wondered why she didn't see his manipulations before now.

Footsteps echoed off the walls, and someone sat on the bench behind her. Amelia barely acknowledged them. Her mind was lost is a fog of betrayal and pain.

"You should get some sleep," Homer spoke softly from behind her. "This fight's just getting started."

Amelia's breath came in shallow gasps. "How did I not see what he was? What he was doing?"

"This isn't your fault, Amelia." She felt his hand on her shoulder. "Henry is powerful, and thanks to Lyla, his skills at manipulation are just as strong."

She turned and gazed into his eyes. "But to harm his own children? What kind of person could condemn their own child to the fate like that?"

He lowered his head, taking his hand off her shoulder and played with his fingers. "This is all my fault."

"None of this is your fault. You've both been incredibly helpful. We're safe because of the both of you."

His gaze darted between her and his hands. "Not safe enough. Maybe if I'd looked harder, been more careful, I could have tracked him down sooner. I could have stopped all this years ago."

Amelia frowned. "What are you talking about? You said omens led you to Henry."

Homer raised his head, but didn't meet her gaze. He shuffled in his seat. She didn't like the way he refused to look at her, and then the fog began to clear from her mind. "Wait, he called you by name. He knows you."

An awkward look washed across his face.

Amelia had seen this look before. The boys gave her that look when she'd caught them in a lie. "What is it you're not telling me, Homer? How do you know Henry?"

Slowly, his eyes met hers. "Henry's my younger brother."

It felt as though the air had been ripped from her lungs. Amelia stared at him, stunned, unable to find the words she needed to yell at him for not telling her before now.

"Younger brother?"

"Half-brother, actually," Homer stammered. "My mother died when I was about six—car crash—and my father never really knew how to raise a child, so he married the first woman that came into his life." Homer leaned back against the pew. "Unfortunately, that woman happened to be Lyla."

Amelia's mind instantly focused. "Wait, she's his *mother?*"

Homer nodded. "Yup. I don't remember much from when I was young, but I remember the day she showed up at our house. There to babysit, and the next thing, she and my father were married. Then Henry came along. She didn't stick around after that."

"Does Henry know?"

"That she's his mother? Oh yeah. The old man was always nasty to him. Blamed him for her leaving, so when she showed up out of the blue one day when he was a teen, promising to make his life better, he jumped at it."

Amelia let her gaze fall away. "Henry never mentioned his family. He told me once that his father was hard on him and always said he wouldn't amount to much." She looked up at Homer. "I always figured it was the reason he was so driven to succeed."

"Yeah, Henry and Dad had some nasty fights." A smirk crossed his lips. "Chad reminds me a lot of Henry at that age."

Amelia ran her hands through her hair, feeling her anger rise to the surface. "And you neglected to tell me this because?"

"Because at first I thought you were in on it."

Amelia slammed the back of the pew with the palm of her hand. "Dammit Homer, I can't believe you didn't tell me until now."

"Sorry, Amelia, but I've been a bit busy trying to save your lives. Besides, I wasn't even sure any of you would survive."

"Oh, thank you for your confidence." She rubbed the red part of her palm, and her anger began to dissipate. "He's had this planned for years, hasn't he?"

"I don't know. Yes, no, maybe. I lost track of him just before he went to college. Must have been when he changed his name."

Memories of her and Henry on dates floated through her mind. "He said he was an only child, so he wanted to have a big family, but after Chad was born, that was it. No more."

Homer frowned. "What about the twins?"

Amelia smiled. "Too much alcohol at a Halloween party." She turned around in the pew. "He could have planned this whole thing years ago."

"It's possible." Homer leaned forward and braced himself on the back of her pew. "One thing I do know, there's a lot more going on here. The creature nesting inside your son is a powerful demon by the name of Korthos. He's the right hand of Satan, and he needs Korthos on this side for his plans to take hold."

Amelia gently shook her head. "The idea that Lucifer is real . . ."

"Lucifer has nothing to do with this."

Amelia frowned. "What . . .?"

"Lucifer and Satan are two different beings." Homer rubbed his face. "I'll explain later. Right now, we need to focus on Chad."

She nodded. "I overheard Henry talking to this Lyla about performing a ritual once the minion was in control. Does that mean something?" She looked hard into his eyes. "Tell me what you know, Homer. All of it."

"I have friends who feel very strongly that everything happening here is a catalyst for the apocalypse."

Amelia smirked. "You're joking."

"I wish I were."

Soft footsteps came up behind them as Father George walked toward the pews. "Might I have a word with you, Homer?" Amelia saw the priest's eyes darted quickly between her and Homer. "Privately."

Homer turned around in his seat. "Whatever you're going to say, you can say it in front of her. Probably has to do with her family anyway."

"That may be, but considering what we must discuss, I doubt her opinion would be much good to us."

Amelia sat up in her seat. "Excuse me?"

Father George clasped his hands in front of him and took several steps forward. "Please don't be insulted, Mrs. Saint, it's just that Homer and I must decide what's to happen to the vessel, and considering you're his mother, your opinion might not be what's best."

Homer chuckled and shook his head. "Excuse Father George, he knows not what he says."

Amelia glared at the priest. "Well, the *vessel*, has a name and there's no way I'm going to let you make any decisions about him without me present."

Homer grinned, looking back at the priest. "You really want to argue with her?"

Father George wasn't impressed. "What I want is irrelevant. My concern right now is for the innocent souls that have taken refuge in this holy sanctuary. They must be protected."

"They are protected," Amelia snapped. "They're here, aren't they?"

Father George focused on her. "And so is the minion."

"He has it under control."

"But for how long?" the priest argued. "Your son is proving his will is strong, but sooner or later it will break, and when that happens, we must be prepared."

Homer sighed. "He's right, Amelia. It's been hours since the minion rose, and even now Chad's struggling to keep control. We have to figure out a plan if he loses it."

"But what about that shroud around him? I thought you said that would help."

"To get him into the church, yes, but to keep the minion under control . . ." Homer shook his head.

"The shroud is a sacred artifact of the church. The more your son wears it, the more it becomes contaminated."

Amelia's narrowed her eyes. She couldn't believe what she was hearing. "Contaminated? My son is struggling for his life, and you're worried about the contamination of some old cloth? You do realize, Father, there is a life at stake here? A living, breathing person who has a right to exist in this world." Amelia stood and tried to calm her anger, but her body trembled too much. "If that shroud is the only thing that's keeping him in control, then there is no way *in hell* I'm letting you take it off him."

She didn't wait for a response as she marched out of the room. She could hear them, but as she headed down the stairs to the basement, their voices gradually diminished.

The rectory below was small and sparsely decorated. Amelia stopped by the entrance. Watching Chad, she could see the caring look on his face as he and the twins sat on the floor talking.

"You should be sleeping," she said, walking toward a table off to the side. Liam turned to her. "I don't think I'll ever sleep again."

Amelia grabbed a couple of sleeping bags that were sitting on the table. "We're safe here. You don't have to worry about anything getting through. This is a sanctuary, remember?"

"That's what I've been telling them," Chad said. "I can hear those creatures in my head, and I don't think they're very happy we made it here."

Amelia untied one sleeping bag and spread it on the floor. "And if they're not happy, that means we've done something right." She looked back over at the twins, and for the first time, noticed the white ring that encircled Chad. "You don't need to be in that circle."

"Mom, it's all right." Chad smiled. "I know what's at stake, and if this," he pointed to the salt circle, "makes Father George happy then I'm willing to do it."

"You're not a minion, Chad," Amelia forcefully worked the strings on the second sleeping bag. "This isn't your fault, and I don't understand why Father George doesn't see that."

"Mom, it's all—"

"No it isn't." Amelia threw down the sleeping bag. "You're innocent, and yet you're the one being punished. How is that all right?"

Morgan's eyes went wide. "Mom, calm down."

"No I will not calm down!" Amelia ran her fingers through her hair. "I am sick and tired of this mess. Sick and tired of the secrets, the deception, and people thinking they know what's best without giving any consideration as to what I think or how it will affect my family."

"Mom," Liam's voice was soft, "what are you talking about?"

"I don't know," she said, placing her hands on her hips. Her anger slowly deflated as she saw the confused look on the twins' faces. "Maybe that's the problem. I don't know what I'm talking about, what I'm doing, or how to deal with any of this."

"Who would?" Morgan said. "Give yourself some credit, Mom. I mean, it isn't like this sort of thing happens every day."

Amelia smiled at his sarcasm, but it didn't help alleviate any of her helplessness. She was the parent, the one who was supposed to protect her children; how could she do that when it felt like people were keeping things from her?

Footsteps from the stairwell focused her attention away from the conversation. Homer looked tired as he strolled to the rectory. In her anger, Amelia forgot she wasn't the only one caught up in this mess; she wasn't the only one in pain over a family member's betrayal, and she wondered how anyone could continue on, knowing the realities that Homer did.

He smiled as he came closer. "Morgan, Liam, why don't you two go check on Jared?"

"Why?" Liam asked. "Is something wrong with him?"

"No." A flash of awkwardness crossed his face. "I just thought it would be nice if you two went to see how he was doing."

Liam raised his brow and stood up. "Oh, okay."

Morgan stayed where he was.

"Aren't you going too?" she asked.

"Both of us don't need to go."

Amelia saw Homer's subtle motion toward the stairwell, and tugged on the sleeve of the teen's shirt. "No. I think you both should go and check on him."

"But I want to stay here and talk to Chad."

Amelia pulled him to his feet. "It's not like he's going anywhere. You can talk to him when you come back." She pushed him toward the stairs.

Chad stood. "Since when did you want to start hanging out with me anyway?"

Morgan looked back as he walked. "Since you got interesting. You know, holding off that minion and all."

Amelia waited until Morgan was up the stairs before turning her attention to Homer. "Okay, why did you want them gone?"

"We need to talk, and I didn't want to scare them any more than they already are."

Amelia crossed her arms over her chest. "I think, after what we went through getting here, they can handle it."

Homer walked past her. "Don't be too sure. They're just kids, Amelia."

"And I think I know my children a little better than you."

Homer sighed. "Look, I don't want to argue about this. We have to stay united."

"All right, fine, but you're not going to keep anything from Chad. If anyone deserves to hear everything, it's him."

Homer faced her. "I agree. That's why I came down here. Father George still isn't convinced Chad can keep the minion at bay for the next few days, and to be honest, neither am I."

Amelia frowned. "But he's doing it. You can look right at him and see that it's Chad, and not that . . . that thing."

"For now, but what about tomorrow, or the day after that?"

"He can do it."

Homer sighed. "Amelia, you're not listening. Minions are powerful creatures, and the one that's inside Chad is focused only on one thing—having complete control over his body."

"So why is it calm now?" Chad asked. "Is it because of the shroud?"

Homer shrugged. "Possibly, but I think there's something more to this. Something about Chad is helping him to stay in control." He looked inquisitively at Amelia. "And you've never had any other dealings with the occult before now?"

"None at all," she said. "I didn't know anything about amulets or signs or herbs before you and Jared showed up."

"Speaking of herbs, do you still have them with you?"

"What herbs?" Chad asked.

"I gave your mother a small bag of protective herbs," Homer said.

"They work too," Amelia continued. "When that creature was inside you, back in your room, it jumped at us, and something forced it back."

Chad frowned. "I felt that. It hurt."

"How much did you use?" Homer asked.

Amelia shook her head. "I don't know, the whole bag? I made four sachets, and there was barely enough left for a fifth." Amelia frowned as she looked down at her open palm, remembering back. "I put some in my hand, just to see what they were like, then Henry came home so I . . ."

She turned and looked directly at Chad. "I dumped them in your cake batter."

Chad gave her a disapproving look. "You laced my birthday cake?"

Amelia shrugged. "Sorry, but these two had me so worried about what your father—"

Chad's eyes flared in rage. "Don't call him that."

The ground trembled as the overhead lights flickered. Amelia froze to her spot, astonished at the intensity of Chad's glare as the air around her grew cold. Even the shroud that hung over the teen's shoulders lost some of its brilliant colouring. Amelia shot a worried look at Homer as everything returned to normal.

"STOP IT!"

Footsteps pounded the ceiling as Father George ran to the top of the stairs. "Make it stop. Don't let it through."

Homer frowned. "Stop what?"

The old priest hurried down the staircase. "This is what I was afraid of. The minion is rising. The vessel has compromised the safety of this sanctuary and contaminated the shroud."

Amelia looked over at Chad. He was calmer now, and looked stunned by the priest's outburst. "He looks fine to me."

Father George's breath came in heavy gasps as he looked over Chad. "No, no, that's impossible. I saw it with my own eyes. The statue of the Apostles became disfigured. I could feel the evil reach out from the darkness . . ."

Chad shook his head. "Sorry Father, I feel fine."

Homer took a step toward them. "The boy was upset, angry that his mother referred to Henry as his father."

Amelia saw Morgan's grubby sneakers suddenly appear at the top of the stairs. "What's going on? Is everything all right?"

"Everything's fine," Amelia called out. "How's Jared?"

"Fine. Can we come back down now?"

Amelia saw Father George shake his head.

"Maybe they should, Mom," Chad said, in a low voice. "This affects them too. It doesn't seem fair to keep them out of the loop."

"They're too young," Amelia argued.

"They're fourteen," Homer said. "And like you said, they dealt with the trip here pretty well. I think they can deal with the rest."

Amelia clenched her jaw and faced him. "Oh you do, do you?"

Chad frowned. "What are you talking about? The rest of what?"

Amelia raised her eyebrows as she turned to walk away. "Fine Homer, you tell him."

She could hear Homer's low voice stumble over his words as she picked up the sleeping bags and headed for the stairwell.

**

Saturday, 9:15 a.m.

A few hours' sleep did little to improve Amelia's mood. She wrestled with the blankets on an old couch in Father George's office. She held a mixture of emotions at the knowledge of Homer's relationship, and she was sure it was exhaustion that provided the fuzziness that still gripped her mind. Not to mention the unsettling fact that she and her family were locked up in a church for the next seventy-two hours. Amelia sighed and looked at her watch.

Correction: sixty-two hours.

She stared at the wooden cross that hung on the wall. The church office was sparse on decoration with its lone picture of the Virgin Mary and Baby Jesus. She rubbed her eyes as she sat up. Even with two blankets underneath her, she felt the lumps in the cushions no matter which way she lay. Which was fine by her. Questions filled her mind, and she knew she had to find answers before they drove her mad.

The church was still as Amelia shuffled through the barren halls toward the rectory. She walked past the entrance to the worship area, noticing the twins still sleeping on the floor in front of the altar. Father George said it was the most sacred part of the church. The place where the Holy Light originated, and she knew, despite their pleas otherwise, both of them were glad to have that extra bit of protection.

Muffled voices floated softly to her as she reached the top of the stairs. The conversation was still hard to follow even as she entered the rectory. Her attention immediately went to Chad, lying on the floor with a blanket and pillow under his head, staring up at the ceiling. Amelia felt a huge weight lift from her shoulders; he'd lasted the night without turning. That had to be a good sign, but as she watched him, she noticed his eyes darting from side to side, his forehead wrinkling every few moments, as though he was trying to comprehend something he didn't quite understand.

"Don't you look all chipper," she said, walking toward him.

His expression changed when he noticed her. "Yeah, never thought I'd be so happy to be in a church." He got to his feet and stretched. "But I could have used something softer to sleep on."

Amelia smiled. "Not exactly your bed back home, is it?"

Chad chuckled. "Never thought I'd miss that room."

The muffled conversation continued from a room just off the rectory. Amelia focused on the single doorway next to a serving window. The window was closed, but she could still make out the distinct voices of Homer and Father George. She grew apprehensive, knowing they were probably discussing her family, and that they, again, didn't include her.

"So," she said, trying not to focus on the voices, "did you and Homer have a little chat last night?"

"You could say that," Chad crossed his arms over his chest. "I still can't believe Homer's our uncle."

Amelia gazed at him sympathetically. "So, he told you."

"Yeah, he explained after you left." His gaze became inquisitive. "Have you told Morgan or Liam?"

"No, not yet, and after the last twenty-four hours, I wouldn't know where to begin with that new piece of information."

"But they have to know. You know that, right?"

She nodded. "We all have to sit down and discuss what's been going on. I don't want your brothers accidentally doing something that would put them, or you, or any of us for that matter, in more danger."

Chad's expression hardened. "I don't think we could be in any more danger than we already are."

Amelia reached out, but her hand was repelled by the invisible barrier. Chad exhaled slowly. "We will get out of this. I know we will." She gave him a reassuring smile.

Murmurs from a room off to the side continued to draw Amelia's attention. She motioned to the room. "How long has that been going on?"

"Not long. My new uncle seems pretty excited about something."

Amelia walked toward the side doorway and peeked inside the room. She was astonished to find a large kitchen with several working appliances and a large centre island. Two small rectangular windows close to the ceiling allowed the morning sun to radiate in, with dust-illuminating sunbeams hitting the wall.

It was an interesting sight. Homer stood in front of the island, staring at several sheets of paper, with Father George and Jared drinking coffee at a small square table at the far side of the room.

"Good morning," she said, keeping her focus on Jared. "Nice to see you up and about."

Jared smiled and straightened himself in his chair. "Could say the same thing about you."

Amelia looked down at his bandaged legs. The dressings wound up to his knees. "How do you feel?"

He gave a small chuckle before taking a sip from a mug. "Like I've been in a battle to save my life."

Amelia stepped up to the counter. "You and me both."

"There's fresh coffee on the counter." Father George motioned to the other side of the room. "Help yourself."

She eyed Homer carefully as she walked around the centre island. "What are you reading?"

He didn't look up at her. "It's a cake recipe."

Amelia took a mug from the shelf. "Are you serious? Why are you looking at that?"

"I've never made a cake before. Need to know what to buy if we're going to make one."

"Homer has a theory," Father George said. "He's under the impression the protective herbs you dropped in your son's cake, could be the reason he's been able to keep the minion at bay."

"It makes sense," Jared continued. "We know the herbs work, so if they're good at keeping the minion away on our side, what's to say it couldn't block them from coming through."

Amelia frowned. "I don't understand."

"Right now, in this state, your son is an open portal," Father George began. "A gateway between our world and Hell. Homer thinks the ingested herbs are acting like a plug, a barrier across this open portal that is keeping part of the minion in Hell."

"But the shroud—"

"Is only a temporary solution," Father George interrupted. "And it's only as strong as the person who wears it."

Amelia walked over to the doorway. "Chad, can you hear this?"

The teen was back lying on the floor, staring up at the ceiling. "A little."

"Homer thinks it's the herbs I put in your birthday cake that's helping you keep control, and keep that thing from taking over your body."

Chad frowned and sat up. "That would explain how I can hear them talking."

"Did you eat any cake?"

He nodded. "I think I had a small piece. Wasn't really that hungry."

She watched him as Chad's attention drifted away. "He's right. That can't be it. I saw that thing trying to come through. I don't think an herb-laced cake is our answer."

"Maybe not," Homer said, straightening up. "But unless you have another idea, I'm opting we at least try this."

"Amelia," the priest held a gentle tone in his voice, "there's something else I want to discuss with you."

"He's not taking off that sash."

"No, I understand that, but if the boy continues to draw on the energy of the minion again—like he did last night, it will deteriorate the shroud's effectiveness, and weaken any other defence we've placed to protect your family."

"Defences? Like the herbs?"

"It's all connected," Father George said. "Anything that is used against the powers of Hell, is strengthened by the Light and love of God. It's the reason it works."

The room was quiet. Amelia exchanged glances with Jared and Homer, and then looked back at Chad lying on the floor.

"Homer, are you sure this cake thing will work?"

"Not really, but if does we'll have a new weapon against these things. Something that could help save lives."

Amelia felt the muscles in her jaw clench. The idea of using her son as a guinea pig—helpful or not—didn't sit well.

She took a sip from her mug. "So, apart from the herbs, how do we keep it strong?"

Father George smiled. "By doing what you're doing now. A mother's love is incredibly strong. The bond it creates is strengthened by familiar memories of family and home. Anything that reminds him of you will go a long way to keeping him with us."

Homer walked toward her. "I'm going into the grocery story to pick up some cake ingredients. I know a shop that has the supplies we'll need to wait out this weekend." He put his hands on Amelia's shoulders. She twisted a bit, a little uncomfortable with his touch. Whether it was recent events or the fact he was Henry's brother, she was unsure. It just didn't feel right to be touched by another person.

"I have a good feeling about this," Homer said, trying to make eye contact with her. "This could be the break we've been hoping for. All we have to do is keep Chad safe for the next couple days, keep him surrounded with as much protection as we can find, and keep an eye on the clock."

Amelia pulled free of his embrace and turned back to watch Chad. He held a bemused look. Was he listening to the demons again? A thought flashed through her mind: if Chad could hear the minions communicating, did it go the other way? Could the minion that hid inside him, hear their conversations? Amelia took another sip from her coffee, and for the first time, feared maybe she'd done the wrong thing by bringing Chad with them.

***

Saturday, 2:38 p.m.

Homer rubbed his eyes as he flipped through the pages of the worn, leather-bound book in front of him. Fatigue had set in. He could feel the irritation in his eyes from lack of moisture and too much strain. He put the book down and leaned back in his chair, taking a quick glance at the stack of books on the table in front of him. He couldn't stop now. His instincts told him he was on the right path; he was close to something, but what, he didn't know. He just knew that somewhere, in the pages of one of these old books, was the key to saving Chad.

Maybe Henry as well.

Homer closed his eyes. How long had he been chasing that dream now? Years? Decades? October 10, 1980, the day Lyla forced her way back into their lives. The image of a young Henry, flush with anger, flashed through Homer's mind. A wave of guilt washed over him. He never should have pushed Henry to learn more about his mother. Sure, hindsight gives you twenty-twenty vision, but what kind of a parent deserts their infant? He was the older brother. He should have been more protective.

Homer's memory of Henry merged with one of Chad, and he smiled. Chad was a good kid, and had a good family despite the ancestry. Amelia was turning out to be a stronger person than he originally thought. A good thing, considering what she was up against. Another smile lit up his face as he envisioned an enraged Amelia going after Lyla. The demons wouldn't know what hit them.

There was a rustling sound of beads behind him. "Nice to see you smile, for a change."

Homer relaxed as the gently sound of footsteps came closer, followed by the female voice again. "How goes the search?" Her tone was soft, and as she spoke, she placed a black mug on the table in front of him.

Homer reached for the mug. "Not good. I can't find anything on the potency of protection herbs in food." He took a sip, savoring the bitterness of the hot liquid. "Doesn't it seem strange to you, Brianna, that no one thought to put them in food before now?"

The middle-aged woman strolled away from him, picking up one of the larger books from the table and giving it a quick once-over. Her long blonde hair cascaded down the front of her ornate dress. "Oh, I don't know. Most of the literature here was written by monks during the Dark Ages. The Church was very strict on how things should have been done back then, and no one questioned them about their methods."

"And not one single person ever thought of putting herbs in the food?"

She raised her eyebrows and placed the book back down on the table. "Maybe they did, just with no results."

"That can't be right."

Brianna turned and walked past him. "Well, Homer, I don't know what to tell you. You asked to look at all the books I have on herbs, and here they are. That's everything that's ever been written on the subject. And I know Aslin told you how extensive my library is."

"I know, and I do appreciate you accommodating me like this, it's just . . ."

"Just what?" she asked, from the other room.

"Frustrating." Homer gave a deep exhale. "I really thought I was on to something."

He closed the book in front of him and stood up. His back ached from sitting in one position for so long, and he stretched the muscles, trying to alleviate the pain.

"Why don't you take a break for a bit," Brianna said. "You're no good to anyone worn out."

"Yeah, I know." Homer walked toward the small library hidden off to the side. "But I can't stop. I have to find something to save Chad."

Homer could hear her shuffling around in the kitchen. "I understand you want to save him because he's your nephew, but you're taking an awful risk, Homer."

Homer walked toward a table full of occult paraphernalia. He picked up a small ceramic dragon holding a large glass marble. "I can't let this happen, Brianna. Everything that's happening is my fault. I should have been there to protect Henry."

"Your brother made his own choice. You're not responsible for his actions."

"You can rationalize this all you want. Doesn't take away the fact that I could have stopped him a long time ago." He traced the tail of the dragon with his index finger, only to have the tip snap off and fall to the floor. Homer rolled his eyes and bend down to pick up the piece.

"I wonder how much this'll cost me."

"Pardon?"

He scanned the floor for the broken tip. "Nothing. Just talking to myself."

He got down on all fours and crawled along the floor toward the table. The small blue piece had rolled close to the wall, and he had to stretch to get it.

"Lyla is a powerful overlord," Briana continued. "You know she'll get her way in the end."

"Not if I can help it." Homer turned his body to one side, hoping to get a better reach, and noticed the corner of a book stashed meticulously behind the bookcase. He reached for the book and carefully removed it from its hiding spot.

"She has command of some of the worst creatures in Hell. Even with the herbs, you won't be able to stand up to her for very long."

"That's why we're at the church," Homer said, leafing through the pages. "I'm thinking that between the herbs, the protection of the Church, and his ties to his family, we should be able to ride out the weekend."

The book was old, older than anything he'd already seen, and he was amazed at the information it held. There was a whole section on herbs, with combinations he's never seen. Homer suddenly realized this could be what he was looking for.

Why wasn't it in with the other books? Homer stepped out into the small living room, the book open to herb combinations.

"Even the church has its limits," Briana said, walking out of the kitchen.

Homer stood next to the table, and then turned his head toward her. "I found this book stashed neatly behind the bookcase. You weren't trying to hide it, were you?"

Briana frowned. "What are you talking about? Why would I do that?"

Homer slammed the book closed. "Why don't you tell me? You said this was all the information you had." He motioned to the stack on the table. "Then I just happen to find the exact book I'm looking for, tucked neatly out of sight."

Homer watched as Briana's once-friendly expressions turned to disgust.

"If it was out of sight, then how did you find it? Snooping through my things?"

Homer was taken aback by her sudden shift in attitude. "No, I would never go snooping through—"

Briana rolled her eyes. "Oh shut up, Homer. You have no idea how pathetic you sound right now, but that's always been your problem, hasn't it? You never knew how to take the initiative. Always apologizing for the slightest bit of backbone you might have grown. I'm amazed you're still alive."

A feeling of dread came over him, and he clutched the book to his chest, keeping his focus on her. "Who are you?"

The room grew dark as the shadows stretched outward from corners and under furniture. Long, inky tendrils slithered toward Homer, lashing out as they tried to rip the book from his grasp.

Briana walked toward him, her torso melting and contorting until Henry stood in front of him. Looking younger than he did the night before.

A sly grin crossed his face. "Hello, Homer. Nice of you to drop by."

Homer turned to the left and then the right, but was blocked by shadows. He watched as Henry motioned toward a stack of books, but couldn't move fast enough as they pummelled him one by one, throwing him off balance.

"Henry, stop this," Homer said.

"Why? I'm winning."

"You're being influenced by Lyla, and no one wins at her games."

Another stack of books flew off the shelves and toward Homer. "How would you know? You've never bothered to play."

Homer felt an icy grip as shadows wrapped themselves around his arms and legs, restraining him as he struggled to keep a grip on the book. "I don't have to play, I've seen the aftermath."

The air around them began to chill with each step Henry took toward him.

"Go ahead, Henry, kill me. I don't care."

"Sure you do," Henry said, stepping past him. "You always care. That's why you're here. You're Homer the hero, here to save the lives of innocents, and to stop bad old Henry and send him to Hell."

A numbness from the icy grip inched its way up Homer's arms. "That's not true, Henry. I don't want you to go to Hell. I just want you away from Lyla's influence."

Henry raised his arm slightly, and the tendrils pulled at Homer, forcing him to release the book and raised him a few inches off the ground. "Why? Does it bother you that someone else is getting all the attention? We're not children anymore, Homer. Dad's not around to throw constant adoration at you."

Pain seared through Homer's arms as his own weight pulled on his invisible restrains. "I know you're upset because of something Dad did years ago." Homer saw a flash of pain in his brother's eyes. "But Henry, Dad was a drunk, you know that. He was a good-for-nothing alcoholic, who was bitter at the world long before you were born."

Henry's face softened, but his expression didn't last, and he raised his arm a bit higher. "Easy for you to say, he didn't make your life miserable."

The restraints pulled at Homer's flesh, straining his muscles, making his arms feel like they were being torn from their sockets.

"So you're destroying your family in retribution? Is that it?"

Homer saw another flash of what looked like remorse. A small wisp of hope brought a smile to his face. Maybe, just maybe, he was getting through to him. Homer struggled under the restraints. "Do you know what you've done to your family? Do you know how much pain they're in because of your actions?"

"Well then, it's a good thing they won't be alive much longer." Henry made a sweeping motion with his hand, throwing Homer up against the wall. "I'd really hate to see them suffer."

Another gesture sent Homer flying across the room, and he was thrown up against the opposite wall. With nothing to brace him from the impact, Homer's body slammed into the wall, sending fixtures crashing to the floor.

"They're good kids, Henry," Homer said, reeling from the impact. "They don't deserve what you've done to them."

"What I've done?" There was an ominous tone to Henry's voice that sent chills through Homer. "I haven't even started."

Homer felt the tendrils pull at his body as he flew through the air and slammed into the far wall again. His head collided with something hard, and the searing pain caused his vision to blur.

"No," Homer said, barely audible. "You've already done enough damage. You've cursed Chad. Leave Amelia and the twins alone. Find another sacrifice for—"

"Not likely. I need their deaths to jump start my political career."

Homer coughed out a laugh. "No one's going to vote for you. You're a lawyer."

Homer felt the pull of the tendrils lower him closer to the floor, and to Henry.

"That may be, but I'll have the sympathy vote all tied up. See, everyone likes an underdog, especially one whose kids were murdered when his deranged wife went on a killing spree. It'll bring credibility to my tough stance against crime." Henry's grip was cold as he forced Homer to look into his eyes. "Fear always brings in the votes." He turned away. "You and Amelia are going to leave a nice trail of bodies in this town, and when the dust finally settles, all the public will see is a heartbroken widower hoping to make things right in memory of his dead family."

Homer locked eyes with Henry. "Don't do this, please."

Henry smiled as he threw Homer back toward the window. Glass and wood shattered instantly as Homer's ragged body impacted the frame, throwing debris down to the alley below. Homer's body slumped to the floor as the shadowy tendrils released their icy grip and scattered back into the darkness. Homer opened his eyes, barely able to focus on the outline of his brother as Henry walked back into the kitchen. There were a few mechanical beeps, and the sound of a microwave starting up.

Homer tried to pull himself up, but his muscles were weak from the restraints and beating he'd received. He heard footsteps approach and tried to move again, only to have his body forcefully thrown onto his back. Henry was staring down at him.

"You won't win," Homer said, barely able to speak. "There are others—"

"What? That sniveling jar-head, side-kick of yours? Please, he has even less of a backbone than you."

Homer's eyesight improved enough for him to watch Henry walk away.

"Besides, once the fire department pulls your charred body from the wreckage, he'll think twice about getting in my way."

Homer watched as the shadows engulfed Henry, and disappeared into the debris. His muscles allowed him to move slightly, just enough for him to get a good look into the kitchen and see the oven door open and long cylindrical cans in the microwave.

Pain wracked his body as he pulled himself toward the broken window and forced his body through the debris. His arms were weak and barely able to hold his weight, as he lowered himself out of the window. A flash of orange filled his view and the intense heat forced him to release his grip. The impact was hard; his legs buckled under his weight, and he collapsed to the ground.

Debris rained down as Homer dragged himself across the alleyway. Several fiery shards landed on him, touching off small fires that quickly burned through to his flesh. The searing pain of his flesh burning cleared his mind, and he rolled to the far side of the alley before succumbing to the black of unconsciousness.

9

Amelia paced in front of the church exit. Her mind reeled with thoughts she didn't want. Doubt clogged her mind, reinforced by the strange way Chad was behaving. He hadn't talked to anyone in hours, not since breakfast. He just lay on the floor staring up at the ceiling with his arms resting behind his head.

He wasn't looking healthy either. This, above everything else, worried her the most. He looked thinner, pallid, almost death-like. If it wasn't for the fact she'd seen his chest rise and fall with his breath, she would have thought he was dead. On top of that, it was taking far too long for Homer to return. Just a few hours, that's what he'd said. How long did it take to buy a few groceries and read a few books? Why couldn't he bring the books here to look over?

She stopped at the far end of the hall in front of Father George's office. Jared was lying down on a dusty cot the old priest dragged out of storage. The astringent aroma hung in the air as he applied a homemade ointment to the wounds on his legs.

She leaned against the doorframe. "How do they feel?"

"Sore, still." He placed the lid on the container. "But my legs don't hurt as much as before, and I can walk a little better now." He looked up at her. "How's Chad doing?"

Amelia shrugged. "Fine, I guess."

"Haven't you been down to see him?"

She kept her gaze on the floor. "Not in a while."

He paused for a moment. "What's wrong?"

"What do you mean?"

123

Jared leaned back on the cot. "This church is like a tomb. Every little noise echoes. I've been listening to you pace back and forth for almost thirty minutes. What's bothering you?"

She slid along the wall into the room. "Maybe you were right."

"About what?"

Amelia couldn't bring herself to look at him. "About not bringing Chad."

"Are you serious?"

The admission felt good, as though a weight had been lifted from her shoulders. "I don't know. I can't help but feel like I made a big mistake. Maybe you were right. Maybe we should have concentrated on keeping Morgan and Liam safe."

Jared sat up. "Think about what you're saying. How do you think he'd feel, knowing you were having second thoughts about trying to save him?"

Guilt surged through her. "Don't lay that crap on me. Don't you think I've been thinking the exact same thing? I've been tearing myself apart, worrying that bringing him here was the wrong thing, that I've put Morgan and Liam's life in danger by keeping them together." She walked over to a couch across from cot and sat down. "It's just, seeing him down there, looking the way he does. It makes me wonder if you weren't right."

There was another long pause before Jared spoke. "Father George told me he's not looking too good."

"The twins are afraid to go near him."

"He must feel like shit knowing that."

Amelia gave a weak smile. "I didn't tell him. I don't want him to think they've lost hope. He knows the shroud isn't the only thing helping him. I don't want it weakened any more by his own self-loathing."

Father George entered the room and went immediately behind his desk.

"Problem?" Jared asked.

"Possibly. In all this excitement, I forgot about mass tonight and tomorrow. They'll have to be cancelled."

"Is that necessary?" Amelia asked. "We can all hide downstairs until mass is over."

"I thought about that too, but I would rather be safe than sorry." He pulled out a sheet of paper and a marker. "I'll just put a note on the doors that I'm sick and service is cancelled for the weekend."

"That could raise suspicions."

"Possibly, but by the time someone asks me what's going on, all this will hopefully be over."

Amelia chuckled softly. "Ah, the Catholic Church and its secrets. I wonder what people would do if they discovered that Hell wasn't just a scare tactic."

"It would mean some pretty uncomfortable questions for the Church," Jared said. "Questions I don't think the Vatican would be willing to answer."

Father George became incensed. "It isn't that the Church would be unwilling, Mr. Quinn, but we understand the weight knowledge like this carries, and some people would not, or could not, be willing to accept the truth."

Amelia settled into the couch. "This shroud, what is it exactly? I've been a Catholic all my life, and I've never heard of it."

Father George took a deep breath and sat down behind his desk. "The first shroud is said to have been created shortly after the death of Jesus. There is a legend that states Mary and the first Apostles took the burial dressings of Jesus with them when they left the Holy Land, cut them into pieces, and created thirteen sashes. It was a way for them to carry the spirit of Christ with them when they went forth to teach His word. Then, when each of the Apostles died, their robes were cut and sewn onto the sashes, adding to its strength. For hundreds of years each new Catholic church that was built was given its own shroud, as a form of dedication."

"So there are thousands of these things all over the world?"

Father George put the marker down. "There were, but as the centuries passed, war and intolerance destroyed most of them. There is no reverence, even within the Church itself, for these sacred relics. There hasn't been a new shroud created in over a hundred years, and the ones that still exist, have not been added to since the turn of the last century."

Amelia rubbed her eyes. "Well, whatever the mystery behind this, at least it's doing what it's supposed to."

"Whatever happens," Father George continued, "don't ever blame yourself, Amelia. This was not your fault. Your husband must have been planning this for a while."

Amelia smiled. "Thanks, but the guilt will go away only when this is over. Henry may have started this, but I'm going to finish it."

"Good." The priest smiled. "Stay strong. Stay determined. You've come this far with the odds against you. That has to mean God is on our side."

She nodded and stood. "I hope it stays that way." She walked out of the office and headed toward the stairs. The rectory was dark, even with the afternoon light coming in through the small basement windows. Amelia hesitated by the entrance. Just the feel of the room sent shivers through her body.

"Hey you," she called, into the room, "how are you holding up?"

"Good, I guess." Chad lay motionless on the floor, staring up at the ceiling. "I can still hear them talking, but the thing inside me hasn't moved for a while, so it's not all bad."

Amelia took a step forward, carefully eyeing the shadows cast by darkened corners and the odd piece of furniture. She knew in her heart they were safe, but she couldn't shake the feeling they were being watched.

Chad sat up on his elbows. "Maybe we could leave the church and go home?"

Amelia's heart skipped a beat. "Why would you say that?"

"Well, it doesn't feel like they care about me anymore. Maybe whoever's in charge down there thinks I'm a lost cause and gave up."

Amelia walked cautiously up to the salt circle. "Feel?"

Chad sat up and crossed his legs. "Yeah, it's weird, y'know. I know when they're focused on me, and when they're not, and right now, they're not." He frowned and tilted his head to one side. "Homer's not back yet, is he?"

Amelia made herself comfortable on the floor. "No, not yet, but he shouldn't be long."

He looked surprised. "Really?"

A shiver raced up Amelia's spine. "Why?"

Chad shook his head. "Nothing."

"No, it's something. What?"

Chad hesitated. "The minions, they're excited. That's the only way I can describe it."

"Excited?"

"Yeah, like the way you get when your team wins the big game." His gaze drifted past her. "Like a hysterical frenzy almost, and it's focused away from me . . ."

Amelia jumped to her feet. "That can't be good."

Chad stayed seated, shaking his head slowly. "No, I don't think it is."

She made it to the stairs in three long strides, her mind raced as fast as her heart. She knew something was wrong. There was no reasonable excuse for Homer to be gone so long. She was winded by the time she got to Father George's office.

"Homer's in trouble."

"We know." The priest walked past her, taking his coat off a hook by the door. "Jared's talking to him now. He was ambushed by Henry."

Amelia felt cold. "Is he all right?"

"He's injured, but alive." Father George took a set of keys from the front of his jacket. "I'm going now to pick him up."

"It could be a trap," Amelia said. "If he ambushed Homer, what's to say he won't be ready for you?"

"It's a risk I'm going to have to take."

Amelia held out her hand. "Give me the keys. I'll go."

"Don't be silly Amelia, you can't go. It's probably what Henry wants."

"He's right," Jared said, placing his hand over the cell phone. "Homer, myself, Father George, we're nothing. You and the kids are the main prize."

"And what happens if Chad turns while Father George is gone?" Amelia argued. "I don't know the first thing about fighting these things. I can't even shoot a gun, and you're in no condition to take one on by yourself." She grabbed the keys out of the priest's hand. "Besides, Henry is after the kids, not me. I'd rather have the both of you here watching over the twins, just in case something does happen."

The silence between them was full of tension but Amelia knew she was right. As it was, she was no good to them now, but it was something she planned on rectifying as soon as she could.

Jared exhaled deeply and put the cell back up to his ear. "Amelia's on her way." Then he lowered the cell phone. "Brianna's house is near that new strip mall right next to the main highway."

"It's the blue minivan at the back of the church," Father George said. "And there's a first-aid kit under the driver's seat. Be mindful of the accelerator; it's touchy."

Amelia's hands trembled as she headed toward the front of the church. With each step, her mind argued that she should stay, not go outside, but she couldn't leave Homer injured someplace. Not after all he'd done for her and the kids.

She took a deep breath and pulled open one of the heavy wooden doors. A gust of warm air blew past her, along with the scent of wildflowers. A nice change from the musty air of the rectory.

"Mom," Morgan said, behind her. "Where are you going?" There was a hint of fear in the tone of his voice.

"Homer's been hurt," she said. "I'm going to get him."

"Hurt? How? By Dad?"

Amelia turned to him. "I'm not sure of all the details, but the important thing is he's okay." She cupped his face with her hands. "I'll be fine. Father George and Jared are here, and those things don't bother people during the day."

Morgan looked back at Father George, then at her. "Just hurry back, okay?"

"Don't worry, I'll be as fast as I can."

"You promise?"

Amelia pulled him to her. "Listen to me, everything's going to be fine."

"I know," Morgan said. She could hear the slight crack of his voice. "But I'm just—"

"Scared, yes I know, hon. We all are, and there's nothing wrong with that. After everything that's happened, you're allowed to be scared, but if we're going to get through this, we have to be strong, especially for Chad. It's why he's still with us, and he's depending on us to help him through this."

Morgan pulled away, and hid behind his blonde hair, but Amelia could see him fighting back his tears. "All right."

She smiled and gave him a kiss on the forehead.

Tightness gripped her throat, and she headed out the door before anyone could see the tears in her eyes.

It felt like years since she felt the warm sunlight rays on her face. It energized her and helped a little to push back her anxieties, but she kept a close eye on the shadows as she walked toward the back of the church. Everything looked different to her now; every tree or shrub could be a potential hiding place for a minion. Even the neighbourhood looked different. The familiar buildings brought back flashes of the night before, with minion's scampering across the rooftops in an effort to capture them.

Amelia found the strip mall, but the parking lot was clogged with emergency vehicles. She scanned the area for any signs of Homer, but the crowds were too thick for her to see from the safety of the van. Once face, however, did look familiar, and she waved to the bearded face of the grocery store clerk.

Amelia rolled down her window as he came toward her. "What's going on?"

"Cops are saying a gas line exploded," he said, but Amelia noted a hint of disbelief in his voice.

"That must have been a hell of an explosion." Amelia looked around. Debris littered the ground with several buildings missing windows. "What building was it?"

"That one right there." He pointed to the remains of a stone house that was completely engulfed in flames. "They said it doubled as some kind of New Age shop. Really weird stuff inside."

"Was anyone hurt?"

"One person is dead. They say it's the owner. Blast threw her through the window."

Amelia scanned the area again. "Do they have the whole street blocked off?"

"Pretty much. You need down there?"

"Yes, I have to pick up a friend."

"Well, you're going to have to back up and take one of the side streets. It'll take you down by the highway, but it's the only other way around."

"Thanks."

With the help of a police officer, Amelia got the van turned around and headed back down the street. She turned down the next street and continued, growing angrier by the moment. Another person was dead because of Henry.

She had only driven a few minutes when she spotted Homer sitting on the side of the curb. His clothing was ripped and burnt in some places, and his skin showed signed of being singed by the fire. His head hung low, but as she pulled up behind him she noticed a bloodied wound on the side of his face.

She parked the car and jumped out. "Homer, are you all right?"

He smiled up at her. "I've been better, thanks."

She helped him to his feet and into the back seat of the van, climbing in after him and shut the door.

"I'm going to take you to the hospital," she said, searching under the seat.

"I'm fine, nothing a few hours of sleep won't cure."

Amelia pulled the white metal box out from its hiding spot. "Bullshit, you're not fine. You just survived an explosion. You could have internal injuries."

"Actually," Homer leaned forward, "I got out before the place went up."

Amelia's shoulders slumped. "I'm sorry about your friend."

Homer frowned. "My friend?"

"The owner of the shop? They found her body outside of the building. They think she was thrown out in the explosion."

"No, Henry killed her long before that. Then assumed her identity."

She poured a small amount of antiseptic on a gauze strip. "What do you mean?"

Homer winced as she gently touched his wound. "I mean, he can make himself look like anyone he sees."

Amelia froze. "Are you serious? Since when?"

Homer shook his head. "I don't know, but he was good enough to make me believe it was her until the last moment." Homer reached up and took her by the wrist, pulling her arm away. "I'm sorry, Amelia. I told him what we were planning."

Amelia hesitated for a moment, trying to digest the severity of his words. Henry knew their plan now. All this time she was worried about what would happen if he knew, yet as she sat there, looking at the gaping wound in Homer's forehead, it didn't bother her. It was almost a relief.

She looked into his eyes. His apologetic gaze marred only by the black marks of soot and blood that streaked his face. "At least you're still with us. That's all that matters." She continued dabbing his wound. "I know Jared and Father George are experienced at this, but I feel a lot better with you around."

Homer's gaze drifted to the back of the seat. "Maybe because we're family?"

"Maybe," Amelia searched the first aid kit for more gauze. "But if you give away our plans again, I'm going to have to shoot you." She saw a flash of confusion in his eyes, and smiled. "Oh relax, I'm kidding."

She handed him the first aid kit and moved into the driver's seat. "So where does that leave us now?"

"Same as before," Homer said. "We're still safe as long as we stay inside the sanctuary. We just have to ride this out."

She turned the key to the engine. "Do you think Henry will try something again?"

Homer chuckled. "Oh hell yeah, he's getting desperate. He has, what, two days left? Nothing he's done so far has had any effect on turning Chad." Homer leaned forward. "Whatever supplies we need, we better get them now. I don't want to be anywhere but inside the church when night comes."

Amelia pulled away from the curb. "Would it be safe to stop by the house? Just for a few minutes?"

"I don't know. With all the damage from the storm, and the cops showing up, your neighbours probably have their eyes trained on your house."

"Probably, but right now I don't give a rat's ass what they think." Amelia felt her anger build. "I just want this whole thing over with. Too many people have died already. I don't want anyone else dying."

She drove Homer to the far side of the city to buy supplies. Homer waited in the van as she took his list and ran in to buy what they needed. He wanted to go with her, but his wounds would make him stand out. None of her neighbours shopped in this part of town, so she hoped she didn't have to worry about appearing in public, considering her neighbours talked and probably already gossiped about the police car being in their driveway. Not to mention the squealing tires and their hasty departure. As she walked toward the store exit, she noticed one of the store employees stapling something to a public bulletin board.

Amelia's eyes went wide as her driver's licence mug shot stared blankly out at the world. She kept her head low and calmly headed out into the parking lot.

"What's wrong?" Homer asked as she quickly got into the car. "Didn't you get all the stuff we needed?"

She dropped the few plastic bags in the back seat. "The police are looking for me," she said, as she turned the ignition. "They're putting my picture up, probably all over town, with an Amber Alert for the twins."

"That's not good," Homer said, putting his cell phone into his pocket. "Probably because of the fire too."

Amelia frowned. "What fire?"

"The fire at your house." Homer looked out the window. "Jared called while you were inside. It's on the local news. Apparently your house is burning down."

Amelia stepped on the gas and the van lurched forward. It didn't take long to see black smoke rising above the canopy of the neighbourhood trees. Amelia's heart sank.

She stopped at the corner of Belvedere Road. A large crowd stood on the opposite side of the street and watched as the flames engulfed the building. She yanked on the steering wheel, but felt resistance as Homer reached across and pulled the wheel forward.

"You can't go down there," he said, keeping a firm grip on the wheel. "We shouldn't be here."

"My house is on fire," she said. "All our things are in there!"

"Amelia if you run over there, you're just going to have to answer to their questions, and right now, we can't afford to have any more people know what's going on." He grabbed her by the wrists and forced her to look at him. "It's too risky. Henry has no problem killing anyone who stands in his way. If you go over there, you'll be putting your neighbour's lives in danger."

Amelia felt her breath catch in her throat. "But that's my house. All of our things are in there."

"Yes, I know. All your material possessions are in there." He kept his eyes locked on hers. "All of Chad's things are in there too. Other than you and the twins, anything that could tether him to this world, is in that house. Do you understand what I'm saying?"

Amelia broke free of his gaze and stared at the burning building. "Henry did this."

"Henry knows Chad's will is strong. He has to make Chad feel isolated, alone, and the only way he can do that is to destroy his support system. And that's you. If Henry can break you, make you feel hopeless, that will have a direct effect on Chad." Homer slumped back into his seat. "Once that happens, Chad will be too weak to fend off Korthos, and not even the sanctuary will be able to protect him."

Amelia's body felt weak as she watched more of her home succumb to the flames. "Everything's gone."

Homer reached across and held her hand. "No, it isn't. Your life is back at the church, waiting for you to return safely."

She looked at him, her mind numb from shock.

"Material things can be replaced, Amelia. Your children can't. You need to be stronger than ever now. Your love for your children is the only thing that's going to keep Chad with us now." He gripped her hand. "Don't let Henry win."

Amelia turned and faced the fire again. He was right, and she wasn't about to let Henry win. It was a quiet ride back to the church. Amelia wrestled with whether or not to tell the kids what happened. It would be hard for them to hear everything they owned was gone, and she struggled with whether or not telling them was a good idea. They pulled up to the side of the church and a few moments later; both Morgan and Liam ran out the side door. She hugged them both tight, and took a few deep breaths before facing them.

"Get back inside," she said, and pushed them toward the doors of the church.

"Are you all right, Uncle Homer?" Liam asked.

Amelia stopped and turned around when he didn't reply. Homer stood by the side of the car, looking oddly calm.

"Homer?"

He shook his head and smiled weakly. "I'm fine. I just . . . he called me uncle."

"Yeah," Morgan said. "Chad told us while you were gone."

Amelia tilted her head to one side. "Does that bother you?"

"No." Homer took a few steps toward the church. "It's just going to take some getting used to, I guess."

Father George suddenly appeared at the entrance.

"Amelia, Homer, good you're back. And just in time."

Even in the warm afternoon, Amelia could feel a cold presence sweep over the yard. "It's Chad, isn't it?"

"We're running out of time."

Amelia raced into the church and followed the priest down to the rectory. The back part of the hall was dark; the temperature was much cooler than before. Amelia felt her heart beat harder as she focused on the red glow from across the room. Chad lay in a heap in the centre of the circle, growling and snarling like a wild animal.

"Not again," Morgan whispered, from behind Amelia.

"Boys, I want you upstairs," she said. "You don't need to be down here."

"Remember where I said," Father George spoke softly. "Behind the altar upstairs. You'll be safe there."

Amelia didn't take her eyes off Chad as she cautiously stepped forward. "How is it still in him?"

"He's an open portal, Amelia. Remember?"

"The herbs must be wearing off," Homer said, coming up behind her. "You stay with him, try to bring him back."

"Is there any more of that herb mixture? Maybe he can eat some and—"

"Mom?"

Amelia saw Chad's face had returned to normal. Her heart ached as she saw the fear in his eyes.

She got down on one knee near the salt ring, and tried to keep him from seeing her own fear. "I'm right here, hon." She spoke in a calming tone, trying to make her voice as soothing as possible. "I'm not going anywhere."

"Careful, Amelia," Father George said.

"Don't tell me to be careful. I know what I'm doing."

Amelia kept her eyes trained on Chad. Small shadows darted across this face, twisting his features, making him look grotesque, but his eyes were the key to who was in control, and when they became black and cold, she knew her son was buried.

She pulled back from the circle as a wicked smile formed on Chad's lips.

"Chad, can you hear me?"

A low growl came as a response.

"I want to talk to Chad."

"No," he said, snarling.

Amelia clenched her jaw. "I don't want to talk to you. Go away and let me talk to my son."

Father George came up behind her, softly whispering a phrase over and over again in Latin.

A spray of water hit the side of Chad's face. Immediately the minion reacted, pulling away and shielding its body as the water bubbled on the skin. Amelia caught a flash of panic in the creature's eyes as the black pools gave way to the soft brown hues and the frightened look of her son. With everything they were doing to protect Chad, she realized she may have to deal with the minion as well, if she wanted any connection to her child.

"Chad? Are you with me?"

"It's too strong," he gasped for air, slumping toward the floor. "And I feel so weak." He looked up at her. "What's happening? Why is it getting stronger?"

Amelia hesitated, and glanced back at the priest.

"Mom?"

"It's Henry," Father George said. "He knows he can't touch you, and he's getting desperate."

Chad frowned. "Getting desperate?"

"He attacked Homer and killed a woman." Amelia looked away. "That's probably what you picked up on earlier."

"Is Homer all right?"

"He's banged up, but fine."

"And that's making the minion stronger?"

Amelia made herself comfortable on the floor. "It's all part of a plan."

"What plan?"

"Henry's trying to make you feel isolated and alone."

"Why?"

"Then you'll be more receptive to the minion."

"That'll never happen, will it?"

"Only if Henry has his way, and I don't plan on letting that happen." A feeling of pride washed through her. "You're ruining his plans, and we all know how much you love to do that."

Heavy footsteps bounded down the stairs as Morgan hastily moved toward them. He held out his hand, a cell phone rested in his palm.

"Leslie is on the phone."

Amelia's eyes went wide. "Who's phone is that?"

"Mine," Morgan said. "I had it in my coat pocket."

Amelia jumped up and grabbed it from him, placing a finger over the receiver. "Have you been calling people?"

Morgan's familiar sarcastic expression came at her full force. "No. Stupid thing hasn't been working right since we got here."

Amelia put the phone to her ear. "Leslie?"

"Are you all right? Where are you?"

Amelia relaxed her stance. "We're fine. We're at the church down the road from our place."

"Bloody hell, Amelia, I've been worried sick about you and the boys. I've been trying your cell number for hours, with no answer."

"Yeah, I must have left my cell at home. We had to leave in a hurry."

"So what happened? How did the fire start?"

"Not sure. Probably something with the electrical system."

There was a long silence on the other end.

"Amelia, what's going on?"

"What are you talking about?"

"Why did you go to the church? Why didn't you come to me?"

Amelia paused. What could she tell her?

"And there's something else."

"What?"

"Henry called me this morning. Wanted to know if I thought you'd been acting strange lately."

Amelia frowned. "Acting strange? How?"

"I don't know, he didn't really say." There was another long pause. "Amelia, are you sure everything is all right?"

"Yeah, everything's fine. Look, I have to go. I'll get in touch with you as soon as things have calmed down."

"Okay. Be careful."

She flipped the phone shut and faced Father George. "I didn't like the tone of her voice. I don't think she's buying it."

"Well, you're going to have to work harder at convincing her." Father George moved toward the salt ring. "The fewer people who know, the better."

"What about the electrical?" Chad asked.

Amelia ignored his question. "You don't understand, Father, she thinks Henry is cheating on me. I thought I had her convinced otherwise, but me being evasive like that, will make her think I don't trust her."

"Maybe that's for the better," he said, spraying water around the circle.

"She's my best friend."

Father George stopped blessing the circle and looked up. "Which would you rather have, Amelia, a best friend who thinks you lied to avoid being embarrassed, or a best friend who's dead?"

Amelia clenched her jaw. "That's not fair. She's only trying to help."

"Then let her help afterward, when all this is over." He began spraying water down on the floor. "You're going to need her help more after all this. Let her think Henry is being unfaithful. When he's gone, you can just say he left you for the other woman."

Amelia folded her arms across her chest. She was going to need Leslie's help afterward, lots of it, and she knew Henry wasn't above killing at random to get what he wanted. As much as she needed to talk to her friend, Amelia conceded that keeping Leslie out of the loop was, for now, the only option.

She exhaled and relaxed. This day was already too much for her, and they still had the night to contend with. She rubbed her temples with her index fingers, hoping to ease the pounding that was slowly building in her head.

"So," Chad's tone was slightly indignant. "Are you going to tell me or not?"

Amelia frowned. "What are you talking about?"

"You told Leslie something about the wiring in the house?"

Amelia thought back to what Homer said in the van. "It's nothing, don't worry about it."

"Bullshit it's nothing. Leslie wouldn't be calling you if it was."

Amelia kept quiet and just looked into his eyes.

"Something else happened that you're not telling me about."

"Yeah, but like I said, don't worry about it."

He rolled his eyes, and Amelia felt her anxiety rise as that old confrontational expression washed over him.

"This is my fight too, and I can't protect myself if I don't know what's going on."

"I don't think that's a wise choice," Father George said, standing next to her. "Every time the minion takes control of his body, we run the risk of it learning everything we do."

"Fine, then don't tell me everything," he looked helplessly at Amelia, "just the stuff I need to know."

She took a couple steps toward him. "Just remember, we are going to get through this."

Chad straightened up. "What did he do?"

"We think, we're not quite sure, but we think he set the house on fire."

"What?" The air around her grew cold as the shadows stretched out toward the circle. "Our house caught on fire? You gotta be kidding me!"

"Homer and I saw the smoke as we were heading back, but by the time we got there, the house had pretty much burnt to the ground."

Chad ran his fingers through his hair. "So we have no place to live?"

"Calm down, it's all right."

She saw him make a conscious effort to reign in his temper, returning the room to normal.

"How is it all right?" he asked. "You said everything burnt to the ground. We have nothing."

"We have each other, and that counts for more in this fight than any stupid material objects." Amelia reached out and gently touched the barrier, causing it to flash. "Henry will not win as long as we have each other."

Amelia's worries lifted as a gradual smile inched its way across Chad's face. She hoped he believed her.

***

The grocery store clerk stood on the opposite side of the street, hiding in the shadows of a storefront entrance, watching the fire department put out the flames. The corner of his mouth curled upward as a stretcher draped in a white sheet left the alley next to the decimated building. A long shadow inched its way up the side of the entrance, and he turned, allowing the shadows to partially cross his face.

Lyla appeared within the void. Her cold stare focused directly on the clerk.

"This is taking too long." Her mouth barely moved as she spoke. "You promised me his transformation would be soon."

Henry's face appeared within the partial shadow. "Don't worry, it'll happen."

"My Master does not share your enthusiasm. He is most . . . displeased at this setback."

"Maybe this would go faster if I had more help from you."

Her eyes glowed crimson. "Watch your tone. I spared your life under the premise you would offer a vessel before the appropriate time. If you are unable to fulfil your promise—"

"I'm going as fast as I can, but she has allies. Homer's found her, and he's being annoyingly helpful. Not to mention resilient."

"Then go after the boy directly. Find his weakness, and use it against him. Our Master needs Korthos in this realm. Only their fused blood will open the gateway."

Henry glared at her. "I know the plan."

"For your sake, I hope so."

The shadow cleared and skulked back into the ground, as the face of the shop clerk returned to normal.

10

Morning came too soon, but Amelia was grateful. Another night without incident and they were one day closer to the deadline, but she knew the calm of the previous night would give way to another attack. She doubted Henry would give up now. Not when his life was at stake.

The night's calm didn't allow her a peaceful night's sleep either. Shadows dancing across the walls kept her mind occupied with thoughts of demons, along with the constant fear of Chad turning. The cake Homer made was keeping the thing at bay, enough so that Father George allowed Homer to break the protective ring around her son. Chad was grateful he could go to the bathroom by himself again, but the added protection wasn't enough to calm Amelia's nerves. If anything, the rapidly approaching deadline, mixed with the calm night, fueled her anxiety. The walls were closing in around her, and she felt helpless. She'd developed a case of cabin fever after being cooped up for only two days.

The mid-morning sun shone through the stained glass windows, reflecting a kaleidoscope of colour on the walls. The multicoloured auras gave a mystical feel to the hallway, which seemed to lighten her mood as she headed toward the kitchen.

She felt tension the moment she stepped through the entranceway into the rectory, but it had nothing to do with demons. The calm had reopened the sibling rivalry between the twins, and she could hear their muffled bickering in the kitchen. Her attention shifted to the empty salt ring on the floor when she heard Chad trying to play mediator between his brothers.

"Don't you two ever stop?" Amelia asked, as she walked into the kitchen toward the pot of coffee on the stove.

"I will if he will," Liam said, swiping a small chunk of cake from a platter.

"That's not for you." Morgan reached for his brother's arm. "Put it back."

Amelia hid her smile as Liam licked one side of the cake piece. Even the blast of name calling that followed made her heart feel lighter. Things were normal, and for a brief moment, she wasn't worried about what might come.

She wandered over to the kitchen table and made herself comfortable in the chair next to Chad. He still wore the sash around his shoulders, but she could see it had noticeably dulled in the last twelve hours. She wondered apprehensively if its special ability would last the entire weekend.

Amelia watched her boys interact with each other. It was especially good to see Chad smile again, but she knew deep down he must be feeling betrayed. Why wouldn't he? Why wouldn't they all? It would be a long time before she would trust anyone again.

"Did you get some coffee?" she asked. He looked older than his eighteen years now, and in many ways he was.

"You call that coffee?" he replied, smiling. "It's more like liquid mud."

Amelia pretended to be insulted. "Well, I'm sorry it isn't up to your gourmet coffee house standard," she teased. "But for now, it's the best we have."

"Well then," he picked up his mug, "who am I to slam the crap?"

Morgan's cell phone rang, and at once the room went quiet. It sat in the middle of the table, the annoying ring-tone blaring a hip-hop tune. No one moved.

"That's a really stupid ring tone," Liam said, picking at cake crumbs.

Amelia picked up the phone. "Unknown number. Any of your friends have number block?"

"No, but it came up like that last night when Leslie called."

Amelia flipped open the phone. "Hello?"

"Is there anything in particular you or the kids need?" Leslie's voice was loud over the receiver and Amelia held the phone a few inches away from her ear.

"Leslie, where are you?"

"Outside my house. I picked up a few things at the thrift store this morning. I figured you'd need it since all your clothing went up in flames."

Amelia felt her face grow warm with embarrassment. "Leslie, you don't have to do that. We're managing fine—"

"Stop it, Amelia, you're going to need these, and since you didn't come to me in the first place, the least you can do is take this stuff now."

Amelia smiled. This was typical Leslie, and she knew better than to argue with her. "Fine, and thank you. I don't know how I'll ever repay you."

"Don't worry about that, but you're going to have to come to my place to pick it up. I'd drop it off, but I have a meeting in the city and I'm already late."

"Not a problem. I'll head over now."

Amelia took a deep breath and put the phone back on the table. "Leslie bought us some new clothes. They're over at her place now."

A wide grin broke across Morgan's face. "Sweet!"

"You say that now," Amelia teased, "but she bought us secondhand clothes."

"I don't care," Morgan said. "I'll wear anything as long as it doesn't smell like it's been sitting in a church basement."

Chad didn't look so happy. "Are you serious? Why would she do that?"

"To help," Amelia said, and took a sip of her coffee. "Why do you look so shocked? She's helped us out before." Amelia was hit with a sudden fear. "Wait, you don't hear something, do you?"

Chad furrowed his brow. "No, and I know she's helped us out before, but . . ."

Amelia smiled. "Let me guess, it's a nagging feeling that you're missing something. After this weekend, I'm surprised we're not all jumping to conclusions." She stood up, bringing her coffee cup with her. "I'm going to head out now. I shouldn't be gone that long."

She felt the anxiety in the room grow as both the twins and Chad went to her side.

"You can't go by yourself," Morgan said. "Those things—"

"Don't come out in the day." Amelia tried to reassure him. She glanced at Chad, motioning him to validate her. "I was fine yesterday. Nothing is going to happen to me today."

"She's right," he said, but he didn't look as though he wanted her to go either. "The minions are weakened by sunlight." He focused on her. "But that doesn't mean they won't try to find a way to interfere."

"I have to go," she argued. "If I don't, she'll only end up here and start asking questions. The less she knows the better. Might even save her life."

"Then I'm coming with you," Chad said, and grabbed a chunk of cake. "I can at least warn you if those things start acting up."

Amelia shook her head. "I don't think that's a good idea. You're safer in here, and—"

"Mom, I have to get out of here." He grabbed his coffee mug and took a gulp before continuing. "They're not going to harm me. If anything, it's you and those two," he motioned to the twins, "they're after."

A hundred responses piled into Amelia's head, but not one was a truly valid reason for him to stay. He needed to have some time out of the church as much as she did, and it would be nice to talk with him about this, without the others around.

"Okay, I get the message, but you're taking that sash with you. Just in case." She faced the twins. "Try not to kill each other before we get back."

The day was already warm when they stepped outside. A light breeze played with dried leaves on the ground, and the excited snickers coming from Chad made Amelia smile. Maybe his being outside was a good idea after all.

"Where do you two think you're going?" Father George asked, as he and Jared walked to the church steps.

"Leslie called," Amelia replied, stepping down to meet them. "She has some things for us, clothes and stuff, so we're going to go and pick them up."

"I don't think that's a wise idea. We have plenty of extra clothing here, I'm sure you can find something—"

"I know that, Father," Amelia interrupted. "But she's on her way out of town and—"

"So pick them up when she returns."

Amelia was taken aback but his rudeness. "I also want to talk to her."

"About what? I thought we'd decided you weren't going to say anything?"

"I know, but I think Henry is trying to mess with her mind. He was asking her questions about me, if I've been acting strange. He may be trying to plant some kind of doubt in her mind."

"Sounds like he's trying to break another bond," Jared said. "She might end up believing him."

"That's what I'm afraid of too." Amelia gave a feeble smile. "I don't know what he's said to her, but if I can convince her that he shouldn't be trusted, she's apt not to believe anything he says."

"Can you do it without giving her too much information?" Father George asked.

"Shouldn't be a problem. She already thinks he's cheating on me, remember?"

Jared motioned toward Chad. "So why is he going?"

"Because if I don't, I'm going to go fucking stir-crazy"

Amelia clenched her jaw. "Chad, please don't swear."

"Mom, I'm eighteen."

"You're also in front of a priest. Have a little respect. Just because you're a legal adult doesn't mean I'm going to stop being your mother."

"Father George, please," Chad's tone was more respective this time, "I have to get out of this church. I've done everything you've asked of me, without argument. I just need this."

"We're not going to be gone long," Amelia continued. "I promise."

"Do what you want," Father George said, as he stepped past them. "And I'll pray for your safe return. Hopefully, the forces of evil will be as lax in their judgment as you seem to be in yours."

Jared pursed his lips. "What are you going to say to her?"

"I don't know." Amelia thought about it for a moment. "I don't know if there's a way I could tell her Henry was dangerous without freaking her out. I guess it all depends on what she tells me first."

The mid-morning sky seemed to darken as they drove off church property. Amelia kept a close eye on the scenery, and looked for any signs they were being followed.

"Is it me, or do things seem—"

"Darker?" Chad finished.

"Yeah. Hear anything?"

Chad shook his head. "Nope."

"Well, keep your ears open. I don't want any surprises."

Amelia kept quiet all the way across town. She didn't want Chad distracted. He was her early warning system, and she needed him focused.

Amelia's anxiety grew as they turned down a small side street. Leslie lived in a smaller house at the end of the road. Her heart raced as they pulled into the driveway and parked behind a Lexus.

Leslie suddenly appeared in the picture window at the front of the house; a look of confusion on her face.

Amelia stepped out of the van. "Anything?"

Chad shook his head as he walked up beside the mint-green car. He took a quick look in the window on the passenger side. "Where are the clothes?"

Amelia took a quick look. "In the trunk, maybe?"

She hurried up the driveway to the side entrance of the house. She barely had a chance to knock when Leslie swung open the inside door.

Before she could speak, Leslie reached out and pulled her into a strong hug. The embrace felt good and the warm feelings melted away some of her tension.

"You have no idea how worried I've been since I saw that news report," Leslie said. She let go of Amelia and went for Chad. She noticed the strange sash around his neck and played with it a bit. "What's this? Some new style?"

"I don't know," he said. "It just something I found in one of the old boxes at the church." He picked up one end of the stole and flipped it over his opposite shoulder. "Kinda cool looking, isn't it?"

"Well, it certainly is interesting."

"What are you doing here? I thought you had a meeting in the city?"

She turned to Amelia. "That's not for a couple hours. Come on inside. I'll make some coffee. I want to hear everything."

Amelia took one more look around the property, then followed Chad and Leslie into the house.

The house was small but cozy and felt more inviting than the basement of the church. Amelia glanced around the kitchen and all the pattern knick-knacks on the shelves. Leslie never had any children, so she didn't have to worry about any of them getting broken. Amelia picked up a small ceramic cow and chuckled.

"What's so funny?" Leslie asked, pouring water into a kettle.

"I had one of these when Henry and I first got married."

"What happened to it?" Chad asked.

Amelia put the ceramic down and looked at him. "You."

Chad slumped down into a kitchen chair. "Sorry."

Amelia put the trinket back, and joined Chad at the table.

"So what exactly happened to the house?" Leslie asked. "Have you heard anything from the fire marshal?"

"No, not a word," Amelia replied.

"What did Henry say? Is he coming home?"

Amelia tensed. She felt her palms grow sweaty as she tried to think of a something that sounded reasonable. "He doesn't know yet."

"Are you serious? Why haven't you called him?"

Amelia looked at her puzzled. "With what? I told you, we had to get out of the house fast. I didn't even know Morgan had his cell until you called."

It was Leslie's turn to look baffled. "What are you talking about? I didn't call you."

"Yes you did. Yesterday."

Leslie chuckled. "You must be under a lot of stress. I didn't call you yesterday. As a matter of fact, I didn't call anyone. My cell's disappeared." Leslie's raised her eyebrows. "Wait, you're staying at a church? Why didn't you go to a hotel?" She looked away from Amelia. "Chad? What are you doing?"

Amelia whipped around. Chad sat with his head bent toward the table, his eyes racing back and forth.

"Mom, I think we have a problem."

Amelia's blood went cold. "Shit!"

Leslie reached out to Amelia. "What's going on?"

Amelia jumped up and was at the back door within seconds. She turned the knob, but the door wouldn't open. Frantically, she turned back around and went to Chad's side. "Anything?"

"Amelia what are you doing? What's going on?"

"You're in danger, Leslie. We all are. We have to get out of here now."

She grabbed Chad by the arm and yanked him out of the chair. It was a trap, it had to be, and she swore softly, angry that she'd fallen for it. She pulled Chad into the living room, headed for the front door, but froze as a shadow moved quickly up the length of the door.

Leslie came up behind them. "What do you mean, in danger? From who?"

Henry stepped out from the shadow. His eyes firmly locked on Amelia. "From me."

Leslie stepped up beside Amelia. "How the hell did you get in here?"

"Leslie," Amelia reached for Leslie's arm, "keep away from him. He's dangerous."

Leslie yanked her arm away. "Maybe in the courtroom, but this is my home, and he has no right barging in like this."

"Leslie, please, you don't understand."

"Amelia, relax, you're safe here. Let me deal with him."

"Deal with me?" Henry said, amused. "Just who do you think you are?"

Leslie moved in front of Amelia. "Listen to me, you sonofabitch, I know you're cheating on Amelia, and if you think you can just dump my friend and walk off into the sunset with some young bimbo scot-free, well you've got another thing coming!"

Amelia tugged on Leslie's arm. "Leslie, stop!"

Henry took a step toward them, clearly amused at her outburst. With a flick of his hand, Chad was thrown up against the wall, pinned down in a spread-eagle position. Leslie griped Amelia's arm, and this time it was Amelia who went on the defence.

"Bastard. Leave him alone!"

Amelia took a step toward him and was thrown back against the wall.

An icy hold gripped her from behind, pinning her body in place.

The weight of his glare was strong. "You don't ever tell me what to do."

Amelia focused on her friend. Leslie didn't move, and Amelia could see her body tremble as Henry moved closer. "What's going on? How is he doing that?"

"Leslie, get out of here."

"I don't think so." Henry grabbed Leslie by the hair and dragged her over to Chad.

"You have us," Amelia pleaded. "Let her go."

"I don't think so." Henry held up his hand in front of Chad and the teen's chest began to glow. The smell of burning flesh permeated the room as small flames lit up on the front of Chad's shirt, burning away the material and exposing the amulet underneath. Chad's eyes grew crimson red as his face twisted and contorted into that of the minion. This time more of the creature immerged, and the stole began to smoke as Chad sank to the ground.

Henry pulled Leslie closer to Chad. "Do you see this? This is what I can do, and you want to deal with me?"

Leslie struggled, trying to break free of Henry's grasp. "What the hell are you?"

"What I am, is powerful, and unless you want to end up a charred pile of bones, I suggest you shut your mouth and do as you're told."

Amelia could only watch as Leslie struggled against Henry.

"Never," Leslie said, trying to break his grip. "You're an asshole, Henry, and I don't listen to assholes."

There was something about Henry's sudden calm demeanour that frightened Amelia, as his other hand went to Leslie's chin.

"Fine, Leslie. Suit yourself."

With a quick yank, Henry twisted Leslie's neck, snapping the bone with a grinding sound, and her limp body fell to the ground.

Amelia heard a piercing cry and realized she was screaming as she stared at the body of her friend on the floor. Leslie's eyes were open, a calm reflection on her face with her lips slightly parted. There was no fear, no pain. Only peace.

Amelia's eyes stayed on Leslie as Henry stepped over the body and came toward her. The air around her grew colder with each step he took, his face only inches away from hers. Wisps of steam escaped from her lips as she trembled from fear, her tears cooling as they trickled down her cheek.

"I kind of like you this way," Henry whispered into her ear. "Completely under my control."

A thousand words raced through her mind, as she contemplated a comeback as icy as the grip that held her in place, but nothing she thought of could properly express the hatred she had for him.

Except for two words. "Fuck you!"

The smell of rancid meat enveloped Amelia as Henry chuckled at her response. "Where did all this defiance come from?"

Amelia turned her head as his smile revealed a forked tongue that flicked against her cheek, lapping up her tears. She closed her eyes as he moved closer, feeling his icy touch against her skin as his hand found an opening between the buttons on her shirt.

A low growl came from the floor on other side of the room. "You really are an asshole."

Amelia's eyes snapped open. Chad sat, hunched over on the balls of his feet, eyes focused on Henry. His smile sent a chill through Amelia, as two rows of sharp fangs and the emaciated skull of the minion took over.

As Chad stood, more of the minion revealed itself as the stole continued to smolder around his shoulders, but Amelia could still make out features that belonged to her son.

The air warmed slightly around her as Henry stepped away. "You should have turned."

Half human, half minion, Chad hooked his thumb in the belt loop of his pants. "I should have done a lot of things, like kill you when I had the chance."

"You don't have the power," Henry said as he and Chad circled each other. "Even with Korthos inside you, you're just a weak little shit."

A sly grin appeared on Chad lips. "Care to test that theory?"

Father George's words leapt into Amelia's mind. "No Chad! Don't let him goad you into—"

Another wave of Henry's hand and an icy shadow reached out from the wall and down Amelia's throat, choking off her words, barely allowing air to travel to her lungs.

"LET HER GO!"

Chad leapt at Henry, claws extended, aiming straight for his throat, but Henry flicked his wrist, and the young man was sent flying backward into a pile of knick-knacks.

"You're pathetic," Henry said, turning back to Amelia. "Almost as pathetic as this useless corpse on the floor." Henry kicked at Leslie's limp hand as he walked past her. "I was hoping she would see just how crazy you are, Amelia. Too bad she had to ruin everything by being so loyal." Henry stopped directly in front of her. "Now, where were we?"

Amelia struggled against the invisible restraints as Henry groped around the buttons on her jeans. "Maybe just once more," he said, sniffing her hair, "for old times' sake."

Bile stung the top of her throat. She closed her eyes as Henry's cold touch sent a wave of repulsion through her body. His icy strokes caused her abdomen to contract, limiting even more air into her lungs. Growls echoed from every part of the room as something brushed past her, taking Henry with it.

Amelia opened her eyes and found Chad standing several feet away. His stance was shorter, almost by a foot, and more of the minion's features were becoming prominent. She whimpered as the creature looked back, its eyes full of rage, but she could still see a small hint of Chad's dark brown eyes through all the anger.

She shook her head, but the creature only smiled and focused back on Henry, who was holding his side, blood oozing through his fingers from two sets of claw marks.

"So there is still some human in you after all?" Henry said, bracing himself against the wall. "But you're still not strong enough to take me out. If you want to kill me, you have to let the minion take control to access its power, but then, you'd be gone, and I win."

Amelia's emotions burst and the tears flowed down her cheeks. She wanted to scream, curse, spit, but all she could muster was a frantic thrashing against the wall. Her bond to Chad was strong, and she thought it would be the way to save him. She never thought it could also destroy him.

The creature turned back to her and gently stroked her wet cheek. "Don't worry," it said, the gruff tone held hints of Chad's voice. "I'll be fine."

It turned and focused on Henry, who struggled to walk past the picture window at the front of the room. Amelia watched as the creature took aim for him and leapt into the air, coming into contact with Henry, and they both crashed through the window and onto the front lawn.

Immediately Amelia fell to the floor as the shadows retreated back into the wall. She gasped for air; her body ached from the cold restraint as she crawled over to Leslie's body. Amelia knew her friend was dead, but she touched the side of her neck along a purple vein, and waited for some sign of a pulse. It was a desperate act, but she had to do it. She reached out and closed Leslie's eyelids then placed her lifeless hands across her stomach.

Anger boiled up and forced Amelia unsteadily to her feet, heading to the broken picture window. She didn't know what she could do against Henry. The power he wielded was impossible for her to fight, but she had to try something. She wasn't about to let Leslie's belligerent attitude die in vain.

A strong wind blew in through the opening, bringing dried leaves and dirt into the house, mixing with the debris on the floor. The sun was gone, replaced by an eerie grey that blanketed the neighbourhood and sent a shiver up Amelia's spine. The clouds were coming in too quickly, creating shadows that grew long and stretched out toward the middle of the lawn, where Henry and Chad stood frozen, locked in each other's gaze.

"You can't beat me," Henry said, his forked tongue poking between a sly grin. "No matter what you do, I win."

"Don't be so sure. You have a weakness, and we know it."

Deep cracks opened in the earth and rapidly spread across the lawn in every direction. A wave of nausea swept over Amelia as the orange glow of hellfire added to the chaos unfolding before her. She flinched as intense flashes of lightning lit up the sky, illuminating the band of scrayling that encircled the tree tops.

"Chad," she called, but her voice was too weak to overcome the wailing of the torrent of wind that assaulted the neighbourhood. Amelia headed for the front door, but the handle refused to budge. Her hands only glided over the knob. She let out a steady stream of swear words and ran back to the window, contemplating climbing over the shards of glass.

A strong gust blew directly at her. She lowered her head and tightened her grip on the broken window frame, trying to steady herself against the gale. Shards of debris sliced into her hands and legs, and her jaw clenched as she quietly absorbed the pain.

"Leave her alone," Chad yelled. "You kill her, and she becomes a martyr, and you can't kill a martyr."

The winds died down and Amelia eased her grip. She raised her head and watched the cracks reseal. She pulled herself the rest of the way over the window frame and ran to Chad's side. Henry backed away, and Amelia kept her gaze solely on him, waiting for him to make his move.

"Not to worry," he said, as green flames leaped out from the trunk of a tree. "There are others that you care for. I'm sure killing one of them will be just as satisfying."

Chad lunged forward, but Henry slipped into the flames and disappeared. At once, the sun broke through the dark clouds and the colour returned. Chad let out a yelp and crouched to the ground, writhing in pain.

Amelia ran to his side and bent down, cradling him in her arms. She let out a long and deep exhale, trembling slightly as a steady stream of tears streaked down her face.

"I'm such an idiot," she whispered into a tuff of Chad's hair. "I should have known this was a trap."

Chad looked her in the eyes. The features of the minion were slowly blending away. "You can't blame—"

"Yes, I can. Father George warned us not to go, but I didn't listen. I've been sitting in that church, smugly thinking we have Henry beat, when all along he knew how to get to me. We didn't need to leave the church, the clothes could have waited. We left because of me. I needed to get away from anything that reminded me my life is a walking nightmare. I wanted just a few moments of normality, and now Leslie's dead and you're a lot closer to becoming that thing." She brushed away her tears and stood up. "We're going back to the church, and I'm locking the doors. No one else is going to die trying to help us."

Chad bolted to his feet. "Tony!"

"What about him?"

"That's who Henry meant." He took the sash off his shoulders and threw it at Amelia. "I have to get to Tony before he does."

Amelia took a quick glance around the neighbourhood as green flames suddenly appeared around Chad. An uneasy feeling crept over her. A few of Leslie's neighbours stood on their lawns, staring in her direction. When one pointed to her, she grabbed the shroud and turned toward the house, then hesitated. Leslie's body was inside. If they saw her go in . . .

She lowered her head and headed for the van, hoping no one recognized her.

***

Multiple cityscapes flashed before Chad's eyes as he tried to focus on a memory of Tony's home. It was hard to pinpoint the exact location. His mind was filled with horrible images of what Henry could do, and he couldn't focus on where he needed to be. He couldn't let that asshole hurt Tony or his sister. His mother was too guilt-ridden as it was, and Chad knew she would never forgive herself.

He felt a heat pull at him from behind, trying to draw him deeper into the darkness, but there was something else. The scent of charred flesh and blood exhilarated his mind. It took all of his strength to concentrate on keeping just on the edge of the shadows. Any deeper and he could lose himself in the vastness of the hell that waited for him. Chad closed his eyes and pictured Tony's face: his bashful smile and the way his eyes seem to light up whenever Chad was around. The thought that those eyes might never look at him again sent a wave of heartache through him and helped him to focus.

Then he heard it. A woman's scream from somewhere off in the distance. Frantic shouts and crying that sounded too familiar. He closed his eyes and focused on the noise, blocking everything else from his mind. When he opened his eyes, the familiar sight of a white-sided house and a young girl cradling the body of a young man stood before him.

He took a step out from the flames, his legs buckled under him as he tried to walk forward. A ray of sunlight through the trees caught him in the shoulder, burning his skin and forcing him to retreat to the safety of the shadows, but the young girl's sobs forced him back out. He stumbled across the lawn, jumping from shadow to shadow, and with each step Chad knew he was too late. Blood was everywhere, soaked into the grass and clothing. It still ran out from gaping wounds that covered the body of a young man. The closer he came, the stronger the scent of blood became, until the metallic smell was too overpowering, and he dropped to the ground trying to control the urge to attack.

"This is her fault!" The young girl cradled the body of her brother in her arms. "Tony's dead because of her."

Chad crawled along the ground, the pain in his chest felt like a vice grip. He reached out to touch the side of Tony's face. "This isn't happening." His voice cracked as he brushed his cheek. "I wasn't that far behind him."

He felt her small hand grip his arm and push him away. "You did this," she screamed. "You told your hateful bitch of a mother that you and Tony were lovers!"

Chad crouched low to the ground. The smell of blood mixed with the musty smell of earth excited him, and he grabbed a handful of bloody soil and smeared it over his face. A tightness in his chest grew; a mixture of anger and pleasure washed over him as he watched the young girl cry. He smiled and crawled back, skulking along the ground, revelling in the smell of blood. He stretched out his hand as his nails tuned into claws. The tightness spread as he reached out to touch the side of Tony's face. The body was still warm, despite the rosy colour quickly fading from his flesh.

Tony's flesh. Tony, his boyfriend. The only one who knew his secret, apart from his mother.

Memories of his mother flashed into his mind. Her understanding gaze that night on the balcony when he confessed his secret. Her pain-filled cries into the night when he'd run off into the woods. Her tight embrace when he returned. He knew her, but more importantly, he knew her scent, and it wasn't anywhere around.

"She didn't do this." Chad pulled his arm back as the tightness began to subside.

Tina pushed him away. "Don't touch him! You have no right to touch him."

Chad crawled a few feet back, never taking his eyes off Tony. The smell of blood diminished as his body returned to normal. He felt helpless, worthless. All this power coursing through his body, and he still couldn't save anyone. Not his mother's friend, not his boyfriend. Henry was right; he was nothing more than a weak little shit.

"Pathetic."

Amelia's voice came from a group of bushes next to the house. Chad turned to see his mother hiding just beyond view, but as he raised his head into the air, it wasn't her scent he caught.

Chad stood, stretching out to his full height. He came eye to eye with his mother, as a sneer formed on his lips. Before he could say anything, she stepped back into the shadows and disappeared.

Sirens wailed off in the distance, and Chad took one more look at Tina and her brother. He wanted to stay, wanted to comfort her, but he knew she'd never accept anything from him. He ran to the shed but stopped just before entering the shadow. It had been too challenging travelling here, too much of a temptation to step beyond the boundary. He would have to return to the church the normal way and try to keep hidden from the neighbours.

11

Amelia didn't like the scene unfolding outside the church. Beyond the old limestone fence, several police cars were parked along the side of the road. The officers were huddled in a group, talking among themselves and occasionally focusing their attention toward the church. Amelia anxiously nibbled on her fingernail, rubbing the rough edge along her lip. One cop car she could deal with. This was a whole squad.

"Father George is heading out to talk to them," Homer said, stepping out from the office. "Find out why they're here."

"They think I murdered Leslie and Tony," she said, keeping her gaze on the commotion outside. "Can he keep them from taking us to jail?"

Homer raised his hands. "Calm down. No one's said anything about going to jail."

"But that has to be why they're here."

"Amelia, relax. All we know is there's a pile of police cruisers outside. There could be any number of reasons why they're here."

Amelia rolled her eyes. "Homer, there have been four murders in this city in the last twenty-four hours, and all of them can be linked back to me. Not to mention my house going up in flames." She moved away from the window and rested up against the wall. "If I were a cop, I'd want to arrest me, too." Amelia tilted her head to one side. "How are you doing? Feeling better?"

Homer winced as he stretched his arm over his head. "About as good as I can be after falling out of a two-story building."

Father George stepped out from his office and came toward them. "I've been on the phone with the police station. They want to bring you,

152

Homer, and Jared in for questioning."

Amelia nodded her head. "For all those murders, right?"

Father George let out a sigh. "It would appear so. They have witnesses that put Amelia at the scene of the last two, and they're saying the fire that consumed the house was deliberately set."

Amelia frowned. "No shit."

"We can't leave the sanctuary," Homer said. "Chad's barely keeping it together as it is. If we leave, he could spiral out of control. We need to keep him here, away from his father."

"That's going to be a problem." The priest let out a heavy sigh. "Henry's at the police station with Child Protective Services. He's claimed Amelia is mentally unstable and has demanded she turn the boys over to him."

"But Chad's eighteen," Amelia argued. "Technically he's an adult now."

"But you've brainwashed him," Father George said, with a hint of sarcasm. "So he's not in his right mind, and Henry has applied to the courts to be his legal counsel."

"Guys," Jared called, as hurried footsteps came from the stairwell. He was out of breath by the time he reached the top step. "They just broke in with a special news report. They found the remains of those two cops the scrayling killed."

"Great," Amelia said. "Two more murders to pin on me."

They all scurried down the steps and into the dark rectory. The light from the small screen television barely registered in the gloom as Morgan and Liam sat in front of it. Amelia raced across the room, giving a quick glance to the dark corner and the ring of salt on the floor. Chad was back in the centre, his legs crossed, and his head on his hands. Amelia hesitated, then changed direction and walked toward him.

"Chad?"

"Go away."

She bent down on one knee, her gaze resting on the long claw-like nails on his fingers.

"Don't do this Chad. You have to keep fighting."

He raised his head, and looked woefully up at her. His eyes were bloodshot, and Amelia knew it had nothing to do with the minion.

"What's the point?" Chad's voice cracked, his bottom lip trembling. "He's too strong, and everything I do to try and stop him just works to his advantage."

"We'll figure something out." She reached out to him, but a white flash forced her hand back as it came in contact with the invisible barrier.

Chad shook his head and lowered it back into his hands. "Leave me alone."

"Chad—"

"Please! Just go away."

She reached out again, but paused as a hand rested gently on her shoulder.

"Leave him be, Amelia," Homer said.

Amelia clenched her jaw and roughly shrugged of his hand. "Don't tell me what to do." She stood, glaring at Homer and trying to keep her anger at bay. She wanted to slap him hard, punch him until he hurt the way she did. "I've followed you from the beginning, and it's gotten us nowhere. This wouldn't be happening if it wasn't for you, so don't you dare tell me how to deal with my son."

"Amelia, I—"

"Shut up! I don't want to hear another word from you."

She stormed over toward the twins. She knew it wasn't really Homer's fault. The only person to blame for all of this was smugly sitting at the police station, thinking he was going to win. She'd apologize to Homer later, when she could really mean it.

Morgan looked up at her as she approached, but said nothing. His sad eyes told Amelia all she needed to know. Chad wasn't the only one losing hope, and her outbursts of anger weren't helping.

She didn't hear the reporter's disembodied voice-over as the television displayed two stretchers leaving what used to be the front exit of her home. A picture of her appeared on the screen, along with some statistics. She crossed her arms over her chest and stared hard at the screen.

"The detective on the case is on his way to the church," Father George said, coming up behind her. "He has a warrant for everyone's arrest, and he's bringing a social worker for the twins."

Jared let out a deep sigh. "We're dead. The moment we're in custody, those minions will be all over us."

Amelia looked at him. Jared wanted nothing to do with this plan from the beginning, but she guilted him into it. Suddenly her anger with Homer wasn't so justified.

"Fine then. We do what we did before."

Jared frowned. "What are you talking about?"

She looked back at Homer. "We make a run for it."

Homer raised an eyebrow. "Again? Are you sure?"

"Well, so far it's been the only tactic that actually worked. If we can keep one step ahead until tonight, I think we might make it."

"You can't leave the church, Amelia," Father George said. "Look at your son. He won't survive without the protection."

A flash of light lit up the far corner. Amelia gasped when she turned. Chad stood tall, his hand out to his side, and the stole, draped over his palm, slowly going up in flames. No one spoke as the fire consumed the relic, and in the firelight, Amelia could see a maniacal grin on his face.

"Chad?"

He turned toward her, but didn't take his eyes off the flames. "I don't think this is going to work anymore."

Morgan stood up next to her and slumped to one side. "It was an ugly looking thing anyway."

Amelia clamped a hand over her mouth before she burst out laughing; she wasn't the only one. Both Homer and Jared turned away from Father George, as the priest looked on, horrified.

"You have to leave now," Father George said. "That relic was the core of this church. It's what gave the sanctuary its strength. Now, we're like any other building in town."

A whiff of sulfur caught Amelia's attention. From the corner, a shadow stretched out toward the salt ring, sending flashes as it poked around the protective barrier. More shadows reached out from dark places, engulfing the television, warping it into a hunk of twisting metal and melted plastic. Amelia grabbed the twins as sparks shot out in all directions. The back end of the rectory was quickly becoming an inky black shadow.

"Quick," Homer said, heading toward the salt ring. "Get upstairs before they cut us off."

Amelia shoved the twins toward the stairs as Jared and Father George ran for the stairwell. Homer threw something at the ring, causing it to go up in a blue flame and evaporate the salt on the floor.

Chad frowned. "What are you doing? It's me they're after! You guys can—"

"Your mother said we're leaving." Homer grabbed the teen by the front of his shirt and dragged him toward the stairs. "That means you too."

Amelia waited for them. The back end of the rectory became twisted and warped as the shadows drew closer. They raced up the stairs, barely ahead of the advancing shadows. She let out a small sigh as the sunlight slowed its progression.

Homer looked at Amelia. "If we're going to leave, we'd better do it now."

She nodded and headed to Father George's office. Jared and the priest were already shoving supplies into several knapsacks on the floor.

"We'll head up north, to Pike Lake," she said. "We have a cottage up there, and it's pretty secluded."

"How are we going to get out of the church?" Liam asked. "The cops are at the front door."

Jared handed him one of the bags. "Looks like we go out a window."

"Then what?"

Homer grabbed the straps of another bag. "Then we do as your mom says and make a run for it."

"But those things—"

"We're fine as long as the sun is out," Jared said. "But we're going to have to move fast if we're gonna get to this place before sundown."

Amelia took the last bag. "It's a few hours out of town, and we'll have to head into the woods behind the church and go around the cops."

Chad took the bag from his mother. "I know the streets like the back of my hand," he said, throwing the bag over his shoulder. "I can get us around the cops in a few minutes."

Amelia nodded and headed out of the office and down the corridor. She paused to take a quick look outside, to see what the cops were doing. "We're going to need a car."

Jared passed her. "No problem. I can hot-wire anything."

She motioned Chad and the twins to follow Jared and then smiled at Father George.

"Thank you for your help." She reached out and embraced the priest. "I hope I see you again."

His embrace was strong. "Likewise."

Amelia stepped back and took a look around the church. She'd wanted out of this place so bad, and now that she was forced out, she wanted nothing more but to stay.

"Don't call," Father George said. "If they ask me if I've heard from you, I don't want to lie to them."

"I don't think the damn cells work anyway." Amelia tried to smile, but it was choked off by a tightness growing in her throat. "Do you want to come with us? You're vulnerable now and in serious danger now that the shroud is destroyed."

"Don't worry about me. There are still places in this building that can protect me."

Jared's voice echoed off the walls. "Amelia, come on!"

She gave him one last embrace, then turned and ran down the hall toward Jared. There was a preparation room just off the main altar room, and she found them stuffing the knapsacks out through an open window.

"Looks like Father George is going to try and keep their attention occupied," Jared said, walking up to her.

Amelia looked out the window and saw nothing but woods behind the church. "We're not going to have much time to do this. If they think he's stalling they could rush the building." She turned to Chad. "I know you don't like going into the shadows to move around, but we need to spy on those cops."

Chad smiled. "It's all right. I was thinking the same thing."

"Can you handle it?"

"We'll find out." He stepped back into a shadow and disappeared.

Her heart raced as, one by one, the twins jumped to the ground and ran to the safety of the woods. She went next and grabbed a knapsack as she ran off. The twins were waiting for her a few meters away from the tree line, crouched down between dense underbrush.

"Where's Chad?"

"I don't know," Liam said, keeping his eyes on the back of the church. "Probably still keeping watch."

"I'm right here." Chad stepped out from the shadow of a large oak tree. "I went a little farther up the road. More cars are on their way."

"Might be Henry," Homer said, breaking through the brush. "Which way, Chad?"

The teen motioned to the left and marched through some smaller underbrush. Amelia kept silent as she followed behind, afraid one word might betray their position. She smiled as she imagined the look on Henry's face when he showed up and they were gone, but her smile faded as she thought about the retribution Father George might receive because of it. She wondered about what other protection the church could offer and prayed it was strong enough to ward off Henry's anger.

She smiled again. Henry would be angry. Very angry.

After what felt like an eternity, Chad stopped and crouched to the ground. Homer and Jared came up behind him and knelt down on either side of the teen.

"Where are we?" Amelia asked, looking out across an embankment.

"Walmart is right over there," Chad replied, and motioned to a long strip mall. "There are a couple car lots just on the other side. We can hot-wire a ride there."

Amelia looked out across the dry riverbed to the row of red-bricked buildings on the other side. There was something unusually disturbing about the stillness for this time of day. Amelia couldn't help but fear Henry knew they were gone and had set about killing the whole town just to find them.

With a nod to Jared, Homer walked out from the bushes and down the side of the road, followed closely behind by Jared. Amelia's pulse quickened as Homer and Jared quickly crossed the parking lot and headed for the street.

"Shouldn't we go too?" Liam asked.

"It's not safe," Amelia said. "We'll wait until they're ready for us." She looked over at Chad. He still wore the same shirt with the burn hole in the front. "Maybe you should find something to cover you."

Morgan took off his jacket and handed it to him. "It still smells, but it's better than nothing."

Amelia smiled and tousled Morgan's hair. "That's very kind of you, Morgan."

"That's okay, just get me an expensive hoodie when this is over."

Liam frowned at him. "With what? Dad was the one with the money."

"Then maybe Chad can do that shadow thing and steal me a new hoodie."

Chad zipped up the front of the jacket. "I'm not stealing for you."

"Why not?" Morgan asked. "It's not like you could get caught or anything. You'd be in and out before anyone knew."

Amelia shook her head. This was becoming more surreal by the moment.

She focused again on the other side of the parking lot. Why was it taking so long for Homer and Jared to find something? How hard could it be to steal a car? Images of both men being hauled away by the police flashed through her mind. How would she know if they were caught? How long should she wait here before going to check? She nibbled on the edge of her thumbnail again as she scanned the buildings for any sign of movement.

A cold gust of wind blew over them and Amelia shivered. This didn't feel like a normal cool summer breeze.

"Henry knows we're gone." Chad's tone was as icy as the wind, and at once Amelia knew what it meant.

Morgan motioned toward a large clump of maple trees. "Look."

Shadows from the trunks melted together, forming a large black hole on the ground. An orange and yellow glow emanated from deep inside, as the smell of sulfur carried on the breeze.

"Okay, we're not waiting anymore," she said, standing and grabbing one of the knapsacks. "Car or no car, we're outta here."

The sunlight felt warm as they stumbled out onto the roadway. The smell of hot dirt and wet sand quickly overtook the putrid smell of sulfur. Amelia kept her head low as she crossed the lot, growing angrier by the moment. This was degrading—hiding in bushes and skulking around like a criminal—but she had no other choice, and that bothered her more.

She followed the boys across the street and along the rear end of the shopping mall. The shadows were darker and stretched out toward them even in the daylight.

"They're getting stronger," Morgan said, stepping quickly to one side to avoid a shadowy arm from a dumpster. "I thought the sunlight was fatal for them."

Amelia pushed him forward. "So did I."

The parking lot held only a few cars and a large white cube van. Only when Amelia saw Homer and Jared, did her anxiety lessen.

"Come on," Homer said, sliding the side door open. "The cops are going to shut down all roads out of town in a matter of minutes."

Amelia slid the door shut behind her and leaned up against the wall of the van. She closed her eyes and took a deep breath, listening to Jared's voice as he instructed the twins how to make a protective barrier around Chad in the cargo hold of the van.

"Amelia?" Homer's voice was soft.

She didn't open her eyes. "What?"

"Where am I going?"

"Take Bridge Street east, out of town. Then follow it until you hit the highway." She opened her eyes and smiled. "Then two hours north."

She frowned as Homer's eyes darted back and forth between her and the back of the van where Chad sat, legs crossed in the middle of another salt ring, looking about as miserable as he did before. The fact he didn't look up at anyone bothered her. Not that there was a lot she could do about it. He was feeling responsible for what happened to Leslie and Tony, and as much as she wanted to comfort him, she knew this was something he'd have to deal with on his own.

Or at least, she hoped he was feeling miserable.

"That'll put us at the cottage in the middle of the afternoon," Homer said, starting up the van.

"Sunset is around nine thirty-six. We should have enough time to set things up."

Jared climbed into the passenger seat. "Sounds like you've already got a plan."

"Not really," she said, resting her head against the van wall. "We just need to get away from people."

The floor of the van was hard and cold, and Amelia did her best to stay comfortable. It was a going to be long trip, and she needed to figure out a plan before they arrived at the cottage. That was harder than she thought, even with the van completely silent.

She focused on everything that already happened: the attack on the way to the church, the ambush at Leslie's home. Each time, they thought they were getting away, beating Henry at his own game, until he swooped in and blew everything all to hell. This seemed to be the way he operated, and maybe something she could use against him, but how?

She got to her knees and looked out the windshield then the small windows on the back doors. Odd, they hadn't run across any police yet. Did Henry know they'd left the church, or was he allowing them to escape? Leading them into another trap?

"Hey, look outside."

Amelia leaned forward and glanced out the front windshield. Billowing clouds formed on the horizon and pushed forward over the skyline.

"That's not a good sign," Liam said, next to her.

Jared leaned forward in his seat. "Wanna bet that's a shit-load of scraylings on our ass?"

"Oh yeah," Chad said. "That's a whole pile of nasty things following us."

Amelia turned her head slightly. Chad still had his head bent. His eyes weren't even looking forward. She focused back on the cloud formation, then back at him.

"Don't worry," she said, her eyes darted across his body as she looked for some sign of possession. "We're safe. It's still bright out, and they can't touch us during the day."

Chad raised his head. His eyes were dark and vacant. "Okay . . . Mom."

She pulled one of the knapsacks close to her and unzipped it. "Here, eat this."

She threw a bag of herbs at him, but it hit the invisible barrier and bounced back.

Chad looked down at the bag sitting just outside the ring. "How?"

Amelia frowned and reached for the bag. She'd forgotten about the barrier, and from the way Chad looked, it was a good thing it was there.

She sat back down on the metal floor, crossing her legs, trying to make herself comfortable. She wasn't stupid, not anymore, and she wasn't about to let Henry trick her again. They were going to have one last confrontation, and this time, she would be ready.

***

3:05 p.m.

It was past three in the afternoon when the van finally rolled to a stop. They'd only made one bathroom break during the whole trip. Not bad, considering how long they'd been on the road.

The scent of pine needles flushed out the stale air of the van, as Jared opened his door and stepped out. It was quiet, with only the sound of the breeze whispering through the canopy of the trees.

Amelia slid open the side door and hung her legs over the edge. It had been at least a year since the family vacationed here. Back when she thought her life was perfect. There were still remnants of their time spent here, scattered along the clearing next to the forest edge: a few pieces of garbage, old broken toys, things that brought back pleasant memories.

"Why aren't there any bird sounds?" Liam asked, stepping out from beside her.

Amelia glanced at Jared and caught a flash of concern between him and Homer.

Morgan stepped out next. "That *can't* be a good sign."

She stood and stretched her legs. They were stiff and sore from sitting for so long. The lack of animal noises was unsettling to say the least, and it confirmed in her mind that Henry expected them here.

She walked to the edge of the clearing, to a small stone ring with a makeshift grill built over the centre. Images of the boys and midnight marshmallow roasts flash in her mind, and she suddenly realized, Henry hadn't been involved in any of the fun family times.

"We should get inside," Homer said, walking up behind her. "We have to seal the cabin up tight before nightfall."

Amelia crossed her arms over her chest. "Henry never came with us up here. Said being in the woods wasn't his idea of a vacation."

"He never was one for camping when we were kids either."

Amelia shook her head. "No, I think he didn't want to. Didn't want to make any bonds he knew he'd have to break."

Everything about this place brought back memories of happy times. Amelia could point to a spot and recall some kind of pleasant memory from the boys' childhood.

"That's why you brought us here, wasn't it?"

Amelia sighed. "Apart from the twins and me, this is the last connection Chad would have to this world, and I think it's the strongest."

"Why?"

Amelia smiled and faced him. "Because there are no memories of Henry here." That little piece of information put a skip in her stride as she walked to the front steps of the cabin. *Bet he didn't think of that!* Amelia tried to keep her anxiety level down. The last thing she needed was to be smug about this. Henry still had the upper hand.

***

7:35 p.m.

Amelia watched from the porch as Jared showed Liam and Morgan how to fire a gun. Jared was a professional in every sense, he knew how to treat firearms with respect, and she knew he would teach them the proper way. Still, the idea of her children wielding guns bothered her. They were *children* for crying out loud; they should be playing video games or soccer, not out in the middle of the woods shooting garbage off a rotting log. She jumped at the sudden sound of a gun going off, shook her head and went inside.

The cabin was rustic in a comfortable sort of way. She liked the fresh scent of pine and cedar, but now it was replaced with the more obnoxious smell of burnt herbs. Chad sat, cross-legged and his head bent low in the middle of the floor, encircled yet again by a salt ring. He didn't look up at her as she walked past, and a part of her was glad. His stares sent a chill up her spine every time he looked at her. Even the twins were keeping a good distance away.

"So," Chad's voice startled her, "how goes shooting practice?"

Amelia hesitated. He'd barely spoken since they arrived. She took a cautious step toward the circle, keenly aware this could be more than just her son.

"Fine," she replied, examining him for any new minion features. "Apparently, it's just like the video games."

His shaggy black hair fell across his face as he turned toward her. "Really? That is interesting."

"Yeah, who'd have guessed they'd actually be learning from first person shooter games." She leaned forward slightly. "And they're pretty good with real guns, too."

Chad's head returned to its bent position, and Amelia felt her body relax. Whether or not they were a good shot was a moot point, there was something about the way he spoke that reminded her too much of Henry.

She strolled over to a window, careful not to disturb a line of salt and herbs that ran along the edge of the wall. Dark clouds on the horizon were getting closer, and a few times she thought she saw a stray scrayling appear from the billowing formations.

Homer came around the side of the cabin and immediately glanced her way. Amelia crossed her arms and looked at her watch. A few more hours and one way or another, this would all be over.

"I am sorry about all of this," Chad said. "Perhaps, if things had turned out differently."

Amelia frowned. "Differently? How? Henry had this planned for years. You were always meant to be sacrificed. I doubt anything you or I, or anyone, said could have changed that."

"He was not expecting your love for Chad to be so strong."

A chill ran through her. She turned slowly, and found Chad staring at her. His dark eyes focused on her, but it wasn't her son.

Her heart sank. "Korthos . . ."

He turned his head and looked around the room. "You are a brave woman, Amelia Saint. Most simply give up and die, but not you. You are willing to sacrifice your very life for a creature that will undoubtable kill you all." He faced her. "Why is that?"

She clenched her jaw to hold back her emotions. "Chad is my son. He's a part of me."

"Is? You believe his soul still resides in this body?"

She swallowed. "I do."

"And if I were to tell you otherwise?"

"It would be a lie. I'd know."

"A mother always knows."

She nodded. "Yes. Besides, you still look like him."

Chad turned to her. His eyes glowed a dark crimson. "You are not what I expected. Your desire to protect him is . . . strong, despite the fact you will die in the attempt."

She stepped away from the window, keeping her focus on Chad. "Funny, you're not what I expected either. I thought you'd be some snarling monster, yet you're quite . . . civilized."

Chad gave a curt nod. "Only the minions I command would be so savage and mindless."

Amelia chuckled. "Kind of like Henry."

"We live to serve our master."

"Or do you serve to live?"

"We do not have a choice."

"You always have a choice."

The corners of Chad's mouth turned up into a sick grin. "You chose to die?"

"No, I chose to try. If I die tonight, that's fine. I'm at peace with that. To live out of fear, is no way to live." Her anger rose and she crossed her arms. "I hope Henry gets his just reward when all of this is over. Seems that's all he cared about."

"And you care about your sons."

Her gaze softened. "Always." She sat down on the floor a few inches from the salt ring. "I know you can't free Chad, but can you let my other son's live? I know you need some kind of sacrifice, and you can use me. Just let Liam and Morgan live."

Chad's brow rose. "Bargaining?"

"Pleading. You can take my soul. I'll serve you in whatever capacity you want, just let my boys go free."

"You would willingly give up your soul for theirs?"

Amelia nodded.

The corners of Chad's lips slowly turned upward into a sly grin.

***

<u>10:05p.m.</u>

It was a flash of lightning that caught Amelia's attention, followed by a strong wind that blew branches against the side of the cabin. She jumped up from the table and took a hasty look around the room for the twins.

"Here we go," Homer said, moving to a small window next to the door.

Jared was right behind him, grabbing a shotgun from a chair as he passed.

"Whatever happens," Jared said, looking back, "it's been an honour."

Amelia handed Liam a pistol, and frowned as Morgan grabbed a weapon from the stash and stepped up to the salt ring. Debris smashed against the sides of the cabin blown by the huge gusts of wind. More and more flashes lit up the night sky and caused the lights inside to flicker.

Amelia heard a low chuckle come from Chad. "This isn't going to work."

"Shut up, Chad." Liam said.

"Yeah," Morgan fiddled with his weapon. "You could be a little more grateful."

Chad's head flopped back like a rag doll. "I'm just sayin', is all."

More debris hit the outside walls as an orange glow crept closer to the cabin.

Amelia stretched her neck to see out one of the windows. "The ground's opening up?"

"Yeah," Jared replied. "I can see those slimy little bastards already."

Homer ran to another window. "I surrounded the cabin inside and out with a protection ring." He faced Amelia. "That should keep them from breaking through and buy us some time."

More menacing laughter from Chad sent a chill up Amelia's spine.

"Not really," he said, his head flopping from side to side.

Amelia picked up a gun from the table. "What are you talking about?"

Chad's body rose off the floor, like a marionette lifted by its strings, and stepped over the salt ring. "Protection only works if the minions are on the outside."

A loud crack came from the ceiling as a large piece of the roof ripped

164

off from the beams and disappeared into the night. The wind blew into the cabin, bringing pieces of debris and the strong odour of sulfur. Amelia pointed her gun toward the ceiling as long mutilated arms reached in through the hole, clawing at the remaining support beams.

She turned back to Chad, horrified as he walked toward the exit. He raised his arms and threw back his head, and the windows shattered inward, adding shards of glass to the maelstrom.

More loud cracks came from above as piece by piece, the roof gave way under the constant clawing of airborne scraylings, until there was nothing above them but the night sky.

Amelia was jerked backward as a strong set of arms pulled her and the twins toward the abandoned salt ring.

"Stay in the ring!" Homer said, handing her his shotgun. "Whatever you do, DON'T step outside the line!"

Amelia nodded, and crouched low to the floor, the twins right at her side.

Dirt and debris swirled around the inside of the cabin, as an orange glow from outside grew stronger. Lightning flashed, illuminating the clouds overhead as a large vortex dropped down over the cabin. Homer and Jared crouched outside the ring, but kept their weapons aimed at the sky.

Scraylings dove in and out of the wall of the vortex, screaming as they swooped down over the open cabin. Amelia felt the effect of their cries, and disorientation set in, numbing her mind. She lowered her head and covered her ears, but the screams were carried on the wind and only seemed to intensify. Several rounds of gunshots went off next to her, and she snapped her head up in time to see two imps blown back by the shots, only to be replaced by three more, digging at the window ledge.

Jared turned and aimed at the window. With one shot he took out two of the creatures, splattering black ooze along the inside wall and floor. An angry scream came from above as a large scrayling dove toward Jared.

"Watch out!" Liam's voice was barely heard over the noise of the scrayling.

Jared rolled and fell to the floor, but it was a shot from Morgan's weapon that kept the scrayling from attacking.

Amelia looked for Chad. He stood just in front of the door, arms outstretched, but there was something about him, something about his calm demeanor that wrenched on her heart.

"Chad!"

Slowly he turned toward her, and she could see it in his eyes. Even at this distance the dark brown of his eyes were gone. Replaced with a cold black that reflected the growing crimson glow.

"Chad?" His name caught in her throat. "Chad, please stay with us."

His arms lowered down to his side as black shadows raced across his face. His mouth opened but the sounds that came out only caused the creatures around them to whip into an even more frenzied state.

Homer cocked his shotgun next to her. "I don't think that's Chad anymore."

Amelia gasped for air as the putrid smell of sulfur grew. The ground shook as chunks of the walls began to fall away from the foundation. Imps and minions crawled in through the new openings and headed directly toward them. Amelia grabbed the twins as Homer and Jared fired randomly. The creatures exploded into black ooze that splattered the walls and floor. Amelia looked back at Chad, her eyes burning with tears.

"Chad! Help us, please!"

Chad blinked. "Mom?"

He was confused, she could see a glimmer of her son in his eyes, but then his expression changed as the vortex began to dissipate.

With a loud roar the remaining walls tore away from the floor and were sucked into the vortex. The ground around them was scarred with deep cracks that illuminated the hellfire. Imps and minions scurried past Chad and headed directly for Homer and Jared. Amelia took aim at one of the closer ones and pulled the trigger. Shots rang out, even from the twins, but for every imp, minion or scrayling they took down, several more appeared from the night to take its place.

A scrayling scream forced Amelia to the floor; her weapon dropped from her hands. She raised her head briefly and came face to face with one of the creatures. The stench of rotting flesh from its breath caused her to gag, and she could see her own disgusted reflection in its black eyes. It opened its mouth and ran a forked tongue across rows of fangs. It growled and lunged, only to be thrown back by the invisible barrier.

Screams from the twins brought her up to her knees, as minions and imps overcame Homer and Jared. Amelia pulled her sons close, watching her friends struggle under the grip as the creatures dragged the men off. She couldn't see their faces, only hear their muffled screams as they were pulled off the foundation of the cabin.

The winds calmed and Amelia found herself more focused than she thought she'd be. She was shaking, and her mind raced with a thousand possibilities of what was about to happen, but she wasn't afraid. If anything, she was anxious, anxious to get this over with.

Chad came toward her and reached out to touch the barrier. At the flash of light, he drew back his hand and looked at his fingers.

He frowned. "What an odd sensation." His voice was deep, calm, an almost monotone.

Amelia kept quiet as the twins whimpered next to her.

Chad's blank stare rested on her. "It didn't really hurt. Not like the last time."

Amelia pulled the twins closer. "What last time?"

"In the room, the place where we slept."

"You mean, in your home?"

Chad turned to her. "Chad's . . . our . . . home."

"Yes."

"I was there. You were . . . crying . . ."

"For my son." A rush of adrenaline raced through her. "You remember? You have Chad's memories?"

He lowered his hand as a wave of disgust washed across his face. Chad turned toward the front of the cabin and took a few steps. "What do you want?"

The small campfire burst into a ball of green fire, and Henry and a blonde emerged from the flames. At first Amelia was shocked, Henry looked so young, but the coldness in his glare forced her to turn away.

"Impressive," the blonde said, as Henry walked toward the far side of the cabin. "I would not have thought it possible for the vessel to hold on for so long."

"We are both here, and you will not hurt these people."

Henry walked toward him. "Is this some kind of a joke?"

The blonde eyed Chad. "You have your orders. I suggest you follow them."

The defiant smile of a teenager appeared. "Or what? You lost. Go away," Chad said, stepping out onto the porch. "I'm in control, and there's no way you can make me turn."

Amelia saw a flicker of excitement in the woman's face. "Oh really?"

Henry walked over to the group of imps and minions that held Homer down. Shadows

danced across his smiling face.

"Well, aren't you the wily cat," Henry said, as the majority of creatures backed away. "And here I thought you'd seen the last of your days in that explosion."

Homer struggled against his captors, as Amelia whispered a small prayer.

Henry stretched his arm outward and Homer's body lifted off the ground. Whatever Henry was doing, the excruciating look of pain on Homer's face forced Amelia to turn the twins' heads away.

"How does that leg feel, brother?" Henry asked.

The grinding sound of bone was instantly drowned out by Homer's screams as Henry moved his hand in a clockwise motion. Homer's leg twisted unnaturally, and she felt the twins cower under her embrace.

"Leave him alone," Amelia shouted. "He's your brother for fuck's sake!"

Henry's gleeful appearance quickly changed to hate. "More the reason."

Homer's breath came in short gasps. "I'm not mad at you, Henry. I know you're under the influence of the Overlord, and you have to do this for her."

The look on Henry's face reminded Amelia of that day in their bedroom. "You don't know anything about me," he said, his eyes narrowing into slits. "Don't ever presume to think you know anything about me!"

"I know the real you, the small child that still hides under his blanket when he's scared."

"Shut up."

"The kid who liked to sit by the stream in the summer and just listen to the sounds it made."

"I said," Henry balled his hand into a fist, and Homer screamed in agony, "shut up!"

"Stop!"

Amelia held her breath the moment she heard Chad's voice.

"Leave him alone."

Henry released his invisible grip on Homer, dropping him to the ground in a heap. Amelia felt a tingle of excitement deep inside. If anyone wanted to stand up to Henry more, it was Chad.

"Why are you even still here?" Henry asked, a partial look of disgust mixed with curiosity.

"I'm always here. We both are. Always have been." He took a step toward Henry. "And we've decided you're not going to do this."

"You forget," Henry said, "I never lose."

"Newsflash, Henry," Chad said. "There's a first time for everything."

Homer's laughing cut through the tension. "He sounds like you did at that age."

"You lost," Chad said. "Korthos and I made a deal, and there's nothing you can do. Mom and the twins are safe, and as long as they're behind me, I have all the support I'll ever need."

Amelia loosened her embrace. If this is where Henry went down, she wanted the boys to see it. They had the right to see the end. She kept her focus on Henry, as he moved toward the other side of the porch. He was too calm, considering everything he planned for was falling apart.

"It's over," Chad continued. "Face it, you lost. No more innocent people are going to die because of you."

Henry stopped in front of a pile of minions, keeping Jared secure. "Don't be so sure."

Amelia knew that look, knew what Henry was about to do, and she lunged forward only to be stopped by the invisible barrier.

Henry's outstretched arms raised Jared high into the air, and she could only watch in horror as a horde of scrayling dived on the young man. Amelia turned her head as the twins buried their faces in her shoulder. She didn't want to look; the images of the attack at her front door were still all too fresh in her mind. Amelia felt the air grow cold with Chad's agonizing cry. She lifted her head as her son dove toward his father. With a wave of his hand, Henry sent him flying backward, landing on the ground close to Homer.

"You didn't have to kill him," Chad said, rolling over onto his hands and knees. "He was nothing to you!"

"Exactly," Henry replied.

There was rage in Chad's eyes as gusts of icy wind blew across the landscape. Quickly, Amelia got to her feet and tried to step outside the ring, only to be forced back into the centre.

"Chad, stop," she said. "Remember what happened at Leslie's house! This is exactly what he wants."

Amelia watched in horror as minion features replaced her son. The fangs, the claws, the grotesque face all forced their way to the surface.

"Mom!" A tug on her pant leg forced her to look down.

Liam was pointing to the floor, and to the ring of protections that was slowly blowing away on the cold breeze.

"Chad, stop," she said, as a small group of imps came toward them. "I know you think using the minion's power will kill him, but remember what Father George said about using its power."

The creature took a few steps forward, leaving Amelia guessing on whether or not her son was still here.

"Chad!" Homer called out. "You're not helping anyone but them." Amelia pulled the twins close to her. "Pull the minion back inside."

The twins grabbed a strong hold onto Amelia as more of the salt blew away. Several imps reached out and tested the barrier, watching its strength decrease with each prod. She reached for Liam's gun, firing it at random into the growing circle of creatures as she tried to keep the boys behind her. Morgan shot off a few rounds, but the deaths of the other creatures weren't working as a deterrent.

"Why aren't they backing away?" Liam asked.

Amelia didn't know what to say. "Just don't let them grab you."

It didn't take long for her ammunition to deplete, and with the last shot, one of the minions reached out and tested the barrier.

It was gone.

Amelia felt her heart drop into her stomach as something grabbed her from above and lifted her into the air. Icy claws dug at her mouth, her arms, and her torso as she struggled against it. Below, she watched helplessly as Morgan and Liam were ripped from each other's grasp and pulled off the foundation of the cabin. She thrashed violently as each of the boys disappeared under the hordes of creatures.

Pain ripped through her body as claws slashed at her arms and legs. She heard Morgan and Liam screamed in pain and Homer's desperate attempt to trade his life for theirs.

Then the attack stopped. Amelia froze as the scraylings lowered her to the ground, just a few feet away from Lyla. Up close, the blonde was not at all attractive, but her cold stare was a carbon copy of Henry's.

She also noticed Henry looked worse for wear, and the satisfying look on Chad's face.

"What do you want?" Amelia's throat was raw. "You have what you want, why don't you just kill us and get it over with?"

Lyla moved a few steps toward her. "I am not sure how your son managed to keep Korthos at bay, but it would appear both are stronger because of it."

"So?"

Amelia didn't like the smile that appeared on her face. "So, I am offering a deal."

Amelia snorted. "Sorry bitch, no deal."

Lyla's expression changed. "The offer is not to you." She turned and walked toward Chad. "Korthos is a very powerful creature, and I am most impressed with the fact you both are living within the same body. An added bonus on my part."

Amelia saw some of Chad's features reassert themselves. "What do you mean?"

"You are part of a timetable, a master plan that would be set back if Korthos does not appear." She turned and walked toward Henry. "Since your father could not fulfill his bargain—"

"There is still time!" Henry cut her off.

"Perhaps, but I'm growing tired of this." She faced Chad again. "I'm offering you a deal. Come with me, stand by my side, and I will allow your mother and brothers to go free."

"Chad, don't," Amelia said. "It's not worth it. Look what happened to your father! Don't—" Icy shadows reached down her throat and choked off her words.

Amelia struggled as the grip on her grew tighter. She stared at Chad, shaking her head quickly, hoping to appeal to his human side.

The familiar teenage-stand shone through the creature as it slumped to one side. "How do I know you'll keep your word?"

"If you are as attached to Korthos as I believe, then you should be able to tell if I am lying or not."

Chad tilted his head to one side. "You're scared."

"Hardly."

He frowned and looked off into the darkness of the woods. "There it is again, that . . . aftertaste."

"Do we have a deal or not?"

"Now wait one minute," Henry said, marching toward her.

"Chad, no," Homer called out. "Listen to me! Do you want all those people to die in vain? How do you think Jared would feel knowing you gave up after he gave his life for you?"

Chad motioned to Homer. "What about him?"

"If you want, I will include your uncle." She held out her hand, palm up. "Do we have a bargain?"

Amelia struggled harder against the minions, causing their claws to dig deeper into her flesh. Lyla held up her opposite hand and instantly Amelia froze looking forward. She couldn't move, could barely breath, and was about to watch her son make the same mistake his father did.

Chimes rang out from somewhere near Chad, and the young man pulled out his cell and swiped the front. His eyes turned crimson red as he held up his cell toward Henry and Lyla.

A sly smile creased his lips as Korthos took over. "Time's up."

The wind howled through the trees forming a large black vortex over the remains of the cabin. Scraylings were sucked into the blackness as imps raced back into the cracks in the ground. Minions that held the twins tight now skulled back into their shadows, and Amelia gulped in fresh air as the icy grip in her throat disappeared.

She collapsed to the ground, breathing rapidly as the winds blew and sucked the creatures back into Hell. A large smile forced itself to surface as Morgan and Liam raced to Homer's side and embraced him.

"Wait!" Henry's frantic shouts were drowned out by a rumbling sound as a long crack stretched out toward him. Long black tendrils reached out from below the surface and wrapped around Henry's legs. He fell to the ground, sliding toward the open gap on his stomach and grabbing at anything that would keep him above the surface, as the shadows pulled him toward the fiery opening.

Chad's features reasserted themselves as he went to Amelia's side. He helped her to her feet, as Henry struggled to keep above ground. She didn't take her eyes off her husband and felt Chad's strong embrace as the imps pulled Henry into the crack. She could see the fear in his eyes, but something else as well. A confusion, bewilderment as his frightened glare melted into a plea.

Henry reached out to her. "Amelia!"

Tears clouded her eyes, and she moved to break from Chad's embrace, but he held her tight.

"Don't," he whispered into her ear.

She leaned back against his chest and watched as Henry frantically clawed at the ground. She covered her ears but his screams echoed in the night.

Then it was quiet.

She buried her face in Chad's shirt as the ground shook and the cracks sealed themselves. She burst into tears and grabbed him around the waist. Fear, anxiety, hatred—it all melted away as she wept in his arms. She felt the amulet under his clothing, and stepped back from him, lifting his shirt.

"It's still there?"

Chad looked down. "Yeah, I guess it'll always be there." He turned and looked at Lyla. "Unless you know some way I can get it off."

Amelia stared at the woman with an icy glare that matched the woman's. "Why are you still here?" she asked, taking a few steps closer to her. "Don't you have more innocent lives to ruin?"

"Don't think you've won," Lyla said. "This is just an interesting diversion. The boy is ours. You won't last—"

Amelia's fist made contact with Lyla's face at the jawbone, throwing her to the ground.

"Shut up, and fuck off!" Amelia turned away, but then turned back. "And you tell the others like you that if I see anything that even remotely looks demonic around my children, I will personally come after them." She took a step forward and leaned over Lyla. "I'm not afraid, and I know how to beat you."

Amelia kept her gaze on Lyla as the woman disappeared in a ball of green flames. She took a deep breath and looked up at the stars as Chad wrapped his arms round her shoulders.

It was a beautiful night to be alive.

12

Amelia wiped away the condensation on the mirror with one of the fancy hand towels on the bathroom counter. The steam from the shower quickly formed new beads, and her image disappeared behind a veil of fog. This week had been nothing short of a nightmare, and she was more than happy to see it end. She took another swipe at the mirror, making a mental note to pick up some paper towels the next time she was in the grocery store. This house was going to need a good cleaning after all the crap that had taken place.

She paused halfway down the mirror and frowned. She shouldn't be here. Didn't Henry burn the house down? Her body tensed as arms reached around her waist from behind, and the familiar musky scent of Henry's shower gel filled her nose. She looked down at the hands: strong and manicured with a wedding ring on the third finger of the left hand.

"Maybe just once more." It was Henry's voice, and it sent a wave of panic through her. "For old times' sake."

Amelia broke free of the embrace and quickly turned around. Her breath caught in her throat as the smiling face of her husband looked down at her. Shadows danced across his face, and his eyes no longer held the rich dark brown hue.

"You!" She could barely breathe as her eyes locked in his gaze. "You're dead!"

The one corner of his mouth curled upward. "No. Just in Hell."

Amelia dove toward the bathroom exit, but Henry was quicker and grabbed her by the throat. She struggled against him, clawing at his hand, trying to loosen his grip, as he slammed her up against the counter. She felt his full weight against her as he pinned her down, his face very close to hers and sniffed her hair.

"I kind of like you this way," he said. "Completely under my control." He opened his mouth and slid his forked tongue along her cheek. His touch burned her skin, but her screams did little to stop him. He ran his tongue up to her ear and then stopped.

"You will always be my wife."

A blast of fire blew past her, consuming Henry and engulfing the entire bathroom. Amelia collapsed to the floor, choking on hot air as it seared into her lungs . . .

Amelia bolted upright in bed, taking deep breaths, her body trembling. She couldn't breathe the cool air in fast enough as the images of the fiery inferno burned in her mind. Was it a dream? Felt more like a nightmare, and she collapsed back on the bed, relieved the whole thing was over.

Her head pounded, sending waves of throbbing pain coursing through her skull. She slowed her breathing, trying to bring her heartbeat back to normal and ward off some of the trembling. She forced other images into her mind: two days in police custody, the intense twenty-four hour interrogation about the house fire, the mutilated bodies, the murders, and their sudden flight out of town. She knew the police wouldn't be done with her for a while, but at least she wasn't a prime suspect anymore. She covered her eyes with her hand as tears raced down the side of her face and dripped into her ear. She was relieved he was gone and the pact was broken, but she knew it would be a long while before any of them ever felt safe again.

"You all right?" Homer asked quietly from the entranceway. "I heard you wake up in a panic."

His smile was soft and like a breath of fresh air. She didn't want to think what would have happened if he hadn't been there for her and the boys.

Amelia sat up and hung her legs over the side of the mattress. "At least I got a few hours' sleep." She rubbed the wetness off her face. "Don't know if I care much for the nightmares."

Homer came toward her and sat on the bed. "It'll take some time to get used to the nightmares," he said, bluntly. "But they do become more manageable as time goes on."

Amelia snorted. "I don't want them to become manageable, Homer; I want them to go away."

"Can't help you with that." He rubbed the side of his face thoughtfully. "But I know some people who can help you deal with them."

Amelia sighed. "Henry's in Hell, and somehow he's put me there with him." She stood up and headed to the bathroom. "I have a feeling my life will continue to be a living nightmare."

The lukewarm water of the shower cleared some of the fog from her mind, but she couldn't help but feel like someone—something—was watching her. Her paranoia had her peeking around the shower curtain more than once. The steam played tricks with her mind, and she searched the room for crimson eyes peering at her from partially hidden shadows on the wall.

The mid-morning sun was bright and almost above the motel when she stepped outside. The world seemed a different place to her now, more dangerous than she thought possible, but at least her children were alive. She took stock of where they were. Chad and Homer were sitting on a nearby picnic table, talking and checking over an array of small calibre weapons, with Liam and Morgan walking back from the motel restaurant, several bags in their arms.

"Sorry, Mom, they were all out of muffins," Liam said, placing his bags on the wooden surface of the picnic table. "So I got you some whole wheat toast instead."

Amelia ruffled his hair. "That's very thoughtful of you. Thanks."

Chad opened one of Morgan's bags. "What else did you get?"

"We tried to find something special for you," Morgan said, removing a Styrofoam container from the bag.

"Yeah," Liam continued, "but they were all out of devil's food cake, and it's too early for devilled eggs." He looked at Homer. "Apparently, that's a lunch thing."

Amelia couldn't help but giggle at Chad's blank expression. "Oh they're just teasing," she said, and gave him a slight nudge.

Chad went back to his weapons. "Yeah, real funny."

Amelia helped distribute the odd assortment of breakfast items, watching her family try to be normal, but it was anything but ordinary. How many families held breakfast outside on a picnic table alongside a small pile of ammunition and handguns? It was a far cry from the burnt toast and whining of a week ago.

"Hey Homer," Morgan said, stuffing toast into his mouth, "are you gonna stay with us, now that we know you're our uncle?"

Amelia saw Homer's eyes dart in Chad's direction.

"Well, I could," he said, taking a sip from the Styrofoam cup.

"What is it?" Amelia asked. "What's going on?"

"What do you mean?"

"I know that look, Homer. There's something you're not telling me."

Chad wiped his mouth with a napkin. "I was going to talk to you about it later, but now that it's been brought up . . ."

"What's been brought up? Nothing's been brought up. What are you talking about?"

Chad shifted in his spot on the bench. "Homer and I were talking, and we think it would be better—safer for you and the twins, if I left."

Tightness again formed in the pit of her stomach. "What do you mean leave?"

"Leave, as in, away from here."

Amelia's glance went from Homer to Chad. "Where would you go?"

"I have some friends in Ottawa," Homer said. "People who know how to deal with this sort of thing." He took a sip from his Styrofoam cup. "They deal with it on a daily basis, and I think he being there would benefit the lad and them."

"How so?"

"They're hunters, of sorts. They have abilities that other people don't. There's been some things going on, strong demonic things, and I think Chad can help."

Chad picked up a slice of her toast. "Homer says their boss is a demon."

There was a short outburst of disbelief.

"You can't leave," Liam said. "What if those things come after us again? Who's gonna warn us?"

They're not after you kiddo. They're after me," Chad said. "Don't you remember what Lyla said? It's always been about me. You guys were just an added bonus."

"You don't know that," Morgan argued, getting up from the table. "They could come back and we'd all be dead because you wanted to run off and play demon hunter."

Amelia's heart ached as she watched Morgan stomp away. She hadn't seen him this upset in years, and she clenched her jaw as Liam got up and followed his brother.

"Chad's right, you know," Homer said. "There's something coming, something big, but what we did here, stopping Korthos from completely taking over Chad's body, put a big cramp in their plans."

"It did," Chad said, and stuffed the slice of cake in his mouth. "And someone's pissed too, by the way."

Homer snorted. "What else is new?"

"I don't like the idea," Amelia said, glaring at her son. "Did you even take into consideration how this decision would affect the rest of us?"

"I'm trying to protect you all. You won't be in danger if I'm not around."

"You don't know that."

"Yes, I do."

"Then we'll handle it together. As a family."

"Mom, stop." Chad focused on her. "I've thought this through. I want to go with Homer and work with his friends to try and stop more of these minions from entering our world."

"We have a unique opportunity here, Amelia," Homer said. "Korthos and Chad share the same body. He can hear what's going on in Hell, and Korthos doesn't seem to be controlled by Satan anymore. With his help, we could save more people from his fate. He's a real weapon against Hell."

Amelia shook her head. "No. I don't want him running all over the country shooting at minions. I want him here where I can keep an eye on him and protect him—"

"I'm eighteen, Mom. You can't force me to stay here with you." He took her hand in his. "I want to do this. I have to. Lyla corrupted Henry, whispered things in his ear, and look what happened. I don't want any other families to go through the shit we did." His gaze softened. "I don't want any more kids to lose a parent the way I did."

Amelia kept her focus on Chad. "And what if they come after you?"

"Let them," he said, a look of teenage bravado on his face. "I wouldn't mind another crack at that bitch."

"But this Korthos could turn—"

"He would have done so already, Amelia," Homer said. "It's been two days, and we haven't even heard a growl."

"Korthos is at peace right now," Chad said and took a deep breath. "I know his thoughts, his feelings. He was so angry, so vengeful, but he was scared too, and no one could understand that. They all turned their back on him for what he did, and he accepted that, but banishing him with the rest of those traitors?" Chad shook his head as he looked away.

Amelia looked confused. "What traitors?"

"It's a long story," Homer said. "Needless to say, he betrayed a lot of people. His punishment fit his crime."

"Maybe so, but Mom sticking by me, that calmed him down." His eyes moved from side to side, as though he were listening to some internal conversation. "It was you. You kept me close, even with everything that was going on."

"You're my son. I love you."

Chad smiled and looked over at his uncle. "Maybe if his family had done the same thing, not given up on him, we wouldn't be here now."

Amelia cupped her hand on his face. "I will always love you, no matter what."

"Even with Korthos hunkered down inside me?"

She smiled and kissed him gently on the tip of his nose. "Just make sure he doesn't get you into trouble, or he'll have to deal with me." She leaned back and looked at Homer. "I'm still not happy about you taking him away."

"I know, but there will be more people corrupted not only by Lyla, but other overlords. The minion killings will continue whether Chad stays with you or not." He looked proudly at his nephew. "I'm hoping if he comes with me, and learns how to use the abilities that he has with this pairing, we could save a few more people who wouldn't have had a chance before."

Amelia took a quick glance at Chad and exhaled deeply. "Doesn't sound like I can talk either of you out of it."

Chad smiled. "Sorry, your mom-thing isn't going to work this time."

Amelia smiled at his reference. "No, I guess not."

She reached for him and wrapped her arms around his shoulders. "I guess I had to let go sooner or later." She pulled away and brushed a few stray hairs from his face. "I just wish . . ."

He smiled at her. "I know."

Liam's voice broke the moment. "Hey, Mom!" Amelia looked past Chad and saw Liam motioning to a minivan pulling in on the other side of the parking lot. "It's Mrs. Beatlemire and Frankie."

Amelia's anxiety rose as she watched Morgan run up to the side of the vehicle and interact with his friend. She knew these people and knew they wouldn't hurt him, but she couldn't take the chance they weren't who they looked to be. Not after Lyla's warning.

Amelia got up from the table and picked up one of the small calibre guns sitting on the pile.

"Mom?" Chad said, turning in his seat. "What are you doing?"

She pulled the magazine out of the weapon and checked the ammo. "Just in case."

Chad reached out and took her by the arm. "Put it down. He's safe. Trust me. I'd know if they were anything other than human."

Amelia looked into his eyes. The dark brown hues of his father's eyes looked back at her. "Yeah, well I still need to be safe."

She tucked the nozzle of the gun down the back of her pants and walked toward the minivan. At this distance they looked fine. Apart from the odd sympathetic look, Amelia didn't see anything that would indicate they might be possessed, but then, she was still so new to all of this, and she'd been surprised once before.

Frankie gave her a quick nod. "Hi, Mrs. Saint."

Morgan turned around when his friend's attention shifted to her.

Amelia smiled at the teen and glanced in the car. "Hi, Eleanor."

Eleanor's ruddy face broke out into a bright grin. "Hi, Amelia. Oh

God, it's good to see you again."

Amelia tapped Morgan on the shoulder and motioned to the motel. "There's some open space over by the picnic tables. Why don't you take Frankie over and kick the soccer ball around?"

Morgan's pale blue eyes seemed to sparkle a bit. "Sure, Mom."

Amelia felt a deep weight lift as the boys roughhoused over to the tables. She caught Morgan's quick glance back, a slight worried look on his face, but she nodded and smiled and wondered how much of their lives would now involve these invisible conversations.

"So, Amelia, how are you?" Eleanor's question seemed almost comical.

How am I? Amelia thought. *Well, my twin sons will never have another peaceful night's sleep again, my oldest has a demon inside him with an amulet welded to his chest that's a gateway to Hell, and my husband tried to kill us.* Amelia let her shoulders slump. "Surviving. That's about all we can do."

"Just so you know, I've invited Morgan to stay with us any time he wants to. Despite what his father did, you have to try and resume a normal life again, as soon as possible."

"Thanks a lot. I know Morgan will appreciate the offer." She frowned and tilted her head slightly. "Eleanor, how much do you know about what happened?"

"Honestly, nothing more than the rumours, Hon. Henry took off with some blonde bimbo, set the house on fire, and tried to blame you for it." She shuffled around in her seat. "No offence, Amelia, but that Henry was a real piece of work. Imagine, thinking just because he was a high-priced lawyer he could get away with it."

Amelia smile. "Yeah, he thought he could get away with a lot of things."

"Have the police developed any new leads as to who could have killed your friend Leslie?"

Amelia's stiffened at the mention of her name. "No, not that I know of."

Eleanor shook her head. "All this happening to your family in the same weekend. It's just horrible. Good thing you had Father George there for support."

Amelia slowly nodded. "Yes, yes it is."

Out of the corner of her eye, Amelia saw a police car pulling into the parking lot. She could hear Eleanor rambling on about how the twins would be affected by the actions of their father for the rest of their lives, but Amelia was too distracted by the arrival of the police to pay attention, especially when she noticed Father George sitting in the passenger seat.

Amelia smiled at Frankie's mother. "Excuse me, Eleanor, I think they're here to see me."

She didn't wait for a response and noticed both Homer and Chad heading toward the parking lot as well. Father George looked calm, a good sign something else was going on, but the fact he was here at all, and with the police, bothered her.

"Good morning, Mrs. Saint," the officer said as he got out of his car.

"Amelia," Father George said, exiting the passenger side. "You remember Detective Brice."

Amelia tried to smile. "Yes, and I'll try not to hold that against him."

The detective gave her a curt nod as he walked around the front of the car. Amelia noted a file folder in his hand. "I thought I would come by in person and let you know that I spoke with Tina DaCosta earlier today."

"How is she?" Chad asked.

"Better. They doctors still have her on strong sedatives, but she seems a little more coherent this morning." He glanced quickly at Amelia. "Enough so that she told us who killed her brother."

Amelia's pulse raced. "Who?"

The detective's glance shifted between her and Chad. "She says it was your husband, Mrs. Saint. He lured him out of the house somehow, and then stabbed him multiple times."

Chad's posture slumped a bit, and Amelia reached out and embraced him with one arm. "We thought something like that, but we weren't quite sure."

"We've sent an officer to her hospital room. She's offered to make a full statement."

Father George glanced quickly at the detective. "And Miss Carmichael?"

Detective Brice nodded. "We found your husband's DNA evidence on Miss Carmichael's body."

Amelia swallowed a few times, trying to conceal her relief. "Just like I told you. He strangled her."

"The evidence agrees with you."

"So she's not being charged with either murder?" Homer asked.

"With all the evidence we've gathered so far, it looks like your husband was the main perpetrator in all these crimes."

"Just like she told you."

Amelia exhaled slowly as a lone tear trickled down her cheek. "Hopefully, Henry won't be able to hurt anyone anymore." She looked up at Homer. "Wherever he is."

"Actually, Amelia," Father George reached for her arm, "the police think they've found Henry."

Amelia's heart raced. "Found? What do you mean?"

"Dispatch received a call early Monday morning about a car on fire a few miles from your cottage." He fumbled with the file, opening it and revealing several glossy pictures inside. He picked up one and held it out to her. "Is this your husband's car?"

Amelia took a hard look at the burned out wreck. It looked like his Porsche, but it was so damaged she really couldn't tell. She shook her head. "I'm sorry. I don't know."

Amelia took a quick glance at the other photos. "What's that?"

Detective Brice tilted the file slightly upward, obscuring her view. "Unfortunately, we found this victim in the car." He reached for the top photo and then hesitated. "I don't mean to put you on the spot, Mrs. Saint, but do you think you could identify some personal items we found on the remains?"

"Remains?" Amelia felt several hands on her shoulder, and then nodded. She closed her eyes and took a deep breath. Her jaw trembled as she tried to keep calm. Henry was a horrible person, so why was she feeling any grief for him?

"Mrs. Saint?"

Amelia opened her eyes and looked down at the photo. It was gruesome, but not the worst she'd seen. The burnt flesh and seared bones of the corpse was tame compared to the tattered remains of the police after the scrayling attack.

A second photo showed an expensive watch, a wedding band, and a few other items. Amelia took a deep breath and swallowed. She studied the picture, looked for some hint that they were Henry's, but nothing sparked familiarity about them. Should she say this? Tell the detective these weren't Henry's things? It could force the police to put her and her children in protective custody, in case they thought Henry might come after her again, but she knew that wasn't likely. Henry was burning in Hell, or so she hoped, and the police keeping tabs on her would make their lives more frustrating than helpful.

Not to mention Lyla's warning. They could be attacked again, and Amelia didn't want any more innocent people to die.

She looked directly into the detectives eyes. "That's his watch, Detective."

His eyes narrowed slightly. "Are you sure, Mrs. Saint?"

Amelia nodded. "Positive. It's a one of a kind Rolex. I'd know it anywhere. I saved for close to a year before I had enough money to buy it for him for Christmas."

Chad's arms embraced her around the shoulders, and she buried her face in the sleeve of his jacket. She felt the twins at her side, felt their arms encircle her waist.

Detective Brice sighed. "I'm sorry for your loss, Mrs. Saint."

Amelia nodded, leaned against Chad, and cried softly into his shoulder. Her mind was numb and she couldn't stop crying as Father George and the detective got back into the cruiser and pulled away. She calmed herself as the police cruiser pulled out of the parking lot and onto the road.

"It's over," Homer said and pulled away from her. "At least I hope it is. You can never tell with the overlords."

She stood silent with Chad next to her. It wasn't over. She could feel it in her bones. It might be quiet for a while, but she had a horrible feeling that her family was now a part of something that would never stop.

"It's not Henry. Just another one of his victims," Chad said, when they were alone.

She looked up at him, his eyes were glossy and clear. "What?"

"In the burned car."

"How do you know?"

Chad turned to her. His eyes were dark brown, but there was a crimson ring around the outer edge of his iris. "We know."

Amelia sighed, and brushed some of the wetness from her face. "Hopefully, his last." She blinked back a tear and looked up into the cloudless sky. Already the cicadas were chirping, predicting another hot summer day. She gazed to the woods across the road, and with a deep breath wiped the last of the tears from her eyes. "I suddenly found my appetite. Let's go finish breakfast."

Chad stood still.

Amelia frowned. "Chad? What is it?"

Chad stood frozen to the ground, staring straight ahead and across the road. Amelia's gaze followed his. Two red eyes peered at her from the shadow of a large tree where an unnaturally long shadow ran out from underneath.

She motioned to the shadow. "I see it now. Is that what I think it is?"

The muscles in his jaw tensed. "Yeah, that's one of them."

Amelia pulled out the handgun and aimed directly at the shadow. "Don't even think about it."

~Fin~

ABOUT THE AUTHOR

Darke Conteur is a writer at the mercy of her Muse. The author of stories in several genres, she prefers to create within the realms of Science Fiction and Dark Fantasy. She has short stories published in several online magazines including Bewildering Stories and Aphelion.
A gamer at heart, she also enjoys knitting, gardening, cooking and good music. When not busy writing, she watches over one husband, one wannabe chef, four cats, and one ghost dog.